EVERYTHING

WAS

BEAUTIFUL

AND

NOTHING

HURT

EVERYTHING WAS BEAUTIFUL AND NOTHING HURT

BEN REEVES

Atlantic Books
London

First published in hardback in Great Britain in 2026 by
Atlantic Books, an imprint of Atlantic Books Ltd.

1 3 5 7 9 8 6 4 2

A CIP catalogue record for this book is available from the British Library.

Hardback ISBN: 9781805465799
Trade paperback ISBN: 9781805465805
EBook ISBN: 9781805465812

Text designed and typeset by Tetragon, London
Printed and bound by CPI Group (UK) Ltd, Croydon CR0 4YY

Atlantic Books
An Imprint of Atlantic Books Ltd
Ormond House
26–27 Boswell Street
London
WC1N 3JZ

www.atlantic-books.co.uk

Product safety EU representative: Authorised Rep Compliance Ltd., Ground Floor,
71 Lower Baggot Street, Dublin, D02 P593, Ireland. www.arccompliance.com

For Kelly

A ROLLING BOY

The silver car tumbles end-over-end five times before resting on its roof at the crossroads. A traffic light shifts from red to green, detecting nothing wrong with this arrival, and the headlights glare through the rain, and the wheels keep spinning, flicking their spray at no one in the empty street.

All is quiet. A kebab shop, yellow haze. The stark whiteness of an off-licence and the spatter of residential windows glinting like fairy lights. Faces peeking through the curtains. There's a scent of sparks from the fireworks behind the terraces, and from the car's roof where it scraped along the road.

The car sits steaming in the cold, the upside-down world reflected in the wet tarmac. It was the wetness that made the tyres slip – tyres, illegal, too bald, beige threads – and it was the Jägermeister he'd brought to the party, and the pills still fizzing inside his stomach.

The car's wheels begin to slow, like a worn-out clock.

Nothing moves but everything speaks – the car speaks, the signs speak. It all speaks, so quiet, so gentle – the whisper of a drain, the birdsong of distant sirens. All of it waits.

They arrive, an ambulance and two police response vehicles, flashing blue-red-blue. The traffic light does its best to recite what happened in its light-language, but none of them listens. The paramedics scurry to the scene, urgent and cautious and tired from the long night. The police chatter like budgies into their radios. They await instruction.

But no instruction comes, for the world slows, slows.

It slows and slows and slows to an imperceptible crawl.

Paramedics with their steely faces masking worried ones – paramedics caught mid-stride, the flaps of their hi-vis jackets frozen behind them in the frigid air. The police officer trapped in a half-blink. The rain suspended in space, a billion glass beads reflecting the scene.

I pass through all of it. Through these hanging rain-drops, through the emergency team, and I relish the weight of my body, and the crunch of windscreen glass beneath my bare feet. I tread towards the car, over these fragments scattered like the diamonds of some careless jeweller. A sign reading '30' leans mockingly beside the driver-side door.

And when the driver, twenty-nine, the man who is still a boy, Samuel Preston, sees me through the side window, his eyes are wide. His eyes are wide because he knows who I am and why I've come. Everyone knows, at the end.

He'd planned on proposing to his girlfriend this New Year's Day. Now he's sprawled on the upside-down ceiling, all crushed and crooked, strapped awkwardly in his upside-down seat, legs mangled somewhere above the steering wheel. Arms broken. Neck broken, the column cracked, its wires kinked.

I kneel down, open his door.

His friends are unconscious – one in the front passenger seat, one in the back. Samuel tries to move, but I hush him. I lean into the car, holding his head on my lap, and I stroke his hair, and he's scared, and I tell him it's okay now. It's okay.

He tells me he can't move, and I say I know, it's okay. He says, is this it? This can't be it, can it? And I don't answer because he already knows. And when he asks if this has to happen, I say yes, it's okay. Close your eyes now. He does, and he winces from the pain. I whisper some things. I tell him things a person should only know right before they die. And the pain rushes away, and he relaxes, caught in this motionless double-world where the light flickers from blue, to red, back to blue, minutes in between.

He asks, will you tell my girlfriend what happened?

I can't, I tell him. But someone will.

She's pregnant.

I know. It's okay. Close your eyes.

Oh god, he says. Oh god, I'm gonna miss it. I'm gonna miss everything.

Samuel Preston stares through the shattered windscreen. For eight seconds, he's still. Then he slips the bracelet from his topsy-turvy rear-view mirror – wooden beads on elastic. He holds them to his lips as he cries, and he smells them, and he remembers. His face is tight and brave. And we rest in the stillness, just he and I, silent, and the smell of the bracelet is the last thing Samuel Preston ever knows.

Samuel Preston – 29 years, 5 months, 4 days

Three years tumble away like rolling cars, and in the first quiet hours of another January, I wander. Samuel Preston hasn't left my mind. None of them do.

So I wander – skirting the city and slipping through those in-between places, the jigsaw puzzle of concrete, the trees trapped in brickwork troughs. I like to stumble upon these green nooks in a grey town – nooks hiding away, hoping never to be found by developers, and I watch them dissolve into more flats, more houses. A canal runs along the edge of the town, obscured by train tracks and metal fences, little walkways, alleys, under-passes. It's lined with yellow willows whose weeps drape into the water, and there are bramble bushes tangling, and you could almost imagine you were in some paradise. The illusion is shattered by the rumble of a train, or an island of sewage drifting through the reeds, or the power lines peeking over the tops of the trees. It's a paradise apparent by its own contradictions, all the more precious for its rareness.

I wander the path beside the canal and I pass a teenage couple hand in hand. I don't want to think about who they are or who they'll be – they're a young couple now, and that's enough. There's a man sitting in a green sleeping bag beneath the rail bridge. The arches of the bridge are a patchwork of greys where the council paints over the graffiti, and the graffiti crawls back over the paint, and the paint wipes over the graffiti in an eternal battle where

neither opponent will ever meet the other. There's a
stink of piss. A musky scent of cannabis. The man in the
sleeping bag asks for a cigarette and I tell him I don't have
one. I pass beneath the bridge as the rising sun cuts red and
gold through the willows like a photograph flare in my
little oasis.

This is the park with the playground at one end and the
cemetery at the other, and this is the park where I sit on the
bench and watch John Lamb, the old man on his morning
walk. He dresses the part with his baggy beige trousers and
floppy shoes, his tatty tweed jacket. There was a time he'd
come here with his dog Virgil, a cocker spaniel, and the two
of them would stop to greet every other dog who crossed
their path, and John would smile at the owners and say
g'morning, and sometimes they'd chat about small things,
about dogs and rain, and then they'd all be on their way.
But Virgil died two years ago from old age and from his
broken heart for John's wife who died the winter before.
Now John walks alone, and I watch him toddle the long
diagonal path through the green, away from the brick-wall
alley, through the corridor of trees, past the swings and
springy jeep towards the main road. His stomach is empty
because the bacon was off. His hand is empty with no Virgil
leading the way, and his arm feels too light, like it could
float away and reach his dog and his wife waiting up there
somewhere. He walks past me, this old man, and he doesn't
look at me. I watch the waddle in his step where his knees
are stiff so his hips do the work, and I watch the way his

fingers clench and unclench. I watch the wisp of white hair
on the back of his head, the way it wafts with every step,
and I listen to those flappy shoes squeak and creak on the
tarmac path. I can taste the staleness in his mouth from
the lack of breakfast and no cup of tea. I can feel the socks
about his shins, the itch in his crotch, the belt hanging loose
around his waist. I can hear the way he tries to ignore the
traffic, to better remember how this place felt when he was
a boy. And as I watch him, this dogless old man, I think
of his wife, and I think of bread-and-butter pudding, and
I watch him walk this same walk, alone, week after week
after week.

❧

A MORNING MAN

John will often go a fortnight without anyone speaking
to him. He'll visit the shops just to pass people. He says
g'morning g'morning to each one, and he might receive a
pitying smile, or a mother will shield her son, or a teenager
will tell him to fuck off. But he says it anyway, g'morning,
g'morning, and when a stranger looks at him, he knows
he's not a ghost.

Today he passes the old pasta shop and walks down
an alley with flats on one side and an overgrown garden
on the other. The garden hides behind a wire fence, and

sometimes John peers through the fence and watches the resident goat munching on dandelions and brambles. Today there's no goat, so John keeps walking, through the alley and across the park.

There's a young man on the bench listening to music in his headphones. G'morning, g'morning. John doesn't need anything from the shop, but he's going anyway. If he buys something, he's almost guaranteed a few words – cash or card? Would you like a receipt? They're empty words, but they're words, and John cherishes them like fossils on the beach. A woman walking her dog. John says g'morning, g'morning, and the dog sniffs John's knees. He's unsure of the breed – a shaggy little thing. Oh, he says. Hello there. You're a handsome boy, aren't you?

The woman is in her early thirties. She smiles, and it's a real smile, but she eases her dog away from the old man and disappears down the alley past the goat garden. John's heart knocks against his vest. He checks his watch. He wonders if that lady and her shaggy dog always walk on this path at this time, and if they do, maybe they could pass one another regularly. Regularly enough to say g'morning, and then maybe, how are you? How's the doggy? Lovely day, isn't it? John daydreams a whole scenario in which this woman asks him about his life, and he asks about hers, and eventually she invites him for dinner with her family – a husband and three boys – and he visits every week, even at Christmas. John keeps walking.

At the shop, he chooses things he knows will soon run out. Bananas. Milk. Chocolate for later. And when he brings the items to the counter, he says, g'morning, g'morning, chirpy as if it was the first time he'd said it.

The young man at the counter walks away from the till. A red light indicates that the till is closed. But John hangs around a bit longer before using the self-service.

He walks home without a word. And when he steps through the front door with his bag of shopping, he sees me sitting on his settee with two cups of coffee. I say, g'morning, g'morning.

John's house is dark even when the windows are bright. Dust floats about, settling on the settee, on the coffee table, on the piano with all the darts trophies. The place is tidy but for the dust.

— Thought I saw my old English teacher the other day.

I watch as he meticulously packs his shopping into the cupboards. He tucks the plastic bag into a drawer beside the fridge. He tidies some bowls and plates from the draining board. When he's done, he sits beside me and holds his coffee in both hands.

— Looked exactly like him. But it wasn't him. Yeah, that teacher was a real horrible cunt. Nothing was ever good enough. If you wrote something minimal, he'd say it was basic. Too poetic — he'd say it was overwritten. My dream was to publish an anthology of poetry, then track him down and say, look! I did it, you miserable bastard. Ha!

He nods over to the bookshelf beside the piano. Among the leatherbound volumes and darts books are five fat paperbacks with his name on them. Those aren't dusty, they're shiny as the day they were printed. He's told me this story before, but I'll listen. Some people need my time more than others.

— Sue always said, leave it. You don't need to go tracking down old teachers. You published your poems. You showed him. But I ignored her – I searched through the phone book to find him. I visited the old school, asked about him, but he'd moved away. Leave it, Sue said. Just be proud of what you've done. Leave it. But I couldn't – I wanted to show him. And then one day we saw his name in the obituary – lung cancer. He was only fifty-five. Well, you know all about that, don't you, Mister Death?

John likes to call me Mister Death, like the Cummings poem.

He grins and nudges my knee with an old blue hand. And his smile fades. He's still looking at the books on the shelf, each dedicated to his wife. All five were published while she was alive. He's been working on a sixth anthology for the past three years, but his muse has gone. A pile of loose papers sits on the coffee table in front of us.

John picks up a poetry book from the side table.

— Can I read you one?

— I'd like that.

— Alright. This was my wife's favourite. It's called 'Bread'.

He clears his throat and reads the poem in a stately voice. When he's finished, he sips his coffee. I stay quiet.

— Bear in mind, I wrote it thirty years ago.

— Okay.

— Well, say something.

— What does it mean?

— It doesn't matter what it means. It's not a riddle. How did it make you feel?

— I'm not sure. I'd have to think about it.

— Well, think about it. I've got nothing better to do.

— It made me feel sad. Wasteful. Is that right?

— I told you, it's not a riddle. But sad makes sense. Sue always said it made her sad. She said we've made life more complicated than it needs to be, and sometimes she wished she could live in a windmill in a field somewhere. Maybe we should have. Maybe a windmill would have been nice.

— At least it would be less dusty.

— Cheeky bastard.

I'm serious, but he nudges my knee again. And for a while, John reads his old poems – some aloud, some in his head. Poems about dogs and darts, about trains, about his wife. I don't usually comment unless he asks. But today I'm feeling bold.

— Why was 'Bread' your wife's favourite?

— What do you mean?

— You said it made her sad.

— It did. I suppose sometimes we need to be sad. But she was never one to dwell on things.

He closes the book. He lifts a sheet of paper from the stack on the coffee table, but lays it down again.

— Don't you have places to be? People must be dying every minute.

— They are.

— How does that work then?

— You wouldn't understand if I told you.

— Well, you're nothing if not stubborn.

John Lamb sits up straight and closes his eyes. He draws a long slow breath and holds my hand. It's cold and bony – I can feel each tendon through the loose skin.

— Come on then, Mister Death. I know why you're here. It feels different this time.

— Does it?

— Yes. You never ask me questions.

— Is there anything you'd like to do?

John opens his eyes. He takes off his glasses, folds the arms, lays them on the table.

He glances around at the home that once belonged to him and his wife and his dog. Then he smiles that classic g'morning g'morning smile. Nah, he says. Let's get on with it.

John Lamb – 81 years, 10 months, 6 days

After John, I wander some more. Along the avenue with all the cars, and up to the roundabout with the factory. I find myself drifting towards the industrial estate – not a place of living, but a place of work – with its car parks and building units, vans and lorries and exhaust smoke, but no playgrounds, no schools, no shops. It is the town that thought itself a city. Finished and unfinished, growing like a black hole, denser and emptier with time.

And I walk to the cathedral where young couples huddle on the benches eating supermarket sandwiches, and I step inside to see the woman handing out leaflets and offering a guided tour. I look at the noticeboard where children have drawn pictures of Jesus for a competition, and one of the Jesuses has sunglasses and a skateboard and a flamethrower, and the woman with the leaflets asks me to leave. She thinks I'm homeless because of my coat and the holes in my jumper, and my hair and my boots. I tell her I'm just looking at the pictures. She says, I'm going to have to ask you politely to leave. So I glance up at the decorated ceilings and arches, and I leave the cathedral and walk to the bookshop instead.

An old man drops his wallet on the pavement, but I don't want to scare him by snatching it, so I let him bend over and pick it up himself. He struggles. I wonder if he preferred it that way, grabbing it himself, or if he wishes I'd helped and thinks the world is going to hell. There's a lost teddy on a stone wall.

My flat overlooks a busy crossroad, a KFC, a few pubs. It overlooks the allotments and some newer flats for rich young commuters. It's a quiet place. Mainly old folk.

The living room is white and spotless except for the near-invisible cobwebs in the corners, and the folding table, which is always stacked with photo albums, bottles of deionized water, plastic trays and glues and scalpels, a tin of compressed air. Usually around this time in the evening I would sit at the table and set to work, but today I stand at my front door glancing around the meagre room.

I have no trinkets, no plants, barely a stick of furniture. Only the photographs over there on the table, and I can't bring myself to move from this spot in the doorway. I have felt this before. Rarely, and always unexpectedly. A great emptiness. As though my body were an atom and somewhere deep within me sits a nucleus of a person so infinitesimal I'm surprised the whole thing doesn't collapse in on itself. It almost does, right there in the doorway. But I step inside. I close the door and sit at the table, switching on the lamp.

For a few minutes I just listen to the little girl singing across the hall, and Mr Campbell's television above me.

Mr Campbell is 103 years old. He gave me his photos to restore – a whole book of them. The album is a few decades old – a yellowing plastic binder with garish cartoon flowers in the bottom right. There's a transparent pocket on the front with a piece of card reading *This album belongs to*, but no one has written a name.

Inside, the photographs are mostly black and white – a wedding, a baby, a toddler. Photographs of people in their sixties slacks and dresses, people just standing in kitchens or sitting on floral settees – no occasion, just an excuse to use the camera.

I know, of course, who each of these people is – I have met almost all of them, and over time they have known me by different names, in different shapes. I will meet the rest of them before long. Now, in these photographs, they stare back at me, fresher, carefree.

Many of the photos are stained with brownish clouds. Some are torn, others creased. Some of the oldest – the thicker, squarer ones on papery card – have begun to flake and disintegrate at the edges. A few of them have become stuck to the clear plastic that holds them in the album. And others have paled to where the faces look like ghosts – but it's okay, I remember every one of them. I will restore them until they're as pristine as the day they were developed.

Between the suicides and the heart attacks, I restore the photos. Between the strokes and the car crashes, the ladder accidents, the occasional murder, I sit at my table, buffing, dabbing, scraping, sealing, touching them up and putting them back together, and I focus on the work, on my hands, on the people in the photographs and their voices.

Today I start by cutting one of the clear pockets from the album with a scalpel. With a gentle touch, I try to tease the photo away from its plastic. Too firm, and I'll risk tearing the picture. It's stuck tight, so I fill a plastic tray with the deionized water and submerge the photo.

It's a picture of Mr Campbell – Ronny Campbell, and his sister Lilly Bennett. They're both in their twenties, playing Battleship on a flock carpet. Ron won three times in a row, and Lilly wouldn't speak to him for the rest of the night. The plastic comes away from the photograph with a little help from the scalpel. I dab the picture dry with a muslin cloth, then brush away some dirt with my thumb. And this photograph is saved.

To my right, I hear the padding of small feet and a low purr.

A white cat has come through the window in the bedroom. I don't recognize this cat, but I stand up and walk over to it, and it flirts around my ankle.

— No no, you don't live here.

I crouch, pick it up. I check for a collar, but there's none, so I carry it purring back into the bedroom and lower it out of the window so it can reach the awning it came up from.

Back at my table, I repeat the water process with the remaining stuck photographs. The Christmas jumpers. The naked boy standing in the paddling pool. The school play with the crying girl – this one has completely peeled at the upper corners so I open my little tube of glue and I—

The purring again.

This time her tail curls around the table leg, and I know this means she's about to make herself comfortable. Again, I take her in my arms and carry her to the window.

— I'm sorry, I'm sure you're a very nice cat, but you don't live here and I don't have any food.

I drop her back onto the outer ledge and she watches me as if we've been friends for many years and I'm doing her a great dishonour.

I close the curtains. I get back to work.

Within twenty minutes the cat is back, padding back and forth across the table. She lies among the photos and cleans herself.

— You're sitting on my photos.

I stop working and lean back in my chair. I watch the cat.

This morning I bought myself an apple from the shop around the corner, and I eat it now, trying to savour each bite. The papery, plasticky skin in my throat. The wet, crisp sponge of the flesh, the woody chew of the pips between my teeth. I gnaw on the stalk until it's mush, and the cat springs onto my lap. She rests her chin on her paws and closes her eyes, purring.

— You're not going to leave me alone, are you?

I gently push her off, wipe my hands on my jumper, and walk out my door to the one across the hall.

When Dalia answers the door, she's wearing pyjamas and rubber gloves. She looks concerned to see me, as if the only reason I'd knock would be an emergency – the building is on fire, or there's a murderer running around.

— Do you have any cat food?

— Cat food. Maybe, why?

— A cat has come through my window. She's hungry.

I step aside and we both look into the open doorway of my flat, at the white cat licking herself on the carpet. Dalia says, okay, wait there. She starts rummaging through the kitchen cupboards, first the top ones, then the bottom ones, including the one under the sink. She takes out all the bottles of bleach and boxes of washing powder, cans of fly spray. She places them all around her on the floor.

— I'm sure there are some biscuits somewhere. We used to have a cat, but he got squished the day we moved in.

— I appreciate you looking.

— Mum, what are you doing?

— Looking for cat food.

Their flat is much like mine, except its layout is a mirror image and it's full of ornaments and framed photos. The television is on, but no one's watching. The floor is strewn with toys, magazines, colouring books and a one-year-old pulling cushions off the sofa.

— You're the man who lives over there, aren't you?

I look down at the seven-year-old girl. Her skin is paler than her mother's, her hair fairer. She's pointing across at my living room, where the cat is still licking herself.

— That's right.

— I'm Layla. What's your name?

— Travis Smith.

— Do you want to see my game?

— Your game?

Layla glances at her mother clanking around in the cupboards. She lowers her voice.

— I'm playing a video game in my room. Come and see.

— No, I should wait here.

— Come on, I'll show you.

She takes my hand and leads me through a door to the right. Her room is small – barely big enough to contain the single bed, the wardrobe, the little chest of drawers with the hamster cage and television on top. Her walls are white like the other rooms, but she has some posters of narwhals and llamas – nature photos with facts listed down the side.

She plonks herself on the bed and picks up the controller. She tells me to sit down, and I sit beside her, watching the pixelated man run and jump over pixelated monsters.

— Do you want to try?

— No, I'd better see if your mum has found those biscuits.

— Just a quick go.

She pushes the controller into my hands.

— Press that one to jump. Hold that one if you want to go fast.

— Why do I need to go fast?

— So you can complete the level before Mum says time to get off.

— Alright.

— You died already.

— How?

— You ran into that monster.

— I didn't know it would be there.

— Well, that's the point of the game. You've got to watch out for them. It's alright, you've got two more lives.

Dalia comes into the room with a yellow box of cat biscuits. She says she's not sure how old they are, and I tell her they look fine, thank you. Layla looks at me.

— How come you've got a cat but no cat food?

— It's not my cat. She just keeps coming in.

— Right – time to get off, Stinks. Get your jammies on.

— We haven't done this level yet.

— I don't care, jammies on now.

— Can't we just finish this level?

— No, you've got school.

— Brooke's mum lets her stay up until nine.

— Well, I'm not Brooke's mum.

— Please, Mum. We're nearly done.

Dalia looks at me as if for help, and I look at Layla.

— It's okay with me. But only if it's okay with your mum.

She glances between us, trying to decide what a good mum would do.

— Five minutes. I mean it. Then bed.

Layla whoops and grabs the controller from my hands. She tells me she'll show me how to do it. Dalia shakes her head and leaves us alone.

Now Layla takes her time, collecting every coin, stomping every monster. She explores every hidden area, every power-up. And when she's finished the level, she switches off the console and the television and ushers me out of the room so she can get ready for bed. She says bye and closes the door, while her mother washes dishes at the sink.

— Biscuits are on there.

— Thank you.

I take the box, but I watch her for a moment longer. She looks tired. She grabs a plate and scrubs it with the brush. She doesn't turn her head.

∿

A VERY OLD WOMAN

She rises early, and every morning it's like waking from the dead. Sitting on the edge of her foam bed, she rubs the blood back into her elbows, her knees, her blue-veined hands – she reminds them she's still alive.

Life quickens as you age, people told her. Those childhood years are a lifetime, then things accelerate into your twenties and thirties until each year is a month, each month a week – seasons whizzing like Catherine wheels – Christmas after Christmas – terrifying and impossible and unstoppable. But nobody warned her what happens when your husband dies at seventy-four, when you're seventy-nine. They never told her how those next ten years will last forever. How every day is an exercise in waiting. They never told her that.

She makes the long walk from the bedroom, through the endless hallway, hands brushing the walls for balance, to the kitchen where she carries the kettle to the sink, fills it, carries it back to its base. Her spine is a wooden post she carries like a scarecrow. Tiny shuffle steps, bare feet peeling from the lino. The human life is a cycle, she's learnt. We start pathetic, we end pathetic. Perhaps, she thinks, we weren't meant to last this long.

It's not that she can't live without him. She just never wanted to. She lived a life with the man she chose and now she's in a new phase, a superfluous phase, where his voice doesn't exist, where his smell doesn't exist. They arrived on this planet separately. They found one another. They spent more years together than apart. And when he left her alone, she was halved, and now she's ready to become no person at all.

She debates whether to stand and wait for the kettle to boil or go and sit in the living room. Yesterday she waited until her knees seized up and then she couldn't sit down, but if she goes and sits down, she'll have to get back up again – and now she realizes she hasn't even flicked the kettle on. She flicks it on and shuffles towards the living room.

Maybe she could speak to Mason about buying a walking frame, and maybe a bar stool for the kitchen. Then she could sit while the kettle boils, and it would be tall enough for her to easily slide back onto her feet. Maybe she could watch the garden through the kitchen window, watch the birds.

Some might even think it's weak, to mope about like this. You're an independent woman, love. He didn't define you, dear. There's life in you yet. But she learnt long ago, there's no life better than a life shared. To fully give it, and take it, until one isn't complete without the other. They never told her that.

She shuffles to her armchair in the living room. It's a long way down. And the precise moment her backside hits the cushion, the doorbell rings.

Leave it, she thinks. You're not expecting anyone. They'll go away. Sit in silence. Don't switch the telly on yet. Leave it. The doorbell rings again, and they say her name, and it's a man's voice, and she knows who it is.

With her hands on the arm of the chair, she heaves herself back up just as the kettle clicks off in the kitchen. When she opens the door, there's a tall man who looks as though he's in his late thirties. Average-looking, a little scruffy. Baggy grey jumper, black jeans, old shoes.

I say hello, and she lets me in.

She offers me a cup of tea, and I say yes, I'd love one.

— You know where the kettle is. Just boiled.

Breathless, she sits back down and switches on the telly. She enjoys the holiday and property programmes — all the happy people with too much money — somehow it humbles her.

In the kitchen, I drop a couple of teabags into the cups, pour in the water and let them brew for a minute. I stir in two sugars for her and bring the drinks into the living room, sitting on the pouffe near the television.

— You've never made me a decent cuppa.

And we sit in silence for some time, she and I, watching the beautiful young couples in their beautiful landscapes of palm trees and oceans so blue they hurt your eyes. The young man says, the pool is too small. Couldn't swing a cat in there.

She clears her throat.

— So, is today my lucky day?

I look at her, but I don't answer.

I look back at the television.

— I'm ready, Travis. You must know I'm ready. For goodness' sake, I've been ready for ten years. What's the point in keeping me here, hmm? I'm done. I lived a long and happy life, and blah blah blah, and now it's done. Are you really going to drag it out? Until I'm sick and fragile? Travis, will you bloody look at me?

— How are you feeling today?

She laughs, shaking her head.

— Like a very old woman. Old and brittle as a gingerbread woman in a nightie. Make yourself useful. Go and fetch the biscuits, will you?

I do as I'm told, grabbing the red tub from the cupboard next to the fridge, resting it on her lap. She opens it – the sweet wheaty whiff of malted milks and custard creams, a couple of old digestives. She never cared much for digestives, but she stares at them now. She doesn't move.

— You know, when Nicholas died I wasn't sad. I mean, I was *sad* of course, but it's not tragic, is it? Not in the same way that a young person dying is tragic. Old people are supposed to die. We all know you're coming for us. But Nicholas, he wasn't ready. I think he would have liked to die after me, so I'd never be on my own. I didn't think I was ready either, but when you took him, I knew I was. There's a certain dignity to it, isn't there? Bowing out while you still have all your faculties – while you still know who you are. I expected you'd come for me before long.

Now she looks at me, glossy-eyed.

— You don't know what it's like, Travis. You think you do, but you don't. To lose someone so important, and to live all those years without them.

I know she's not just talking about Nicholas.

— Is it even your decision? Do you choose who stays and who leaves? Do you choose when, and how? Or are you just a servant? Just a force of nature?

I sip my tea. And when she realizes I won't answer, she takes a custard cream from the tub and dips it, watching the young couple drink margaritas on the balcony.

◌

Around the corner from a closed-down pub lies a strip of houses where the front doors open directly onto the road. A ditch runs behind the houses, alongside the little gardens – murky water flowing from a corrugated pipe. Each house is a different colour – a grimy duck-egg, a dripping grey-white, an exposed brick, a flaky pastille yellow. I knock at the brick one.

Inside, the children race up and down the stairs, squabbling over a superhero mask while the mum tries to sleep and the dad dismantles his motorbike at the kitchen table. He yells for the kids to shut the fuck up. They don't, so he says it again and puts a bit more throat into it. He can't even think straight – he was counting bolts, and now he doesn't know what goes where or why he's even dismantling this bike in the first place.

This man, this dad, was the world's best dad for his first and second child. But somewhere around the third and fourth, he grew too accustomed to it. He grew so accustomed to being a father, he forgot himself, and a numbness crept through his muscles and his face until his life was a viscous liquid in which he could barely keep afloat, and now he couldn't love those children if he tried. Of course he loves them. He would protect them with his life. But he doesn't love them the way those kids love that superhero mask. He doesn't feel it. He can't look at these children and feel excited, or proud, or thankful – he's too close, like trying to read the words of a page your nose is touching. Maybe if he could live somewhere else for six months, he'd come back and see them anew. But he'll never have those six months, and he won't feel a thing until exactly one year after the youngest leaves home, his motorbike still in bits in the kitchen.

The little girl is crying now, and the boys give her the mask, and the house is quiet for the first time since dawn. Now the dad hears a knocking at the door.

He answers it, he sees me. A flicker of confusion – am I a delivery driver, a Jehovah's witness? Have I come to pick up the slide? But he sees the photo album in my hands. This one is purple with *Precious Moments* stamped in silver cursive.

— Ah, brilliant. Thanks, mate. Did you manage to salvage any of them, or…?

— All of them.

— Cheers. My mum will be well happy with that.

He takes the album, thumbs through a few pages. He doesn't know most of the people in the pictures – they're his parents' friends and second aunts and great-uncles.

— Brill. How much do I owe you?

— It's fine.

— You sure? Nah, that's not right.

He lays the album on the table near the door and digs into his pocket for his wallet. He pulls out some money and thrusts it at me. I find it's easier just to take it, so I take it, and we both stand there in the doorway. He has that look on his face – a look I've seen many times. Like he met me years ago but can't remember where.

— Do you want to come in for a coffee or anything?

His little girl rushes through the hallway in her mask and nylon cape.

— No.

— Alright. Well, cheers for that. Much appreciated.

He nods at me and gently closes the door. He walks past his daughter, back into the kitchen, back to his exploded bike parts.

A short walk from the flat there's an allotment. A hideout of flowers and vegetables and colourful sheds surrounded by crumbling brick walls. It smells of herbs and compost, sometimes of pollen. I have a plot – a patch of earth the size of a coffee table – bursting with a mishmash of plants, and I sit on the little stool that I keep here, and I watch them grow.

The morning is cold and bright, and quiet but for the muffled traffic beyond the walls. The gardeners smile to one another, but we rarely speak. If someone does talk, it's to congratulate a neighbour on their potatoes or their cherry tomatoes. The compliment is then returned, and that's enough for another year. That's how they like it. Our little sanctuary, our monastery, a temple of quiet in the loudness of the world, and our role is simply to tend the plants.

I don't know the names of these plants, but they're pretty and they grow on top of each other and through one another, and they need very little care. I close my eyes for a few minutes and listen to the gentle clinking of forks and trowels, a crunch of roots, the pigeons in the willows, a shiver of leaves, the purr of engines. The rhythm of the world. It ebbs and it flows and swells and grows like a restless heartbeat.

And when I walk along the river beyond the industrial estate, I count the objects in the water – the trolley, the nappies, the mattress, the bicycle – and it's all so disgusting and gorgeous, so useful, that I construct the items into houses in my mind, a place for me to sleep, a place to hide when it all gets too much, with the brown water, and the fish caught in the car spring, the silt and the sludge and the bridge and the marsh with the seashells embedded in the muck and reeds. These marshes lay beneath the sea until they dug the ditches and drained it off, and now it's a land so flat these humans have forgotten what hills look like. It's all open and exposed without perspective, just a cut-out of a world, and there's the bridge that spins to let the boats pass, and atop the bridge is a wooden hut with nothing in it but a man at a chair, and a lever, and a phone, and a stack of faded magazines. I stay and watch the bridge as it

swivels, clanking and grinding on its axis, before swivel-
ling, clanking and grinding back.

At the train station, everything is normal but for the man
in his thirties, about to jump. People don't know this yet –
they bob around on the platform, they kick the air absently,
they scroll on phones and bloat their brains with anything
they can find in these nothing-minutes. They read the
signs, even the boring ones. They watch strangers, and they
are all strangers, and the strangers watch the strangers. They
think about where they're going. Some of them listen to
music. Some of them talk, but it's filler, it's idle, and there's
a train approaching. It happens so fast, the strangers will
think about it for weeks – the man in his thirties, he jumps
in front of the approaching train. He jumps like a starfish,
and the front of the train hits him. There is no blood, no
guts. The train wasn't travelling fast enough to burst him.
Instead there's a metallic thud, a screech of brakes, and the
man seems to hang onto the front of the train forever. A
cartoon coyote, splatted on the wall. Gasps, a shriek or two.
A teenager in a hoodie shields his girlfriend's eyes. The
starfish man falls and slips beneath the wheels.

Fifteen people saw the man jump. Ten of them ask
themselves why they feel almost nothing – they witnessed
this horrific episode, yet they feel little more than they'd
feel if they saw it on television and knew it was fiction –
and *that* feeling is the one that will bother them for weeks.
The fire engines arrive. The police. The replacement trains
arrive on a different platform, and the people who watched

the man jump, they board their trains and they miss any aftermath. And later when they google the incident, they'll read about the scene they saw with their own eyes, and they'll read that he died later in hospital, and they'll hear rumours that he was a terrorist, he had a USB stick in his back pocket and was running from the police – he ran out of options, chose to end it, served him right, still sad though, no it's not, and they try to picture his mangled legs beneath the wheels of the train.

∾

A FEARLESS BOY

There is a quiet bedroom, and in the quiet bedroom there's a nightlight in the shape of a hot air balloon. The nightlight glows a pinkish red, bathing the room in a rosy tint. White painted clouds. A money box in the shape of a digger. And in the dark wooden cot there is a baby in a blue romper, his fingers curled at his pink lips.

I step across the room, over the rainbow rug, and I sit on the stool where his mother feeds him in those long nights. I can smell him. He smells of her milk. And the sweet smell with the pink glow of the room leaves me drunk like a fly in honey. And I watch him for an hour, this little boy. This little boy with the blue romper and the tuft of black hair.

People will say, he might have done this, he could have done that. Could've been a footballer. Could've travelled the world, got married. Could've been, might've done, would've seen, tried, tasted, loved. But they're wrong, he never could've. There is only this. A short story, without an arc or a resolution. Just a boy who was there one day and gone the next.

They will be sad, because sad is what it is, and the sadness comes in many colours – the vibrant shock and disbelief in a few hours when she finds you, then a more muted colour for many years after that, and finally a subtle, more abstract kind of colour until I come and take them too.

But you, little boy, you won't feel a thing. You're dreaming of floating around inside your mother, and it is warm, and it is safe – you wouldn't change a moment passed. This bedroom was the home they made for you, and it was a good home – familiar, with all its softness, and they tried. They wanted much more for you. They thought you'd be here forever.

Now I'll reach through the bars of your cot and touch your little hand. I won't tell you that it's okay, because you're fearless. You never learnt to be frightened.

And as your breathing slows, and your mouth dries, and your fingers run cold, I'll recite a bedtime story I thought you might like.

Noah Finch – 0 years, 5 months, 29 days

Some nights when my head is loud, I wander the streets
like a stray cat and I try to dampen the noise by humming.
I'm inside everything, everyone, everywhere, between it
and through it, every seed in every pod, every fragment
of gravel, that blade of grass leaning against that blade
of grass, and I squeeze my eyes shut and walk like that,
fists clenched, the beauty of everything, the handprint
on the window, the porch with the flickering light. I am
tired and awake, and I think about the little family across
the hall, the midwife and her girls, and I think about the
rotten bodies, stiffening then loosening, bloating blue,
their skin taut and papery, gums receding to reveal the
longer teeth, the longer hair, the longer fingernails, and
I can feel the man farting as his wife spoons him and she
calls him a smelly bugger but doesn't let go, and how
about the baby who at this very moment almost chokes
on the tiny plastic shoe, but doesn't, and no one notices
so nothing matters, or the woman praying to God that
her husband dies, or the vinyl record buried in the garden
with all the little glass bottles, and the woman who dances
after hours in the hall with the mirrored walls, no, no,
hum hum hum. And I'll walk and walk until the sun
screams over the rooftops, long shadows, and she brushes
her teeth and spits in the toilet because the sink is blocked,
and he measures his penis with his phone, then measures
his phone, and I walk and walk and walk and walk — the
man with the brittle brown Christmas tree in his garden,

he gives it one swift kick and all the needles shower to the
grass, and he saws it up and throws it in the brown bin –
and the girl makes herself sick and weighs herself again.
Someone's spilt white paint in the road. The swept-up
bird bones in the gutter and the lads playing football
on the green. A mattress propped against a paper birch.
The mattress has been there for three weeks, sagging and
weeping with rain, soaked up, swelling, collapsed like
a lung with black spots creeping from bottom to top,
bottom to top, once a warm place, once a sleepy dreamy
dry place. A tyre flat for so long it's adopted its new shape,
all sad and dry and cracked like lips. Roy backhands his
wife in the kitchen, gravy smell, fumbling pans, she spits
at his feet, locks the bathroom door and calls her brother
who keeps his crowbar in the car, and I am everywhere
and always, and it never stops. It never gives me rest, not
even for a second. I rub my eyes until the sparkles fill the
black. There's too much. There's not enough. Take it
away. Give me more.

And when there's nowhere left to wander, when I have no
photos to restore, when there are no more books to read,
I tend to sit on the floor in the middle of my living room
and plug my ears with my thumbs and press my index
fingers into my eyes until everything rumbles. But even
in the rumbling, the thoughts are still there. Even in the
rumbling, I wander.

When I open my eyes, a piece of paper has been slid
beneath my door. It's a hand-drawn invitation – *Come to*

my 8th birthday, with a time, and a date, and a location: *right across the hall.*

The cat crunches her biscuits in my kitchen, and I find that I've been staring at the birthday invitation for close to an hour. Layla has drawn four stick people and there's an arrow pointing to each. 'Mum' is the second tallest stick figure, with scratchy black hair and a triangle dress. Then there's 'Neda', the smallest – little more than a blob at Mum's feet. 'Me' is the second smallest, in the middle. She has a triangle dress too, and shorter, browner hair than Mum, with an orange party hat. To the right of 'Me', is 'You' – the tallest, with scribbly black hair, and what appears to be a games controller in his hand. I'm not sure why I should spend so much time looking at this drawing, except that I rarely see myself drawn as part of such a cosy arrangement. We each have smiles. Our hands are almost touching.

I Blu-tack the invitation to the wall above my photo-restoration station. And as I press my thumb into the final corner, she knocks at my door.

I answer it. The girl with the triangle dress.

— Well?

— Well, what?

— Did you get my invitation?

— I did. It's over there on the wall.

Layla walks in and sees the invitation. It's the only thing hanging on the wall, and she seems proud of that.

— We're having pasta bake. Do you like pasta bake?

— Layla, I'm not coming.

— What? Why not?

— I can't. But I hope you have a lovely birthday with lots of presents and cake.

— But it's my birthday.

— I know.

— Why won't you come then?

I kneel so our eyes are level, rest my hand on her shoulder.

— Layla, please don't come to my door again.

— Mum says it's okay.

— It's not. I'm sorry.

Her eyelids narrow, trying to figure out if I'm joking – surely I'm joking – but when she realizes I'm telling the truth, her eyes shimmer and her cheeks flush.

— What's the matter with you?

— Nothing. I'm just very busy and I have my own things to take care of.

— No you don't. You just sit in here alone all night – we can hear your music. If you didn't like us, why didn't you just say?

— Layla.

She punches me in the gut and snatches the invitation off the wall.

Cheeks wet, she runs back to her door. She slams it behind her.

I stand up and listen to her muffled voice as she curses me to her mother.

At six in the morning, Layla sneaks out of her bedroom. She's wearing her narwhal slippers and her narwhal nightie with the rainbows. She pads into the living room, yawning, and she slumps on the sofa to watch her cartoons. The television beams into the dark room with all its colour – the yellow backdrop behind the TV presenter, and all the drawings the children have sent in. Layla turns the volume down to number three and hugs a cushion and curls her legs, resting her head on the arm of the sofa. The baby kept her up again last night, crying. These short hours between six and school are the rare moments when the world is quiet. Sometimes she even switches the volume down to zero, just watching the cartoon families, the dog mums and dog dads, and she imagines what they might be saying. They're always perfect families, always laughing, never shouting. Layla finds it all a bit silly, but they make her feel fuzzy and calm.

Around seven, Neda starts crying. This is Layla's cue to pour herself some cornflakes with a splash of milk. She sits back on the sofa in time for the next cartoon – the little girl and her pet duck. Layla wouldn't mind a pet duck.

— Morning, Stinks. You been up long?

— Just got up.

— I would have done your breakfast.

— I know. I was starving.

Her mum walks into the little kitchen, divided from the living room by a few cupboards and a countertop. She feeds Neda in one arm and makes Layla's packed lunch with the other. She's not wearing any make-up, and her hair looks crazy – still, Layla is always amazed at how her mum can butter bread and cut off the crusts one-handed. Mum looks at Layla over the cupboards.

— You look tired, Stinks. Did Neda keep you up again?

— No. I just couldn't sleep. I was excited about the Easter stuff at school.

— Where's your bonnet?

— On my floor.

— Silly – I told you not to put it on the floor. You'll end up treading on it or falling on it and that'll be it.

— I won't tread on it.

Layla spoons a heap of cornflakes into her mouth and listens to them crunch in her head. She'd never step on her Easter bonnet. Her mum spent all week putting it together – a straw hat with coloured feathers, daisies, little eggs, and a nest full of chicks on top. Layla didn't want to shove it in the wardrobe with loads of other things. She wanted to keep it in the middle of the floor where she'd always see it. And today, her whole class will see it.

— I've put your dungarees on my bed, and your wellies are near the door.

Layla manages to watch one more episode before she drinks the sweet milk of her breakfast and puts her bowl in the sink. She brushes her teeth, washes her face, pulls on her clothes and looks for the finishing touch – her fairy wings. They're not in the toy box and they're not under the bed. They're not in her drawer or at the bottom of the wardrobe.

— Mum, I can't find my fairy wings.

— Fairy wings? I thought you wanted to be a farmer.

— Yeah, a fairy farmer I said.

— Baby, I think we gave those to the charity shop. You never wore them.

— We gave my old pair to the charity shop, but I've got another pair. I wore them last week, but I can't find them.

— Have you checked the toy box?

— Yes.

— Well, there are only so many places they could be – they're massive. Let me get ready and I'll have a look.

— Alright.

— Go and get your wellies on.

— Okay.

And Layla sits on the arm of the sofa, catching a few more cartoons, but her eyes wander through her mum's bedroom door. She watches her mum pulling on her socks and pants, brushing her hair, brushing on a quick bit of make-up. Neda stands at the bed, gurgling, pulling the covers off, and their mum keeps putting them back. Neda is still in her sleepsuit, and she won't be dressed until it's time for crèche.

— Alright, Stinks. Get your book bag.

— But my fairy wings.

— Fairy wings. Right. A quick look.

Her mum checks in all the same places Layla has – the toy box, the drawers, under the bed. She checks a few extra places, random ones – under the pillow, on top of the wardrobe, in the bin.

— They're not here.

— I know.

— Where did you last see them?

— In here.

— Well, they're not here now. I'm sorry, baby, but you'll have to leave them. We're going to be late. You can be a fairy farmer next time.

Her mum grabs the keys, her phone, her bag. She glances around for anything else she might have forgotten, mouthing the names of the things she's remembered.

— Bonnet.

Layla picks up her bonnet. She looks at it again, but she sees it differently now, knowing the fairy wings are missing. Now she's just a farmer with chicks on her head.

— I really wanted to be a fairy farmer.

— I know you did. I guess you're a dairy farmer instead. Or maybe you're not a farmer who's a fairy, you're a farmer who farms fairies.

— That's horrible.

— Get your book bag.

— Why are they farming fairies?

— We have to go. Where's your lunch bag and your book bag?

— My book bag is broken. The zip fwoinged off.

— You'll just have to carry it as best you can – come *on*.

Layla learnt the art of saying *okay* in a tone that means *that's not okay*, and she says it now as she grabs her book bag and her mum nudges her through the door. They walk down the stairs, the baby in her mother's arms, and into the car park where the little car waits.

Mum straps Neda into the baby seat in the front while Layla straps herself in the back with her bonnet on her lap. A rumble of thunder and her mum glances at the sky.

— You haven't got your coat. Are you going to be alright without your coat?

— Yeah. We don't even go outside when it's raining.

— Wait there, I'll get it.

— It's okay, Mum.

Layla's mum locks the car and rushes back into the flat. From where Layla is sitting, she can see Neda in her baby seat. Neda is enjoying a lovely sleep now, after keeping everyone up all night. Layla knows some siblings at school who are friends, like the siblings in the cartoons, but she can't imagine ever being friends with Neda. She's annoying, and useless, and pretty stupid even for a baby. She doesn't walk properly, she mainly shuffles herself along on her bum and pulls herself up using table legs or chair legs or human legs. Looking at her now, Layla feels nothing.

Her mum comes back, breathless. She hasn't brought Layla's coat.

— Sorry, babies, my phone rang.

Her hair is a mess again, and she slides into the car just as the clouds burst. The rain is loud on the car's roof.

— That was lucky. Just missed it. Got everything?

— Yes.

— Got my purse. Got the baby. Let's go.

She starts the car, backs out of the car park and straight into a queue of traffic.

At the old flat, they could walk to school. But when they moved, Layla's mum gave her the choice of moving schools or staying put. She chose to stay put, and she's felt guilty about it ever since. The journey always makes her want to cry – the congestion, her mum's swearing, the clock ticking away.

But today, Layla's mum turns off the main street.

— Where are we going?

— I think we can miss all that traffic if we go this way.

— Is it a shortcut?

— Not really, but at least we'll be moving.

Layla looks out of the rainy window. A few unfamiliar turns, and the town dissolves into fields and winding roads with ditches on both sides. No traffic in sight. Just a mum, a baby and a non-fairy farmer.

— Mum, do you know where you're going?

— Yeah, I used to bike this way all the time.

Layla smiles at that. She likes imagining her mother younger, doing younger things.

The rain falls harder, and it's soothing. Layla could almost fall asleep.

But the car chokes, rolls to the side of the road, and stops.

— Bloody thing.

— Mum?

— Bloody, bloody thing. Please not again.

Her mum switches off the engine, waits a few seconds, turns the key. The car sounds like it's not even trying – a wheezing, insolent sort of noise. The sort of noise Neda makes when she doesn't want her bath. Her mum tries the car eight times. She waits longer between each try, except for the last couple which are quicker and more hopeless.

— Shit and balls. Absolute piece of crap. Sorry, baby.

— What are we going to do?

— We'll have to walk. It's not far.

— It looks far.

— It's really not. See that church? That's the one right near your school.

— That's miles. I can hardly even see it.

— Well, we don't really have a choice. At least you're wearing wellies.

Layla's mum gets out of the car and walks to the other side to fetch the baby. She pulls Neda's canopy over the car seat, unclips it so it's a carry cot, then opens the child-locked door for Layla. The downpour is relentless. The kind of rain that feels like a bully, like you're being punished for even daring to step foot in it. But they walk the long rural road. Out here in the open fields, the world feels like it goes on forever. The road disappears over the horizon in both directions, and the sky is metal grey.

— My bonnet's getting wet!

— Give it here.

Her mum rests the bonnet gently on top of Neda, below the canopy. Neda wakes and starts grumbling. She doesn't like the bonnet. Mum hushes her, says it'll only be a few minutes.

— It's still getting wet. The eggs are falling off.

— There's nothing I can do, is there? What do you want me to do?

— I don't know.

— Where's your book bag?

— In the car.

— For god's sake, Layla.

— I'll run back and get it.

— Leave it. You'll have to say you forgot it. You've got your lunch, yeah? We're so bloody late. So bloody late. Why didn't I bring an umbrella? I could see it was going to rain.

— You didn't know the car would break down.

— No, that's right. I didn't know the car would break down.

Neda's grumbling builds to a full tantrum and Mum hands the bonnet back to Layla.

— Mum, it's getting all—

— I know! Alright, Layla? I know. I need you to be a big girl here. I know the bonnet is getting wet, but there's nothing I can do. I can't pull a brolly out of my arse. You'll have to try and fix it when you get to school. Stop crying. I mean it — stop crying. Right now. We haven't got time. Your bloody book bag as well, for god's sake. I'm gonna be late for work. I said stop crying, Layla.

Layla stands as still as she can, concentrating on holding back the tears. Her mum stomps off through the sheets of rain. Layla looks at her bonnet, all sticky with wet glue, the feathers all crooked and clumped, the chicks sitting in a pond.

The rain slows. Layla stops crying. She follows her mother.

Now Dalia stops walking. She rests the car seat on the road and holds her face in her hands.

— Mum?

— I'm okay.

— Mum, I'm sorry about being annoying. It's okay about the bonnet. I'll fix it when I get to school – maybe Brooke will let me borrow some feathers. And I remember where the fairy wings are now, I left them at Brooke's. I'm sorry for moaning.

She crouches to Layla's height. She holds her little cheeks in both hands.

— I don't want you to say sorry. I'm sorry. I just wanted you to have a good day, and it's turned into a nightmare, hasn't it?

— I will have a good day.

At those words, Layla watches her mum's lip wobble. She looks like she might cry. But she holds it together, and she smiles, and tells Layla she's a good kid. Then she pulls her phone from her bag.

— What are you doing?

— Calling Neda's dad.

— Why?

— He can pick us up.

Dalia puts the phone to her ear.

— I thought you didn't like talking to him.

— Well, sometimes I have to. Hello? Solomon. The car's— Yeah. Again. I don't know. It made a funny noise and just stopped and it won't start again. I don't think it's the battery. It might be— Yeah, I did. Yeah… Sorry, I know you're at work… Yeah, so if you drive to the flat, then go the way I go to school, but take the first left down Mason Avenue, just keep going down that road and you'll see us… First left… Okay. Thanks, Solomon. See you in a bit.

Layla's mum puts her phone in her pocket.

She kisses Layla's head and picks up the car seat.

Come on, she says. Let's go and wait in the car.

❧

Mother runs with fawn in tow. An acre of woods near the garden centre roundabout – a windy night, harder to hear the cars, but the mother knows only one thing. Find the next home. This one lasted us well, but you've outgrown it, love. I'll find you a new one if it ends me.

She peeks her head from the brambles, almost gets her skull taken off by an articulated lorry. Big yellow lights and a whoosh. Fawn waits. Mother bolts to the roundabout, fawn follows. Three cars pass – each of them lighting up the scene – the mother and the fawn like a Christmas card, but for their white glowing eyes and stark shadows. They stand still, as if camouflaged, but they're not. After the fourth car, she bolts again, fawn follows, lolloping down the bank of the road, through a strip of overgrown foot-path, along the outskirts of a barley field, towards the copse she'd scouted two nights ago.

Fawn watches the barley shimmer in the breeze. The copse on the horizon – black against the brownish clouds. This copse will be their new home. Fawn thinks about the acre he grew up in, and he thinks about his mother. She's all he's ever known. He liked it better before he knew about cars and lorries.

The mother contemplates moving through the barley, or toeing the perimeter of the field. On the perimeter, they're exposed. In the barley, monsters might lurk. She raises her head, pricks up her ears, waits, deathly still.

She creeps along the right edge of the field, and fawn follows. She listens to the traffic behind them, and to the rustle of the barley, she feels fawn brush against her back legs. She doesn't take her eyes from the copse.

They make it halfway across the field before there are lights again. Not from a car or a lorry, but something she's never seen. A hulking, hundred-eyed creature with rumbling turbine mouth chewing up the field. It has spider arms, and it breathes smoke, and it's heading towards them. Again, the mother stops. Fawn stops. If they stay still, per-haps the spider won't see them. It grumbles and shrieks – a slow rampage through the barley, inhaling it, churning it, spitting it out. And when it's obvious the beast won't be stopped, mother deer bolts again, and fawn follows. Now she will not look back. She will not stop until she's reached the copse. Across the lumpy edge, they flee. Fawn falls. Tumbles end-over-end across the dirt.

The mother stops, turns, nudges fawn back to his feet. They're off again, and the mother almost breaks her leg in a rabbit hole, but they prance in the wind with the spider's roar close behind – and they're here. The copse. The next home. They're here.

Fawn's heart flits like a hummingbird's, and the two of them stand in the entrance for a while. But when his heart slows, fawn peers around at this new place. It's larger than the last one. Shadowier. The trees are gnarlier, denser. Instead of the packed earth he grew up with, the ground here is spongy with needles and moss. His mother nuzzles his neck. Fawn bounces on the loamy soil.

Old stag waits in the shadows. Old stag sees these new arrivals and steps from the brush. He bolts forward and thrusts his antlers straight into fawn's belly, tearing him open, spilling his entrails to the soft ground. Fawn buckles to his front knees, gushing, rushing. He quivers, bows his head.

Mother bolts back across the barley field and never returns to the copse.

&

A HELMET HEAD

At eight o'clock, I visit Dan. Dan lives down a street with cars parked on both sides and hardly any road between them. He's thirty-eight but looks fifty, and when he slumps to the door his face brightens to see me. He's skinny-fat – all rib bones and gut, and a head like a miniature version of his torso – shiny, pale, stretched. Running shorts, red vest. He steps aside, ushering me in with one hand clutching an energy drink, and a smile like he's inviting me into a five-star hotel. I wade through layers of pizza boxes, beer boxes, delivery boxes, clothes, rubbish sacks, a toppled chair. Somewhere near the stairs, a vacuum cleaner peeks its sorry head.

I make my way to the living room – a quarry of crap around the computer desk, milk bottles full of dark orange liquid. There's a smell of grease, of piss and shit, and some more complex notes of mould, dust, dead animal.

Today I'm dressed in navy overalls and heavy boots.

— Do you want to start in the hallway? I've got bin bags in the kitchen.

— Bin bags would be good.

— Right-oh.

He coughs a black syrupy cough and sweeps towards the kitchen. I like Dan because he's messy in the same way a monk is tranquil. And while he fetches the bin bags, I lay my sports bag atop the mound of stuff that was once a sofa, and I pull out some rubber gloves. Dan comes back, I hold out a pair for him.

— What are these for?

— For cleaning. I'd appreciate some help.

— I don't really clean. I mean, look at the place. That's why they sent you.

— It won't take long.

Dan looks at the pink gloves in my hands. He looks at me. And somewhere in his helmet head, he knows exactly what today is. He nods.

— There we go.

Together, gloves on, we shuffle back into the hallway and scoop up big bundles of junk in our arms. Heaps of cardboard and foil, cans and bubble wrap and tissues – all of it dumped into the black bags. We hold the bags open for each other. We tie knots in them, sling them out the front door, tear fresh ones from the roll. We uncover plates and bowls and cutlery, we uncover ornaments, like two archaeologists. We use a discarded receipt to pinpoint the exact moment Dan abandoned washing up and began eating from trays. Inch by inch, the carpet is revealed – all stained and discoloured, but it's a carpet. It is a carpet.

Dan wipes his shiny head on his arm.

— Bet this is the worst house you've ever seen.

— It's a good house.

— Upstairs is clean. I don't go up there.

— Okay.

— I didn't mean to let it get like this, honestly. You throw one box on the floor, the next thing you know it's twenty.

I peel another plate from the floor and lay it upon the stack on the stairs.

— It's not like I have anyone to clean up for. Who am I cleaning up for? Friends all moved away, family are useless. Doesn't feel worth it. That makes sense, doesn't it?

He ties a knot in another bag and passes it to me. I toss it through the front door. And we stand in the hallway, marvelling at our good work. It still stinks. It's still dirty and crusted with grime. There's a brown shoreline on

the wall where the rubbish reached, but the place is clear.
There are three other rooms filled to the light switches, but
this one is done. Dan can walk without wading, and I can
see it's unfamiliar to him.

His face turns pink and he bites his index finger.

He tells me he knows who I am. He tells me he knows
why I'm here. He says he's not ready, and he'll try harder.
He knows he hasn't looked after himself. He just needs a
friend, he says. Just one good friend. He's not ready. He's
not ready.

But the rot in his lungs is like a tree, with its roots all
green and dusty with spores and lichen. And as he panics
about what's going to happen next, he coughs, and sits on
the stairs beside the plates.

I sit on the floor, at his feet, my hand on his knee. I like
Dan. I love him.

— If this is the end, why do all this? Why tidy up and
make things better?

I don't answer him because there is no answer. He holds
his head in his hands, and his breath is pizza crumbs and
the fluff down the back of the sofa, it's the silica gel you
mustn't eat and the hairs down the plughole, and the black
mould creeping up the wall behind the fridge. He holds my
hand. He squeezes it as he sobs, and when they find him,
they'll say, poor bloke. Looks like he was trying to turn
his life around. Stinks of shit. Poor bloke. It's bad for you,
breathing all that in.

Dan Harper – 38 years, 1 month, 12 days

In the birthing ward, Dalia remembers the technique her old art teacher taught her. To see the world in shapes and colours. *Values*, he called them — light to dark. The details fade from the white room. A mother cries on the bed, but all Dalia sees is the blue rectangle of the mattress, the figure splayed on top with her legs in an M.

A red shape says something. He says it again and again, and Dalia looks at him. This red shape, the father, he says something in Polish, and his voice is sharp with universal worry — he's asking about his wife. Dalia feels a panic attack brewing in her chest.

The other two midwives mill about at the mother's legs, but Dalia stays at the head, trying to offer comfort. The baby is in distress. The heart rate is slowing. Dalia believes the baby's shoulder is stuck behind the mother's pelvic bone. She relays this to the father in English, hoping some of the tone might carry over in that same universal language.

The obstetrician will be here soon, she says.

Dalia doesn't realize she's trembling until the mother grabs her hand, firm. A mother in pain. She's been in labour for three hours and she's frightened for her child. And the whoosh whoosh whoosh of the ultrasound, with the crying of the mother and the jabbering of the father, and the murmuring of the midwives with their feet shuffling on the tacky floor, it surrounds Dalia's head like a sparkling shadow where there's no air and no exit. The mother

releases her grip on Dalia's hand and grabs her arm instead.
She says some words, but all Dalia sees is a round pale mask
with a black mouth hole. And Dalia disappears.

She tumbles back, back, back – to her first delivery. Five
years ago. A simple hour of pushing, and a healthy baby
at the end. She'd been so confident then, it was simple.
But later that year, one bad birth was enough to ruin her.
Now every time an infant's heart rate drops, Dalia sees that
same purple baby they pulled out – the same agony on
the mother's face, contorted in a way Dalia never knew a
person's face could contort, eyes so distended that it was
like the mother was peering into some extra dimension
where all the dead babies are kept – and Dalia sees all this
now, in this room, with these Polish parents. She can see
the baby in that fleshy tunnel, stuck, believing this is what
life is – nine months of comfort, then you're squeezed into
a tube and you die. The baby will die. It's happening again.

One of the other midwives says her name. Dalia blinks.
They're saying, put pressure on the mother's abdomen.
We'll try to ease the baby around the bone. Dalia does as
she's told, pressing with her palm, just below the mother's
popped-out belly button. She can feel the baby. She can
feel its shoulder. The mother cries out.

The whoosh whoosh whoosh of the ultrasound slows
to a wumph. Wumph. Wumph. Wumph. The father
starts jabbering again, louder now – he knows something's
wrong and he demands answers he won't understand.

Now the obstetrician arrives. No sooner does he walk
through the curtain than his hands are inside the woman,

feeling where the baby is, figuring out what's blocked where. Dalia bolts straight back to the mother's side. The mother is delirious, her face dripping with tears and snot. She stops speaking, her head rolls back, and Dalia knows this woman has given up. She, like Dalia, knows the baby will die.

The obstetrician directs the other midwives.

They hand him the forceps. The mother stares at the ceiling.

Now Dalia takes the mother's head in her hands. Firm but gentle – one mother to another. The mother looks into her eyes. And without a word, Dalia assures her that everything will be okay. Look at me, she says in her silent language – everything will be okay. Everything will be fine. The baby will live. And the mother nods.

Now the shapes and colours sharpen, and Dalia sees the room more clearly than she ever has. Every dial on every piece of equipment, every laminated poster on every wall, each thread on the doctor's coat, every hair on the mother's leg. In this moment, Dalia has never seen the world in such definition. And she watches the boy emerge with the forceps – long-headed, slicked with rhubarb and custard, and very much alive.

Most lunchtimes she locks herself in her car in the hospital car park and this is when she can finally breathe. In this airlock, she can breathe. She doesn't switch on the radio, she doesn't eat anything, she just sits and stares at the hedge outside the windscreen, and her mind is all hush and rush,

all white noise and disjointed thoughts, but she doesn't
fight it, she lets it all happen, just a passenger, a listener.
Her breathing slows. Her hands stop trembling. She thinks
about the happy mother with her suckling baby. And,
by one o'clock, she's ready to go back inside and do it all
again.

In a quiet nook of a lifeless galaxy, two planets collide.
From a safe distance, they appear to be unmoving – two
bubbles sealed together by a halo of blue light. It is a silent
and awesome spectacle, a rare feat of nature witnessed
by no one. Great slow ripples warp across the surface of
each planet as rocks and plasma and dust are ejected into
the void. This debris will become new moons and rings
but not yet. At ground level, the planets blast open. They
quake with pressure and heat and vast clouds of ash. The
smaller of the two planets, the one doing the colliding,
it cracks and breaks apart like a robin's egg. The two
atmospheres haze and blur with beams of white, enough
to blind any creature who might be watching. But nobody
watches. An event so epic and insignificant is not meant
to be watched. It is destructive and it is creative. And it is
happening now.

And even on a Friday or Saturday night by eleven o'clock
the streets are silent, the bars are bright and expectant,
cocktails waiting to be shaken, pumps prepped for
pulling, desserts at the ready, and it all waits, they all
wait, these young business owners with their big dreams,
but they brought those big dreams to the wrong town.
If only they'd have gone further north or south. At this
very moment those cities brim with bustlers from bar to
bar, bustlers dressed and giggling for the crazy golf and
the themed restaurants while the cars go slow for the
pedestrians – but here there is nothing. The residents are
tucked sweetly in their beds, no one willing to make the
first move – why would I explore a town so dead? And the
bars with their faux industrial fittings, their plumbing-pipe
lights, their hammered-metal bar stools and beer-bottle
chandeliers, they close down, only to be replaced by new
ones the following month, refurbished by the next naive
entrepreneur, and this is how the town sustains itself,
feeding on the dreams of strangers.

But there are glimmers of life, for those who look for
them.

Here is a bar, dank and loud, with its inner walls coated
in peeling black paint like a burnt-down house. A sticky
dance floor with a DJ booth. Missing toilet seats, missing
locks, the funk of bile and sugar. And the humans – these
lively humans who dance like mayflies to the same old
songs, week after week.

I stand at the bar, watching them drink their triple
vodkas with bitter lemon. The girl with the pink

dreadlocks woven into her mousy hair, the girl with
the spike-studded boots. The guy with a jigsaw puzzle
tattooed on his neck. They drink and push and laugh and
hug. They take photos. They flutter in the strobe. Without
them, it's just brick and cobwebs.

— Travis? It's Travis, isn't it?

I turn to see a woman in a black dress and flat black
shoes.

— Hello. Yes, it is.

— Dalia. From the flat.

I say hello and ask if she's out with friends. She says
yes and waves over to her friends to show she's not lying.
They're standing at a tall round table near the dance floor,
and one of them waves. Dalia points her can of Guinness
at me.

— You on the vodka?

— Water.

— Right. Driving? Sensible.

— Yes.

— I've never seen you out before.

— I don't get out much.

— No? Oh.

She sips her drink and raises her eyebrows, already
running out of things to say.

We watch the young dancers – the ones who bob their
heads, the ones flailing every limb, the ones standing coolly
at the side. A jarring transition to another song crashes
from the speakers, and some of them cheer and some of
them groan.

— I hope I didn't upset your daughter the other day.

— Layla? What do you— Oh, you mean the birthday invitation. Yeah. I asked her not to, I knew it'd be weird. Sorry about that.

— No, it's fine.

— I think she's worried you're lonely. I don't know if you are.

Her words linger, but I stay quiet. And we stand with our drinks, and she glances over at her friends again, chatting among themselves. I sip my water. It's cold, and the bass pulses through the plastic into my fingertips. Dalia's friends call her over.

— Anyway, have a nice night.

— You too.

Fluorescent drinks tumble inside her. Secluded bars. The stout has gone to her head, and her new friend for the night is called Ant, and Ant buys her even more drinks, and she thinks he's funny, and the drinks tumble. They tumble. A tumbling blur of people who seem to know what they are doing. Loud talking, but distant. Bright colours smooshing past her face – the floor, the toilets, the floor.

The floor. The toilets. The floor.

In the cubicle, she says she'll try it, but not too much, but not so little they'll think she's a wimp. She sniffs it right up. Plywood wall, graffiti. Smudgy telephone numbers. Are you alright, darling?

Fine – I'm fine – fine.

The bar is a boat. Undulating.

Fancy word.

This is the—

I – back in to the –

What?

Ant asks her to buy him a drink, but she lies and says she's run out of money so he gives her some things and she gets them and there is something. There's chewing gum stuck under here. We'll get the cleaners to get rid of it. Well, you should – it's disgusting. Oscillating, spinning. Around and around. Be careful, her friend says. Looks a bit rapey.

Ant and Charlotte and the other—

Are you alright?

Yes.

The other one—

Name is Ant, everyone calls him Spider.

She doesn't call him Spider, she calls him Ant.

And around and around, until they're outside.

Until they're all outside in the freezing night. And the happy people go home, and the sad people stay out for as long as we possibly can. Do you wanna get a blah blah blah la la?

— Dal?

— Dalia?

— Hmm?

— Some food?

— Hmm?

— Do you wanna get a kebab?

— I already said yes.

— No, you didn't.

Fresh air.

Taxis. Snow.

Hot vomit in the cold snow.

— That's it darling. Bring it up girl.

All those wonderful colourful drinks. Brown. Sweet and sour. Ant goes home, Charlotte has gone. They asked if she'd be okay, and she just walks.

And the fresh air rushes into her brain, soothes it.

Phew. God.

Need to get home.

Where is home?

What is home?

Shit. Okay, concentrate.

She wonders, have I ever been this drunk? Must have been. Years ago.

She likes being drunk. Doesn't feel like herself. Muscles don't ache. She's powerful. More observant – noticing things she'd never usually see – like the way the snow-topped terraces look like a tray of iced buns. Or the way the fat snowflakes seem to enclose her and protect her as she walks. Am I hungry?

She clambers halfway across the railway bridge. She peers over the water. The water, the buildings, the orange lights.

She vomits again, over the brick wall – liquid steaming in the bitter air and she imagines she's a dragon breathing fire. Throat croaking, roaring.

And she feels lighter now, having purged herself.

She closes her eyes and breathes the sharp air, and she totters again, to the flat – up too many stairs, down the hall – and she fumbles with the key in the lock. She fumbles, and fumbles, then she stops.

There's music seeping from the flat opposite. Opera, maybe. She listens. And she steps to his door, this man's door, Travis's door, this strange man who keeps himself to himself, who will barely say hello in the corridor, and she listens. She's not sure why she's here – is he handsome? He's kind of plain, isn't he? She wonders what he might be doing in there – did he fall asleep to the music? He could still be awake. She raises her hand to knock.

She could say hi, how are you, do you want a cup of tea? She could say, that's nice music, I have no kids tonight, can I come in? She could. And she stands there with her fist ready at the door. And she lowers her hand and goes back to her own door. She lets herself in and eats toast in bed.

❧

A VERY OLD WOMAN

On her eighty-ninth birthday she's happy to see me because she thinks this will be the day she dies. She answers the door with a birthday grin and a kiss on my cheek, and she says, come in, come in.

— I wondered if I'd be seeing you today.

— Happy birthday.

— Go and make us a cup of tea, will you? Actually, don't worry, I'll do it. Sit there, make yourself comfortable.

I'm holding a supermarket cake and a package wrapped in green paper, but she doesn't look at them — she shuffles to the kitchen in her dusky pink slippers.

I sit on the pouffe beside the television, waiting. The tick of the clock on the mantelpiece. The harsh sunlight beaming on the windowsill. There are some handwritten envelopes on her coffee table, but she hasn't opened them. The empty armchair sits in the middle of the room like a premonition.

And when I'm tired of waiting, I bring the cake to the kitchen, and I take down a couple of mugs from the cupboard. She bats my hand away.

— I can do it. I told you to go and sit down.

— Let me help.

— You can help by letting me get on with it. I've already got a cup, it's there by the kettle. Go and sit down.

As the kettle boils, I lean against the worktop and peer into her garden. It's a bright cold day — the sun blazing white-sharp from the puddles and the washing line and the wind chime hanging from the shed. I cut us each a slice of cake. She makes some tea, then pours it down the sink.

— Actually, bugger it. Since you're here, fetch that whisky off the shelf there.

I do as I'm told, and she pours two Irish coffees. She sets them on the tray with the cake, and I bring the whole lot back into the living room, walking behind her in slow procession. She sits in her armchair with a satisfied sigh, like someone returning home after a long journey.

I'm holding the tray with the coffees and the cake and her present, but she only takes the coffee, so I set the tray on the table and sit down.

— Ah, lovely. Haven't tasted this in ten years. Really warms your cockles.

I sip mine but it makes my jaw recoil.

Dipping the cake in the coffee doesn't help.

— How have you been?

— Oh marvellous, Travis. Cooped in here every day, trapped in a rusty body, no use to anyone. I'm so glad you've kept me alive all these years. But that's alright. Today is a good day.

She dips her cake in the coffee, and she seems to like it. She licks the fondant from her old fingers, and for a moment I can see the smart young woman inside her, and the tomboyish girl before that.

— Where shall we do it? I can die right here in this arm-chair if you like – it really makes no odds to me. I could die in bed. But if I die in the chair, they won't have to carry me as far.

And as I watch her, this very old woman eating her eighty-ninth birthday cake, this person I've kept an eye on since before she could walk, I'm overcome with nausea, though it could just be the sponge and whisky curdling in my gut. This isn't her day to die, and I must break it to her.

I fetch the deck of cards from the drawer and drag
my pouffe so I'm sitting beside her. She shuffles the cards
and deals them onto the arm of the chair, and we play
her favourite game — rummy. As I focus on the cards, my
stomach settles, my head stops spinning. We win a hand
each, then we play a game from her childhood.

She shakes her head.

— Eighty-nine birthdays, eh? Eighty-nine. I still
remember my fifth. It was a school day. But before
I left the house, my father gave me a doll — a Jemima
Patchpocket doll. Or was it Jemima Puddleduck? I can't
remember, but anyway, I didn't call her that, I called her
Freckles. And oh Travis, did I love her. She was made of
cloth and stuffing and she had these tiny flappy ears. Red
woolly hair. Blue dungarees. Yellow wellies. I remember
her like she's sitting right here on my lap.

She smiles at the thought of that ragdoll, and that day,
and she lays her cards face down on the arm of the chair.

— Of course, the more I loved Freckles, the more she
suffered. She grew dirty and worn as toys tend to do, and
that was okay. She was made for that, you could see it.

She closes her eyes, and she's back there in her childhood home with the doll — painting together, gardening
together. She can see it all, and she frowns.

— And when I was ten, I looked at Freckles sitting
on my shelf and I realized I hadn't played with her in
three years. She would just stare across the room with
those beady eyes, and I wondered, was she done? Was
she ready to die? She'd fulfilled her role as a toy, so now

what? Would she just sit on a shelf forever or get packed
into the loft? She was only a doll, but I couldn't stand the
thought of that. So that day I dug a hole in the garden and
I buried her.

Now she opens her eyes. She grabs my fingers across the
cushion. Her voice is quiet.

— Please, Travis. You've got to let me go.

— Let's play another game.

She squeezes my hand.

— Tell me it's today. It has to be today.

— I'm sorry.

At those words, she flips the cards onto the floor.

— Then why the bloody hell are you here?

— Because it's your birthday.

— Useless, irritating man. Getting all my hopes up.

I kneel down and gather the cards.

— Leave them. Leave them for god's sake.

— Why don't you open your present?

— I don't want a present, Travis. You know what
I want. Why are you dragging it out like this? It's bloody
pointless. It's unfair and heartless is what it is.

She sets aside her plate of unfinished cake and holds her
coffee close to her chest. I slide the cards back into their
box. I ask if her family will be visiting today, but she tells
me to shut up. And we sit in a silence only broken by the
ticking of the clock.

When it's clear she won't open her present, I sit on
the arm of her chair and open it for her. It's a photo
album. Pictures of her life – her parents, her children, her

husband – all restored to perfection. I open the first couple of pages, showing her the red and yellow swings, her first bike. I show her the Easter eggs on the dining table, and her father's bigger egg on top of the TV. With every page, the little girl in the photos races towards adulthood.

She closes the album before I go too far.

— Don't you like it?

— What do I need a photo album for? I already know what's happened in my life. I'm the one who lived it. Or maybe you've forgotten.

I glance at her and then at the album. I close it and set it back on the coffee table beside the unopened envelopes. She sips her drink and closes her eyes.

— I'm sorry if I've upset you.

— You haven't upset me. You haven't anythinged me. I've just had enough.

— Is there anything else I can do?

— Apparently not.

I tidy away our plates, the wrapping paper, my half-empty cup. I tidy some other bits in the kitchen – the plates on the worktop, some washing-up in the sink.

Back in the living room, she's pretending to sleep.

I pull her blanket over her and walk to the front door.

— Travis?

— Yes?

— I don't want to see you again until you're ready to do your job. Do you understand? We are not friends. You are not a guest. The next time I see your face, I want to know what day it is.

I take the photo album from the table.

She switches on the television, and I leave her alone again.

~

On Saturday mornings, before the world has woken, I wander the town centre. It's quiet, but not in the same way a meadow is quiet. A town's quietness is heavier. Not simply a lack of sound, but a thing to be noticed and appreciated. The world is switched off, on standby, but I can smell the before-world – the grease from the takeaways, the sick in the doorway, the perfume and cigarettes. A cold scent of dew from unseen grass, the lingering exhaust fumes of a bus. From the smells alone, someone might think the town is in the full throes of an afternoon. But with my eyes open and my ears unplugged, the smells are an after-image. Invisible past-people living their yesterday lives.

Hannah Bruce opens the doors of the bookshop. She will die from a heart attack at ninety-one, and her last thought will be how she never went skiing. Jo Cornish stands her A-frame sign outside the hipster pub: hand-fired pizzas, 2 for 1. She'll also die of a heart attack, and her last thought will be a memory of tracing her fingers along a water-spill on a table at a holiday club at the age of six.

When the pharmacy opens, I buy a packet of pumpkin seeds and sit on the bench around the corner from the bus depot where the pigeons are waiting. They bob their heads at my ankles in unison, these feathered street dancers, and I pour some seeds onto my palm and sprinkle them across the pavement. Some of the pigeons peck at the seeds. The cleverest ones flap up onto the bench, onto my lap. I pour more seeds onto my palm and hold them out, and the birds gather at my hand, they nudge each other, they climb over one another. Somewhere beyond the shopping centre, beyond the flats, a woman unrolls her garden mat in the allotment.

A frothy sky spits over the allotment, but it's not cold. The water has woken the scents of soil and leaves, of slugs and caterpillars. I sit on my camping stool watching my garden tremble from the droplets falling on it, and from the breeze through the gates. A faint hiss of rain masks the sounds of traffic and birds, until all that remains is a comforting tinnitus, everywhere.

A handful of gardeners sit around their patches of earth. Some till the soil, others sit in their raincoats and drink mugs of tea. Dalia from across the hall, she's sitting on a deckchair a few plots away from me, on her phone. She's wearing overalls and a rag tied in her hair. She looks like the photo they'd use on an advert for allotments.

When she sees me, I look back at my garden. But soon she's walking over with her chair in her hands.

— You know you're growing weeds, don't you?

— Weeds?

She sits beside me.

— Ribwort. Chickweed. Couple of nettles.

— Oh.

We stare at my clump of weeds, and we're quiet for a time.

To her, I'm the loner from number 9. To me, she's every school disco she ever danced at, she's the graze on her knee when she jumped from that wall at Plymouth beach. She's the daughter of a breast cancer patient and a stroke victim. There's nothing of value I can say, so I ask if she had a good night last night.

— Oh, you were at the bar! I remember. Yeah, it was a good night. Nice to blow off some steam. It's not often I get a weekend to myself.

— Where are the kids?

— Neda's at her dad's. Layla's with a friend. Better make the most of it, I suppose.

She glances around the allotment, wondering if this is making the most of it. She pulls a flask from a tote bag and pours a coffee. She passes me it, then sips from the flask as we watch an old man, a stone's throw away, picking slugs from his lettuces.

Dalia nods towards the old man.

— See him?

— The old man?

— Killed his wife. Killed her with a trowel and buried her there in the dirt.

— I don't think that's true.

— It could be. You don't know. Your turn.

She points to the woman a few plots away, watering some little green shoots. Her name is Chen Siyu, sixty-eight years old, four children, one grandchild, heart attack.

I tell Dalia I can't think of anything, but she tells me to try. So I fix my eyes upon Siyu and I draw a deep breath and recite every detail of her life – the cottage where she grew up, in Wuzhen, and about the calendars her mother used to make. I tell Dalia about Siyu's chinchillas, and the time she fell off that narrowboat, and her front gate that won't stop squeaking.

Dalia looks at the woman, then back at me.

She shakes her head like I haven't quite understood the game. But for the next half an hour, we make up stories about these elderly gardeners. Mine are uncannily elaborate and specific, and Dalia disagrees with most of them – no, no, no, she says – it's not like that, it's like this. We watch the old man picking more slugs, dropping them into his bucket. I tell Dalia he's a three-time regional bowls champion, married to a four-time champion. Dalia says it's not the lettuces he eats, it's the slugs.

We fall quiet for a while, drinking our coffee.

She points at my patch of soil.

— I can help with this if you want. I've seen you sitting here struggling, not knowing what to do. We can rip all this out and start again. Grow some veggies or something.

She pops an aspirin from her pocket and swallows it with a gulp from her flask. And she tells me small details of her life – her first home, her parents. She talks about hospital dramas, mostly involving the staff rather than the patients.

— Solomon is okay, just a bit posh. That's Neda's dad.
We were hardly together six months. Layla's dad – well,
he needs a rocket up his arse. I dodged a bullet there. Am
I boring you?

— Not at all.

The truth is, she is boring me, and I welcome it.
Somehow, when Dalia speaks, the voices of the world
dampen around me. I forget the clamour of everything,
everywhere, and focus only on the tune of her words, like
a fire blanket over my brain.

— Layla's dad should be dead, really. The amount he's
drunk over the years. Do you know any one who's died?

— A few.

She glances across the plots, towards the road.

— My brother died a few years ago. Car crash. Not
far from here, actually. You know the crossroads with the
kebab shop?

— I think so.

— Twenty-nine, he was.

— I'm sorry.

— I try not to think about it. Drives you crazy otherwise. I don't know if it's ever sunk in – 'my brother is
dead' – my brother is actually dead. I don't know. I cried
when I found out, but I haven't cried since – like a part of
me always knew he'd die young. He had that way about
him. You would have liked him, I think.

Dalia taps the rim of her flask with her nail.

Thunder rumbles over the allotment.

Rain crashes, glass meteorites. The worm crawls pink-bellied among the forest grass. The grass bends and bounces in the wind and the barrage from above. She dips her tip into the black earth then retreats again. Vibrating earth. Moist, slippery, curling. Go this way. Home in all directions, but now to find another part of it – new rooms, new strangers who pass by in the night, evacuate and bump in these one-night stands, fleeting romances before we're on the road again. Rumble sky. Snail huddled in his grotto, dandelion umbrella dripping with collected aromas, the dust wakes. A scrabbling of wings and feet, and the ground disappears with a rush, and she's higher than she ever knew. She's up. Up! She's moving through a thinner place with nothing beneath. No why or where, no who, only this, only now. The pressure shifts, ebbs, the wind rattles. Now there's nothing. No claws, no sound, only the sense of a whooshing from below, and she hits hard ground. She dips, but there's resistance. Slick, craggy. This ground doesn't tremble the way the grass place trembles. It tastes like danger. Louder rumbles, coming, going. She dips again, but it's impenetrable, so she crawls along it with a memory of the grassland so long ago. But the impenetrable desert is endless. For the first time, the eggs inside her feel more urgent and precious.

She crawls on. She knows nothing else.

She tries to get back to wet land.

On the Monday, Dalia delivers three boys and four girls, including a set of boy-girl twins. Textbook births, zero complications. The kind of day that reminds her why she became a midwife in the first place. And that night, still glowing from the day, Dalia runs her girls a bath.

She runs it warm, but not too warm, and she adds bubbles, but not too many.

When Layla steps in, she asks why it's cold.

— It's not cold, baby. I can't run it too warm because of Neda.

Neda sits at the tap end, with her fat belly and fat legs. She splashes the water with her palms, and she babbles like she believes she's making sense. Dalia sits on the damp mat, an arm draped over the side of the bath. She shows Neda the pink rubber duck, and it goes straight in her mouth. Layla ignores them both, playing cars with the soap.

— So, Layla. Y'know that man across the hall?

— Who, Travis?

— What do you think of him?

— He's okay. Neda, budge up.

— He's a bit strange isn't he?

— He's okay. I like him.

— Huh. That's funny – when he wouldn't come to your party you said you hated him.

Layla shrugs.

— Changed my mind.

Dalia dips her fingers into the tepid water. Her bracelets clack against the plastic.

— I was thinking of asking if he'd like to come for dinner one night.

— He'll say no.

— He might.

Layla drives her car-soap along the edge of the bath and up the tiled wall. She makes engine noises and skidding noises, and Neda watches Layla's lips.

— Mum, when Uncle Sam died, do you think it hurt?

— I don't know, baby. I hope not. I like to think it was quick.

— Quick? Quick is bad, isn't it?

— Not really. Something like that, it's better to go quick.

— That's weird. Neda, god's sake, budge *up*.

— Hey, hey. There's plenty of room.

— She's on my side.

— No, she's not. Don't be mean.

The car-soap crashes into the shampoo and conditioner bottles, and they all go plopping into the bath. A fleck of bubbles lands near Neda's eye, and she giggles. Layla tries not to laugh, but she can't hold it in, and suddenly they're friends again.

Layla sits with her head on the arm of the sofa, watching television, while Neda sits propped between two cushions so she doesn't fall. Dalia starts tidying, taking the plates and cutlery to the sink, wiping the worktop – but she stops. Something has caught her eye. Something so simple and obvious, she almost hadn't noticed it. Something so familiar, it's almost invisible.

She has two children.

And they are beautiful.

Dalia lays the cloth beside the sink, and for an undisturbed moment she watches her girls as they stare at the cartoon dogs on the telly. She tries to see them. To truly see them. As if she's woken from a coma, and she realizes now, she has two children, and they are real. They are so much a part of her life, she often looks at them the same way she'd look at a sock or a cereal box. But for these few seconds, she concentrates and tries to see them, and to enjoy it.

Dalia abandons the tidying.

She sits on the sofa between Layla's feet and Neda's cushions. She drapes an arm around Neda and holds one of Layla's feet. Layla shuffles around until she's cuddling her mum. Neda doesn't move – hypnotized by the colours.

There are two girls here, Dalia tells herself. My girls. Look at them. Breathe them in. This is just another school night for them, but for me there's such clarity. I wish I could feel this every day.

She holds them tight. She smells their hair. She remembers Layla when she was Neda's age, when they lived in the old flat, and how terrifyingly fast it's all gone, and she thinks about how old Layla will be when Neda is Layla's age, and how quickly that will go too. And it hurts, and it swells in her chest like the panic of drowning, but she breathes, and she squeezes them tighter. She knows this moment – this precious clarity, this twenty-minute gift – this moment right now, just sitting with her children – is everything she will ever miss.

Layla farts.

— Scuse me.

She farts three more times and says scuse me after each one.

— Layla Preston! Farty bum.

Layla giggles. Dalia kisses her head. She glances back at the cartoon dogs.

And when the kids are in bed, Dalia closes the living room curtains. She switches off the main light and switches on the fairy lights draped over the yucca. She watches her crime documentaries. Although they're full of violence and deception, they relax her – they give her perspective. She didn't make any dinner for herself, instead she eats a Twirl with a cup of tea. And as she watches the police footage, the anonymous interviews, the forensic specialists, she tries to blot out the thoughts of her brother.

She pauses her programme and makes herself another cup of tea. And while the kettle boils, she pokes her head into the kids' bedrooms. Fast asleep. She stands by the front door and listens for movement or music from the flat across the hall, but there's nothing. These hours are the quiet ones. These are the hours Dalia feels separate from the world, outside of it, peering in. Waiting until morning, when she can become a part of everything again.

Nights like this, she wonders if she should have stuck with Solomon. He was always a loving dad to Neda, and a decent role model for Layla, if a little condescending at times. She slips into his old jumper. She pulls on her duck slippers and pours the water into her cup. Waiting for the tea to brew, she hears nothing. No sounds. No movement. Just a woman standing in a dim room, waiting. Even the television is still.

Dalia opens her front door. She peers across the hall.

She's about to close her door, but instead she shuffles to his in her slippers. She listens again. She wants to knock. Say, hey, are you doing anything? Do you fancy a cup of tea? I'm watching that new documentary series, have you seen it?

She thinks of her brother again, imagining his body tumbling around in the car, the burst of glass, the scream of the engine. She imagines him at the party, drinking, knowing he'll soon be driving home with his friends in the back.

And she knocks.

Meanwhile, Debbie sits on the sofa in the dark with a bag of clothes pegs. One by one, she takes a peg from the bag. She holds its legs, pulls, and twists until they pop like chicken bones. The spring drops into her lap. She places the dismembered legs to her right. She picks up the next peg, while exactly a hundred metres east, Logan crosses out all the answers to his history homework and starts from scratch. Across the road, in the park, a dad searches for the football in the bushes. It's too dark and he's looking in the wrong spot. He'll come back in the wet morning, find the ball instantly, and pluck it from the bush like a slippery egg. A cigarette butt rolls into the crack between the kerb and the path. Sammi waters her hanging plants in the conservatory while Graham next door watches porn on his laptop. Callum wonders how much effort it'd be to hoax an alien abduction, and he writes some plans but never looks at them again. Graham closes his laptop and the room goes dark.

❧

A SECRET COUPLE

Enid and Wendy were in love for ten years before they felt brave enough to admit it. Admit it to themselves, admit it to each other. It was another ten before they had the courage to tell their families. Wendy's dad beat her around the head with a spatula and tossed her out in the street. Enid's sister cried and told her she was going to Hell. They never saw their families after that, but they made friends at the car boot sales and they kept their love a secret.

In their fifties, Enid and Wendy tried holding hands in public. That was the year they sent their first Christmas card together. And at fifty-five, after living apart their whole lives, they moved into a quaint bungalow down a winding country road. Fifty-eight, they slept in the same bed. They never allowed themselves anything beyond a kiss, a hug. But they were happy for thirty years after that.

Now they're side by side in that same bed in that same bungalow.

They're holding hands beneath the sheets.

I sit on the edge of the mattress. They look as content and in love as the first day they professed it. They need nothing from me. But I watch them now, these two old ladies, these best friends, these virgins, these car boot veterans. Their eyes are closed, their chests are slow. In a few moments, one will go, and then the other. They have not a single regret between them. Except, perhaps, for the time they wasted being afraid. I sit and watch. And I stay there for hours.

Wendy Lowe – 88 years, 1 month, 22 days
Enid Speck – 88 years, 4 months, 10 days

Seven in the evening, the time Dalia told me to come, I knock on her door. She answers with a smile and tells me to come in. She's wearing an old holiday T-shirt and a bandana in her hair. Her flat is warmer than mine. Cosier.

— The food smells good.

— That's just the oven.

— What are we having?

— Lamb koftas. That okay? You can help me cook it.

I take my shoes off and catch sight of Layla in her bedroom. She's sitting on the edge of her bed with a games controller in her hand, and she waves at me. I wave back.

— Five more minutes, Stinks, then pyjamas.

— Okay.

I follow Dalia into the kitchen. She turns some knobs on the oven and passes me a wooden spoon.

— The meat is there. Stir the sauce into it. You might need to use your hands.

She looks different tonight. Less tired. Often she walks as though she's carrying both girls on her shoulders, but now she's light. She hums to the music from the radio, and she dances a half-dance from cupboard to cupboard.

I wash my hands and pour in the sauce – a thick reddish paste – and I smoosh it into the raw meat with my hands. It slides and squelches between my fingers. This thing that once could see and hear and walk. It changes colour, combines with the sauce, becomes something else. When I lift my hands out of the bowl, my fingers are coated.

— Here, let me pour some soap on those.

Dalia stands in front of me and drizzles some green soap over my red fingers. I wash it all off – the soap and the sauce and the minced-up creature, down the plughole and around the pipes.

— Pyjamas, Stinks.

— That wasn't five minutes.

— No, it was six. Get them on.

Dalia places an empty plate beside the bowl of lamb. She tells me to roll them into thumb-sized chunks. She tells me the chef on the telly says to squeeze them and leave your fingermarks in them, so the ridges go all crispy.

— Alright, I'll do that.

— It's only us eating. Layla had nuggets.

I make one kofta, to check the size is right. She tells me it's good.

— Mum, where are my pyjamas?

— In the drawer, where they always are.

And that's when Dalia's phone beeps.

Her eyes flit towards it, but she ignores it, spooning some mint sauce from a jar into a bowl of natural yoghurt. The phone beeps again, and she swears at the ceiling.

— I know what this is going to be. Yep. For fuck's sake.

— What is it?

— I'm on call at the hospital. Rachel's called in sick.

She glances around at the uncooked dinner, as though she can see it all rotting away in front of her. She swears again.

— That's okay. You need to go. I can look after the kids.

— Travis, I can't ask you to do that. Are you sure? I can ask Lynn downstairs. I can't believe it. The one bloody night. Are you sure? I hate to ask. I don't even know how long I'll be.

— It's fine. We can do this another time.

— Oh god. Thank you.

Dalia washes her hands and pokes her head into Layla's room. She urges Layla to be good, to go straight to sleep, then she disappears into her own room, closing the door behind her. When she comes back, she's wearing a navy tunic.

— Neda's asleep. She's been fed, but if she wakes up there are bottles in the fridge. You can stick it in the microwave for a few seconds, or don't bother, she's not fussy. I completely understand if you want to go home and just check on them every half-hour or so.

Her hospital clothes look strange in the dim light, like a Halloween costume.

— I'll stay here until you get back.

— Okay. Well, the remote's over there. Help yourself to anything. Thank you, Travis. I'm so sorry. I promise we'll do this another night.

— It's fine – go.

She grabs her bag and phone, reminds Layla one last time to behave, and she's gone.

When Dalia leaves, I switch off the rice cooker and wrap the koftas in foil and put them in the fridge. I pull the little poetry book from my pocket and read on the sofa for a while. And while I read, I try not to ask myself how it feels, being here, a stranger in their home, sitting and reading as though I live here. Perhaps this isn't unusual at all. Perhaps I live here, and this is my family. This is a normal everyday life.

Layla pads into the living room.

She stands there in a pale yellow nightie and bare feet, shoulders slumped and head hanging so I'll feel extra sorry for her. She's carrying a narwhal by its horn.

— Can't sleep.

— Would you like some water?

She reaches out a hand and I take it, and we walk to the kitchen and I pour her a glass of water. I swap the water for the narwhal. She's half asleep, her eyes closed as she drinks. When she's done, she passes me the glass and says thank you, eyes still closed. She takes her narwhal.

— Do you feel better now?

— Yeah. Thank you.

Head still hanging, she walks back towards the bedroom but makes a U-turn and goes and sits on the sofa instead. She curls up like a cat, head on the cushion. I sit beside her with my book. We sit like that for half an hour, and she fidgets, and she nudges me with her feet. Eventually, she huffs.

— Aren't you going to put me back to bed?

— Do you want me to?

— It's not up to me. You're the grown-up. I shouldn't really be out of bed this late, should I? I should be asleep, don't you think? I'm only eight.

— Okay, I'll put you back to bed.

— Well, I'm not going.

She squeezes her narwhal tight, closes her eyes and scrunches herself into a ball, as though this will make her heavier. But I don't move. I keep reading, and when she hears me turn another page, she looks at me and sighs. She sits up.

— Mum always does this.

— Does what?

— Goes to work at night.

— She has a very important job. Maybe the most important.

Layla weaves her fingers between her toes and stares across the room. She wants to talk about it more but doesn't know how to start.

— You know she's just tricking you, so you'll babysit. Sometimes Lynn from downstairs comes and looks after us. Or Chris. I like Chris better, he brings games. Did you bring any games? How old are you, anyway?

— How old do you think I am?

— Thirty-five.

— Thirty-five?

— Yeah.

— I like that. Let's go with thirty-five.

— What are you reading?

— It's a book of poems about bridges.

— That sounds boring.

— Nothing is boring.

— Some things are.

— Like what?

— A brick.

I put my book down. I look at the little girl with the mousy hair.

— A brick isn't boring. You could look at a brick and be mesmerized – its texture, its shape, all its cracks and blemishes. The cobweb smell, the smooth powder it leaves on your fingers.

— Maybe, but—

— Wondering what it's made of, who made it, when it was made, how it was brought here, how long it's been here. All the things it's seen, all the people who have brushed past it, sat near it, the arguments across the street, that one quiet street unfolding and jittering like a montage, the cars in the driveway, watching the children grow, watching them ditch their bikes for cars, their shorts for suits, watching the children have children of their own. Wondering how a single brick can help hold up a house. Wondering how long the brick will be here, and how it will end.

Now she looks at me.

— Is that a poem? It's really good how you remember it.

Layla's eyes flit about my face, and she's not smiling or frowning – she has that same look of a child realizing for the first time that they live on a globe, in space, orbiting a sun, and thinking about what that means. She glances up and down at my simple fraying clothes. She takes my hands and inspects my wrists, my fingers.

— You're a bit strange, aren't you?

— I've been told that.

— You don't have any rings or anything.

— No.

— You're plain.

— I suppose I am.

— My mum's got a ring with a mayfly on it. What do you think that means?

I consider brushing the question away, telling her to go back to bed. Instead I draw a long breath and put my arm around her.

— I think it means your mum likes mayflies.

She rests her head on the side of my chest, and she yawns. The fridge makes a noise, the tap drips. Somewhere below us, Mr Northam is polishing his shoes with a black marker pen.

— Travis?

— Yes?

— Are you scared of clowns?

— Clowns? No, I don't think so.

— They're the scariest things in the world. I have nightmares about them every day.

— Why clowns?

— They're just creepy. With their faces. It's not the sad ones – the sad ones aren't creepy – it's the happy ones. What are they so happy about?

— You'd have to ask them.

— No way. I'm not going near one. What are you scared of?

— Grown-ups don't really get scared.

— That's not true. Mum's scared of wasps.

— Everyone's scared of wasps.

— So what are you scared of?

— Clowns.

— Liar.

She closes her eyes and hooks her finger into a loose thread on my jumper.

Her head becomes heavier on my chest. Her words, slower.

— Travis?

— Yes?

— Do you believe in narwhals?

Dalia drives in the opposite direction to the hospital, down
the parkway, to the housing estate. It's the kind of estate
she hopes she'll never end up in – weird brown houses with
weird black roofs, houses with odd proportions and slopes,
as if they were designed ugly on purpose, for those who
can barely afford to live there.

When he opens the door he's surprised to see her.

— Dalia, you didn't have to come.

— You said you were in trouble.

— It's nothing that couldn't wait.

He lets her in and she follows him to the kitchen.

He points at the cupboard above the cooker. She
opens it.

— Herbs and spices?

— Behind them.

She reaches up and feels around, behind the little
glass pots of oregano and dried coriander. She pulls out a
six-pack of beer.

— I don't even remember putting them there. Must've
been for an emergency. But I caught sight of them earlier
when I was making spag bol.

— Right. Don't worry, I'll get rid of them.

— Thank you. I don't even want to touch them.

Dalia considers pouring them down the sink, but she
doesn't want him to smell it. She considers throwing them
in the bin, but she doesn't want to tempt him, so she opens

some more cupboards until she finds the carrier bags. She drops the beers into a bag.

— I'll take them home with me.

— Thanks, Dalia. Sorry, I know it's pathetic.

— It's not pathetic. I told you, I'm here.

— Did I interrupt anything?

— No. You're fine.

He pours himself a glass of water and offers her one, but she shakes her head. He's looking thinner, but it might be because the beard is gone. He looks healthier around the eyes – his skin is no longer grey. Leaning against the worktop, he sips his water, his eyes darting everywhere except to her.

— How's Layla?

— She's good. She misses you.

— Well, only three more weeks and that'll be six months sober.

— Are you still going to your meetings?

— Got one tomorrow.

— They helping?

— Must be.

He tells her to wait there, then fetches something from his bedroom. It's a painting of a closed-down pub.

Dalia recognizes the pub but can't place it. It's not the greatest picture – it's wonky, cartoonish. The perspective is wrong, the colours are too obvious: a flat blue sky, a solid brown tree with green spiral boughs. But it's a painting, and he's done it, and his face is so proud it makes her stomach twist.

— It's really good, Nick.

— Do you think?

— Did you paint it at one of your meetings?

— Yeah, we do all sorts. Embroidery. Poetry. I think it's knot-tying this week. It's like being back at bloody Scouts. But it keeps your mind occupied, you know. Better than sob stories.

— I bet.

He props the painting up against the kettle. He looks at it a little longer, trying to see it through Dalia's eyes. Then he looks back at her. Those sad eyes, the colour of vodka soda lime. He's trying. She can see that. He's trying so hard that she wants to say, forget the six months. I can see you've changed. Come home with me. We'll be a family again. But then she remembers last time, and the one before that. The carrier bag is heavy, the handles cutting into her fingers. No, it has to be six months. It's not fair on Layla.

— Do you need anything else?

— No, I don't think so. Unless you want to stay for a bit?

— I can't. The kids are waiting at home.

— Okay. Maybe see you next week then.

— Okay.

He steps towards her, then stops. Then he steps forward again, and he holds her. He doesn't smell of stale drink or fresh drink – he smells like almost nothing, a faint body odour, and Dalia decides it's a welcome change. He kisses her head.

And somehow, as she smells him, as she stands there in his arms, as she holds that bag of beer, she knows he'll be okay – he doesn't need her any more. He had always weighed on her, like a third child, a sick child who couldn't get well. But now, after seeing him beginning to heal, the weight has lifted. She's done all she can.

I lay my book down a moment before she walks through the door. She's clutching a bag to her chest – a carrier bag of steaming food. It smells of hot pineapple.

— Bloody freezing out there.

She lays the bag on the kitchen side and spots Layla asleep beside me.

— Sorry, Travis, I hope I wasn't too long. Has she been a pain?

— She's been fine. They've both been fine.

Dalia comes and gathers the sleepy girl in her arms. Layla stirs. I want to stay up, she says. I want to watch telly with you. But her mother tells her it's bedtime.

— We need some grown-up time.

— It's not fair.

— It is fair, come on. Your breath smells, did you brush your teeth? You need to brush your teeth.

Layla stomps off to the bathroom and brushes her teeth with furious scrubs. Dalia gingerly lifts foil containers from the bag until Layla stomps back and gives her mother a begrudging hug.

— Hey, little Miss Grumpy. Give me a proper one.

Layla sighs, but she gives her mother a cuddle and a kiss on the cheek.

She looks at me, on the sofa, unsure whether to hug me or not.

— Goodnight, Layla.

— Night.

And she slumps off to bed.

Dalia looks at me, smiling a funny kind of smile.

I stand up.

— I'll leave you to your dinner.

— Don't be silly. I bought some for you.

— Oh. Do you need any help?

— Go sit at the table.

In the corner of the living room is a round breakfast table draped in magazines, colouring, a box of tissues, a hairbrush and a sock.

— You can dump all that crap on the sofa.

I do as she says, while Dalia uncorks a bottle of wine from the fridge. She plates up the rice and chow mein and chicken balls. She brings the food and cutlery to the table, but before she sits down she opens a drawer, pulls out some tealight candles, and lights them at the table. She switches the lamp off but changes her mind and switches it back on.

— You didn't have to do this.

— Well, I wanted to.

— Thank you.

She pours us each a glass of wine, and we eat in the quiet dark, listening to the swell of rain. From where we're sitting we can see the street below – the mini car park and the road, the occasional bus with its yellow headlights illuminating the rain like sparks.

Dalia looks at me in the reflection of the windowpane.

— You're really good with her, you know.

— With Layla?

— Yeah. She can be a handful. She gets moody a lot. But she's really taken to you. I think she might have a little crush. Don't worry – it's normal. I had a crush on one of my teachers when I was her age. It's sweet really.

She eats some chicken and peers down into the road again.

— How was the hospital?

— Huh? Oh, it was okay. Just normal.

— Must be quite stressful sometimes.

— Yeah. Usually. There's all the crying and screaming, there's all the blood. It's tough. But then the baby comes out, and it's all forgotten. And there's calm. Just a family with their new baby. There's nothing better.

She tells me stories of her strangest deliveries, and I try to fix my attention only on her. Not Lynn, in the flat below. Not the fox in the car park, nosing beneath the van. Not all the voices, everywhere – just Dalia, here, now.

— Travis, do you have any children?

— No.

— Ever wanted any?

— I wouldn't be a good dad. I like wandering. I tend to disappear and grow obsessed with small things.

— That doesn't answer my question.

She's teasing, twisting the fork into her noodles like they're the folds of my brain.

— You looked pretty natural with Layla on the sofa there.

— She's a good kid.

— She is.

*

We've slipped into those in-between hours that feel like neither today nor tomorrow, and now we're two people washing dishes, laughing at nothing in the dark with our bellies full of noodles and wine.

— Honestly, I'm standing there in front of this new family, and this is supposed to be a beautiful moment, right? Their first child. And all I can see is this bollock hanging out of his shorts.

— Which one was it?

— Which *bollock?* I don't bloody know! The left one, I guess. I was trying not to look, but it was staring back at me.

Rain falls harder now, hushing, and it helps me forget. I focus only on Dalia wiping the dishes with a tea towel, putting the towel down to hold her wine glass, nudging my chest with the glass as she laughs and tells me stories of all the humans she's welcomed into the world, and the fox is pulling litter from the bin. Dalia kisses me.

It's been a long time since someone touched their face to mine, but I let it happen. I let it all happen, and I taste the wine and spearmint gum on her tongue, and I let her take my hand and lead me to the sofa. She sits on my lap and pulls my jumper over my head. And in these impossible hours where the world doesn't know itself, I am happy to unknow myself. I am a man in a flat, with a woman who is a mother and a midwife, and we are friends, and we are lonely, and she is sweet and she is strong, and her hands smell of medicine, her neck smells of sweat and perfume. I stop her.

— Are you okay?

I sit up, open my eyes. I peer across the room.

— It's okay. We don't have to do anything.

— I'm sorry.

— Don't be silly.

She moves off my lap, sits beside me. She looks embarrassed, but I hold her hand and the embarrassment fades.

— Are you seeing anyone?

I shake my head.

— Oh god, you lost someone, didn't you, Travis? I can tell. You don't have to tell me, but I know. You have that look in your eye – I've seen it a million times. I deal with a lot of broken people at the hospital, and they all have that same look. I had it too, after my brother. You lost someone. Maybe more than one. You don't have to talk about it. But I'll listen if you tell me.

I look at her in the fickle glow of the tealights.

There are no words, so I sit with my hands in my lap, and she rests her head on my shoulder. She brushes my fingers with hers and tells me that it's okay. It's okay. And within ten minutes, she's asleep.

A PICTURE MAKER

On his forty-fifth birthday, Mansoor's wife buys him his first colour television. A 27-inch Panasonic CRT.

He spends half an hour unboxing it, every panel of polystyrene and strip of foam, each plastic strap. He lifts the television from the box like it's some priceless artefact, and he positions it where he spends most of his time – in the kitchen. A spot in the corner, beside the kettle. He studies his curved reflection in the grey not-quite-square screen. And the television watches back.

It watches Mansoor's excitement as he grabs the remote and switches it on. And the television shows him all four and a half channels in dazzling soft-around-the-edges colour. Mansoor switches to the news. He switches to *Countdown*. He switches to the snooker, and the bright green baize almost blinds him. The television listens to every request and is happy to oblige. It is proud to provide one man with so much joy.

Mansoor cooks all day, filling the kitchen with the perfume of cumin and cloves. He's cooked this dish so many times, he barely needs to glance from the screen as he chops and stirs.

When his wife Meera returns from work, and his three boys from school, the family sits around the kitchen table and they sing happy birthday and watch *Coronation Street* while they eat the chicken pasanda. Mansoor chooses the seat with the best view of the screen, and he positions each chair so everyone can see, but no one is in his way.

— What do you think, boys?

— It's good, Dad.

— How many channels has it got?

— Five. When I can get the fifth one working.

— Everyone at school has more channels than that.

— Most of them have got Nintendos, too.

— Well, it's a start.

Meera, with the second-best view in the house, holds Mansoor's hand across the table. She's glad he likes his present. She paid for it with the money she earned from her printing business. Next year, she thinks, she'd like to treat him to a VCR.

And over the next few weeks and months, the television watches this family, watches their lives unfold, watches the boys grow taller – the elder ones stronger, the youngest one thinner – watches Mansoor wipe the screen with a tissue each week, dusting its surface, polishing the remote.

Mansoor's favourite programmes are the game shows, especially the general knowledge questions. He knows the capitals of every country, he knows his kings and his queens, he knows his collective nouns and Olympic gold medallists. The two elder boys show little interest, but the youngest, Krish, loves watching soaps – the bickering, the backstabbing, the affairs. He even loves the adverts – the silly songs, the cheesy characters. And when the television is four months old, Meera discovers the cancer in her left breast.

For weeks, while Mansoor sleeps, I visit Meera in the night-time. And on a Tuesday evening, wearing a tidy black suit, carrying a tidy black briefcase, I visit her in the hospice.

It's a peaceful place. Air-conditioned and full of big leafy plants that climb the walls, and milky light trickling from the windows. Meera sits in bed, crocheting beside a table full of cards and flowers and books.

She's made the place her own, with doilies pinned to the walls, a reed diffuser, her mother's ornate vanity screen. She's brought a portable kettle with her favourite teapot and the china cups with the trees on. She's brought Scrabble. It looks like the perfect place to die.

I sit to her left, laying my case on the bed, pulling out some paperwork while Mansoor watches from the other side. He looks sicker than his wife does.

— Is all this really necessary? Look at her, she's fine.

— Oh hush, Mans.

Mansoor thinks I'm a solicitor, but Meera knows I am more than that. She pours me a cup of green tea from the pot, and the three of us spend the next couple of hours discussing her finances – her will, her assets, her beneficiaries, her printing company. Would everything go to Mansoor? If so, Mansoor should write a will too. And who would look after the children if Mansoor dies? Should we set up a trust fund for them?

Mansoor smacks his palm on the bed. It doesn't have quite the impact he'd hoped for.

— Now stop. You're talking as though she's definitely going to die.

— I am. We both will.

— Rubbish.

— Look at where I am, you fool. I want to be prepared.

I make notes, and file them away in my briefcase. More than once, Meera rubs my papers between her fingers and makes the same printing joke.

— Seventy gram, uncoated. Aren't I at least worth eighty?

— Seventy is standard.

— Oh, I'm joking, you miserable so-and-so.

She nudges my arm and pours me another tea.

We speak a little longer, until Meera tells Mansoor she's tired. He knows what this means. He nods, kisses his wife's hand and says goodbye, reluctantly leaving her side.

Mansoor and I don't speak a word as we walk down the corridor, but he stops. I stop too. He looks at the ground, then eyes me with that same look they all have. He has a question. He wants to ask if she'll be alright, if she'll live, but the words feel so bizarre – why would I, Mr Smith, solicitor, know the fate of his wife? So he stops looking at me, and he shakes my hand and drives home. I head back to Meera's side.

That's when she and I stop talking about death and we talk about more interesting things. Her childhood. Her parents back in Jaipur. We talk about her boys, about how she met Mansoor, about their enormous wedding of every colour, about her job, about her raspberry and chocolate muffin recipe and the school fetes where she'd sell them and all the other parents would grow jealous.

I write none of this down, but I listen, and I learn.

She tells me to come closer. I lean forward.

Closer, she says, and I sit on the edge of her bed.

Now she reaches out and brushes my cheek with her thumb. I lean into her touch. She doesn't look ill — just a little thinner. I close my eyes and imagine I'm her fourth son. Her eldest, come to visit his mother.

— You're a sweet man.

— Thank you, Meera.

— You should find someone.

— It's not that simple.

— No, it never is. But everyone should have someone. Even you. Especially you.

Her floaty home-language, the words drifting like water. She is annoyed to die, she says. Far too busy. It's an interruption, like switching off a film halfway through — the film still exists, other people will get to see it, but you are robbed of the proper ending. She knows she'll die, she says. But Mansoor won't believe it, and that worries her. That worries her more than dying.

Her warmth leaves me as she leans towards the bedside table. She opens the drawer and pulls out a small piece of cloth, laying it in my hands.

— I printed you something.

— What is it?

— Ashoka Chakra.

She sits back against her pillow and I brush my fingers over this beige cloth, this wheel shape printed in royal blue. She tells me it's a symbol of transformation. The spokes, she says, represent twelve causal links. Ignorance, thirst, birth, death…

— It's beautiful.

I fold up the thing and put it in my pocket. And I look at her, this mother in the hospice. Her dark eyes roam my face, and although she's dying, she looks concerned for me. She holds my hands.

Then she smiles, as though she's thought of something. As if everything is beautiful and nothing hurts, and she closes her eyes. She is peaceful.

Meera Gupta – 44 years, 6 months, 19 days

∾

Summer is slow to arrive and quick to leave, but for three weeks the streets bake, the roads sizzle with glittering mirages, and the sky is an oppressive blue, unbroken. People walk about in vests and shirts and flip-flops, and the beer gardens overflow with families and regulars, and the sports-watchers and the pub-crawlers.

Every avenue billows with barbecue smoke, and every cul-de-sac clashes with the tinny beat of stereos and radios, the swish and patter of soapy water across a car's gleaming roof. Last year there was barely a summer, someone says. I'm making the most of it. Do you kids want the paddling pool out? – Hose pipe ban – Get us some chicken thighs while you're there – You're supposed to wait for the coals to turn white – I think it's cucumber, strawberry, orange and mint – We haven't got any mint – Get those back doors open, get some air going through – Oh I love this one,

turn it up – He said it was offside, but I think he's talking
bollocks – Ninety-nine with a flake – No, you're supposed
to keep the curtains closed, then it stays cool inside –
I think the firelighters are in the shed.

During the school holidays, Layla visits me a few times a
week. She brings her beanbag and huddles in the corner
with her homework. She says she can't concentrate with
all the heat and Neda's squawking. Sometimes I'll make
her some toast, and sometimes she feeds the cat, but always
we're quiet and respectful of one another's work.

The man in the photograph I'm working on is called
Walter Laney. He's sixty-three years old and he's sitting
in an armchair with his first grandchild. This photograph
needs very little repair, but as I flick through his life, Walter
ages backwards. He turns from a podgy old bricklayer who
loves bacon sandwiches to a muscled heart-throb with a
thick ginger moustache, to a weedy twenty-something
who's just joined the army. It's this army photo that needs
the most repair – half of his face is water-damaged, the
colours of his skin and his uniform bleeding into the
marbled background. I take a small paintbrush and start
recreating his features from memory.

Before I get too far, the cat meows behind me. I fetch
a packet of cat food from the kitchen and splodge it into a
bowl. She doesn't eat it right away – she pads over to where
I'm kneeling, curls her tail around my knee, a low purr.
Layla crouches beside her.

—— Have you given her a name yet?

— She's not my cat.

— She hasn't got a collar. Maybe she doesn't have a name. We'll give her one. I think she looks like a Tinkerbell. Do you like that, little cat? Tinkerbell. Yeah, she likes that name. You have to call her Tinkerbell from now on.

Layla stands up and brushes the white fur from her hands onto her T-shirt.

— It smells like old people in here.

— Does it?

— You're always working. What is all this stuff, anyway?

She wanders over to my desk and starts leafing through the photo albums, mixing up the ones I've fixed with the ones I haven't. I tell her I'm restoring photos.

— Can't people do that on a computer?

— They can. Some people like to keep the original prints.

— Why?

— I'm not sure.

She picks up the photo of Walter Laney with his baby grandson. It makes her smile. She puts it back and glances around the room.

— Do you have any pictures of your own, or do you just mend other people's?

— I think you'd better get on with your homework.

— Don't worry, I'll take some photos for you.

She runs back across the hallway, slamming doors as she goes, and comes back with a chunky pink camera hanging at her neck.

Now she lies on the floor and takes photos of the cat, each image spooling out in black and white on a little scroll of paper. The cat eating, the cat licking itself, the cat lying on the sofa. And when the cat refuses to move, Layla goes to the window and takes photos of the people below, walking by with their dogs and headphones and shopping.

— I used to have a proper camera that would take colour photos.

— What happened to it?

— Nothing, it's in my wardrobe. But Mum said the film was too expensive. She said I only wasted it taking pictures of pointless stuff. This one prints black and white, but it's better because I can take as many as I want.

She digs into her pocket and pulls out four crumpled scraps of photo paper. She lays them in front of me on the table, among all the other photos. A picture of Neda eating the remote. Two pictures of the toilet. And a photo of something harder to make out – a black pixelated blob.

— Is this a slice of bread?

— Yeah, that's in my wardrobe. I'm taking a photo every day to see what happens. It's turning blue, but you can't see it in the picture.

She looks at the four photos, then at me.

— You think they're stupid, don't you?

— No. They're fascinating. You keep taking pictures of whatever you want.

Layla puts the camera to her eye and points it at me.

— Well, pose then.

— Pose?

I sit up straight in my chair and attempt a smile. Not like that, she says. Put your hand near your face. A bit lower. Like you're having your photo taken.

— Is that better?

— It's okay.

She snaps the picture, tears it off the roll, and hands me two photos – the one she just took, and another she must've taken a couple of minutes ago without me noticing. This non-staged one interests me most. Here I am, in this chair, at this table, dusting a photo with a horsehair brush. Plain background. Simple lighting. A man lost in thought. With little context, this photograph might have been taken in any country at any time. She tells me to keep them.

— Can I see any others?

— No way. I don't show anyone. You're lucky I've shown you these. I throw most of them away.

— Why?

— I don't need them.

— Then why take the picture?

She scoops the four photos from the table and stuffs them back in her pocket. She takes some more pictures of the cat.

When she's sure her mum and sister are asleep, Layla opens her top drawer full of socks and pants. Beneath the socks and pants lie almost a hundred miniature photographs. Some are expensive colour film, others are cheap black and white paper. She pulls them out, all of them, scattering

them over the carpet. She kneels among them – pictures
of ants and sparrow bones. A deflated foil balloon hanging
from the telephone wires. A radiator. A glove. Tactile
paving. She slides the photos around with her fingers,
organizing them by colour, then by outdoors-indoors, then
by age. And when she's sick of the sight of them, she takes
her scissors and snips the photos into little triangles, smaller
and smaller, until she's left with multicoloured shingle. In
a moment she'll scoop it all into her hands and dump it in
the kitchen bin. But first, she'll take a photo of the shingle
on the carpet. She'll look at it for a while, this one mono-
colour photo, then bury it beneath her socks and pants, and
begin the collection again.

And in the summer the sewers bake like furnaces and the
air smells of shit, and I wander the path that is patchworked
from all the times the council tore it up for the cables and
pipes beneath. Life grows in the cracks, grasses and daisies.
Perched upon a low brick wall: a child's stuffed rabbit,
loved, forgotten, waiting to be found. Pale clouds and
creaking fences.

The white houses are yellow in the morning sun, the
windows blazing. A skip spills over with flat-packed
furniture and toys. There's a magazine stand outside
the petrol station but it's empty, and there's a white van
coated in grime. The owner, Paul, used to look out of his

window and see the words CLEAN ME in the dirt. Those bloody kids. It used to happen once a month, but it hasn't happened for years.

On a muggy Sunday, we sit around Dalia's breakfast table and play Monopoly. She's the wheelbarrow, I'm the hat, Layla is the dog. Neda is the car, and she's winning, although she shows little interest in the game beyond scrunching the money in her fists. Dalia rolls the dice and moves Neda's car seven spaces to a Chance card. According to the card, it's Neda's birthday, and we all give her some money. Layla yawns.

— Mum, have you ever had twins?

— Me, personally?

— You know what I mean.

— I've delivered lots of twins. But only one set of triplets, and that was in my first couple of weeks. On Friday we had a little boy come out with a cone head.

Dalia mimes the shape of his head upon Layla's.

— A cone?

— Yeah. He'll be okay. It'll go back to normal.

— How?

— They just do. Your bones are very soft when you're a baby.

— Are Neda's soft?

— A little bit.

We all watch Neda as she chews on a wad of colourful cash.

Layla snatches it from her mouth, and Neda cries.

— You're ruining the money.

— Layla, that wasn't nice.

— But she's ruining the money.

— It doesn't matter, we hardly ever play. Your turn, Travis.

I roll the dice, double ones, and I move my top hat and roll again. Dalia places a hand on mine and asks if I'm okay. I say I'm okay, but when does it end? When does the game end? Layla says it doesn't, you just keep going round and round until everyone gets bored. Dalia says that'll be in about five minutes. And sure enough, within five minutes we all agree that Neda has won, and we congratulate her, and she receives it graciously.

Dalia packs up the game, then starts dinner, and I ask if I can help. She says no, go and sit down, so I sit on the floor with the girls, and they climb all over me and I tickle their feet and under their chins. I lean against the sofa, and Neda flops over my stomach while Layla sits on my legs and tells me how rainbows work.

And when dinner is ready, we sit around the table again, Neda in her highchair to my left, Layla to my right. Dalia is opposite, dishing us each a brick of lasagne beside our chips. She tells us to help ourselves to salad, but no one does. And while we eat, Layla talks about how much she misses school, especially her friends. They live too far away, she says. She stares at her dinner.

— You've only been off a few weeks. What about Thomas downstairs? He keeps asking for you.

— Thomas is a weirdo. He eats paper.

— Well, everyone's a little weird. You should give him a chance. Have some salad.

I eat some chips and help Neda with her mushed-up lasagne. She grabs the food from the spoon and smooshes it into her mouth with her fist, like she did with the money. It looks like the most natural way to eat.

And we eat in silence for some time, except for Neda who slurps and punches the lasagne.

— We had a mini tragedy this morning, didn't we, Layla?

— A *big* tragedy.

— I'm sorry. A big tragedy. Would you like to tell Travis what happened?

— Roly died.

— Roly, your hamster?

— Yes. He died.

— And would you like to tell Travis how you felt when he died?

— Angry.

— And why were you angry?

— Because I don't see why he died when I didn't even do anything wrong. I fed him every day. Cleaned out his cage all the time. Gave him water. Put him in his ball. Stupid hamster.

I try to explain to her why she shouldn't feel angry, but I can't word it right.

Dalia looks at me, but I don't speak. Layla prods her chips with her fork.

— They don't last forever, baby.

— What's the point then?

— You enjoyed having him, didn't you?

— Yes.

— Then that should be enough. Eat some salad, please, or it'll get thrown away.

Layla grabs the tongs and heaps too much salad beside her chips. She chews on some lettuce like a donkey with a mouthful of straw.

— Next weekend we'll go and get another hamster, okay?

— I don't want another one. There's no point. I'll love it, and then it'll die like Roly.

Dalia looks at me again. Then she looks away, abandoning the idea that I could be of any use. I clear my throat.

— So where is Roly now?

— Still in his cage. Mum put a piece of toilet paper over him. She said we're gonna throw him in the bin.

Layla nearly cries as she says that, the injustice of it. The word *bin* comes out like something from a Greek tragedy. Dalia peers at me from beneath an embarrassed hand. She shrugs as if to say, what else was I supposed to do with it?

I rest my hand on Layla's.

— I've got a better idea. Let's take Roly and bury him at the allotment.

— That's what I said, but Mum won't let me. She doesn't want to mess up her flowers.

— Well, that's alright. You can bury him in mine. I've got a little piece of garden that needs a reason to exist.

Layla looks at her mum, wide-eyed, nodding. Dalia smiles.

— You'd better say thank you.

— Thank you, Travis.

— You can come and visit him whenever you like.

— Can we make a tombstone?

— We can make something.

That afternoon, Dalia invites me to the park with the girls. Orange-green trees, Earl Grey sky. Swings, a climbing frame, a zipline.

Dalia pushes Neda on the baby swings while I fetch the zipline for Layla. She bounces along, her legs swinging beneath the round rubber seat. When she reaches the end, I help her drag it back to the starting spot. She tells me to push, so I give her a little nudge. She says no, harder than that, so I hold her shoulders, running, until she almost goes flying off the end. She squeals, giggling. That's better, she says. I drag it back to the start, and this time Dalia records it on her phone.

And when Layla is bored of the zipline, she tries the monkey bars, and when she's bored of those she asks her mum for her camera and starts taking photos of leaves, twigs, a coil of dog shit near the bushes. Dalia and I stand close by, watching Neda toddling about on the wood chippings. Dalia rests her head on my shoulder. She rests it there like she does it all the time.

When Neda grows grouchy, we walk to the allotments and bury the hamster in my patch of earth. It's a drab scene – rusty wheelbarrows, graffitied sheds and wild grass bunched around the fence posts. Layla rests a pebble upon the mound, and she cries. Glossy-eyed, she turns to her mother, but instead she walks to me and holds me tight, weeping into my jumper. Dalia watches us. I hesitate, but I put my arms around the little girl. And as I hold her, as the white sky spits at us, something inside me breaks, and I know I've been a fool. How could I let this happen? Day by day, this little family have sunk their roots into my skin. They've crept up on me like a diagnosis, and there's no hiding it – I have fallen for them.

Dalia says it's time to go. Layla wipes her eyes on my jumper and smiles at me, and I savour it.

❧

A TIME KEEPER

At the end of each day, Mike writes a little X in his squared notebook. He's survived another twenty-four hours, but he's not so sure about his wife. She's in bed now, pale, rattling with phlegm – and although she insists she's fine, it's just a cold, Mike tells her to rest. Four times a day, he pulls on his orange hazmat suit, and he brings her toast and soup and cups of orange juice, and she says, thank you, you didn't have to, I'm fine, but thank you. Four times a day, he leaves her in the room full of germs, and he strips out of his hazmat and steps into a shower so hot it nearly peels his skin.

And between these visits, Mike cycles on his exercise bike, he scrubs the kitchen and the living room from skirting board to coving, behind every unit of furniture, beneath the sofa, behind the oven. He checks the electrical sockets, the fire extinguishers, he performs an inventory of the first aid kits – the one under the sink, the one in the downstairs toilet and the one in the upstairs bathroom. He makes notes, he ticks things off his lists, he checks his watch.

His wife, Tina, once found Mike's habits sweet. She thought they came from a place of love, but ten years ago she learnt what kind of man he is. The kind of man who keeps terrible secrets. The kind of man who abused his two daughters from the age of three.

Now their daughters are all grown up, and the house is quiet. Tina prays that she or Mike will die, and as she stews in this bed, coughing, wheezing, she hopes to god it'll be her.

Mike shows me around his home, his collection of clocks. Cuckoo clocks, grandfather clocks, grandmother clocks. The cat clock with the shifty eyes. There's no ticking or tocking – each of them is stopped at a different time. That one's from Romania, he says, pointing to a walnut clock on the wall, with a pendulum hanging inside a glass case. He stands looking at this one for a while, the intricate carving, the floral details, then he asks if I'd like a drink. I say no, so we sit in the armchairs in the living room. The armchairs are wrapped in plastic. The coffee table is wrapped in plastic, and its corners are taped up with foam. In Mike's house, every pointy object, every banister, door, cabinet, is softened with foam and sponge and bubble wrap. Mike himself sits wearing his red bike helmet and knee pads. He catches me looking at the helmet. He taps it with his knuckles.

— You should get one. Sixty per cent of accidents in the home involve head injuries. Not that you need to worry about that, I suppose.

He's a slim man, athletic. We can hear his wife coughing upstairs. A hacking, bubbling cough. Mike nods.

— I knew this was coming. She's been rough.

— She sounds rough.

— Do you want to see her?

— Not yet.

He nods again, hands on his knee pads. Now that he's given me a tour of his clocks, he's run out of things to say. He's always been quiet. His wife coughs again.

— You will take her gently, won't you?

— Actually, Mike, I'm here for you.

— For me? That can't be right. I'm fit as a fiddle.

— No one lasts forever.

— I'm sixty-one years and forty days old, and there's nothing in this house that could hurt me. I'm clean, I'm careful. I have smoke alarms and fire extinguishers – two for general fires, two for electrical. I have first aid kits. I won't even go upstairs and see Tina without gloves and a surgical mask. You've got nothing on me.

— Well, you've got me there, Mike.

He looks uneasy now. He checks the pulse behind his ears, then checks again at his wrist. He clears his throat, tries not to appear worried.

— So, how much do you know about me? About my life?

— Everything. Every little thing.

— Yeah? What did I have for breakfast this morning?

— A boiled egg.

— And yesterday?

— A boiled egg.

— What do you know about my daughters?

— Everything, Mike. I know who you are.

— So that's it, is it? You think I deserve to die, so that's why you're here?

— I'm here because it's your time.

— So you don't care?

— That's right.

— Horse shit. I bet you've reserved a special place in Hell for people like me.

— Mike, I'm not here to decide what you do or don't deserve.

— Then why are you here?

— I've already told you.

Now Mike stands up. His helmet wobbles on his head, and he tightens the strap. He points at me.

— I've had enough of you already. I want you out of this house.

— Mike.

— I mean it. I don't have to sit here and listen to this in my own home. Come on, out.

— Mike, it's eleven o'clock. Time for your sandwich.

— I'm not bloody hungry.

He's standing there looking at me, his slender arms folded across a tight fuzzy chest. He's trembling, getting himself all worked up.

Mike closes his eyes and checks his pulse, counting, breathing, slow and deep, in – and out. In – and out. He stays like that for a full minute, then he walks to the kitchen, opens the serving hatch and watches me through it.

— You're an irritating sort of man, aren't you? Has anyone told you that?

— A few.

— Do you want a sandwich?

— Sure. I'll have a sandwich.

I stand up and walk to the serving hatch, sitting on one of the bar stools. I watch as he butters the bread and looks in the fridge.

— What do you want in it?

— Anything is fine.

— I've got eggs. Cheese. Marmite.

— Marmite is fine.

He takes the Marmite from the shelf, then butters another two slices of bread for himself. He spreads the Marmite, cuts the sandwiches diagonally, then passes me mine through the hatch. I hold the plate, but he doesn't let go. He looks at the floor.

— I'm not ready to die.

— Few people are.

— Is there anything I can do?

— Sit and eat your sandwich with me.

He lets go of my plate and I set it down in front of me. Mike walks out of the kitchen and back into the living room and sits beside me at the breakfast bar. He takes a big bite of his sandwich, chewing as he talks.

— You think I'm evil, don't you? It's alright, you don't have to answer. I am. I've done awful things all my life. Abominable things, and I've got no excuses for them. I do deserve to die.

He stares at nothing, and he nods.

— I wish you would judge me. Shout at me. Tell me I'm going to Hell, or nowhere, or tell me what you really think. You're supposed to scorn me. You can't just sit there like I'm a normal person.

But I do sit and look at him, and I don't say a word.

He bites into his sandwich again. He chews it, this hunk of bread and butter and yeast extract – the saltiness, the wheatiness, he grinds it between his molars, his wisdom teeth, and he looks almost happy at the simple, bitter, creamy flavours. And as he half swallows, the wodge of food slips past his tonsils and lodges itself somewhere down his oesophagus. It stays there. Eyes wide, he knows this is it. In an instant, he understands.

I watch him. He clutches my shirt, and I watch him. His face turns red, violet, his hands fly to his throat. He stands up and thuds his spine against the wall beside the serving hatch. Bloodshot eyes, half-heave, half-wheeze, mucus and fear, the desperate clawing at himself, at me, and I watch from my bar stool and he sees no smile on my lips, no frown, just me, here, watching.

He drops to the carpet. As he falls, his head collides with the corner of the breakfast bar – the corner padded with foam, his skull padded with the helmet, and he's dead within thirty seconds. I stand up and set the Romanian clock to the correct time. Then I finish my sandwich and wash up his plate and mine. And when his wife comes downstairs to find him dead, she'll call her daughters, and when they learn he died by choking they'll finally be able to breathe.

Mike Rudd – 61 years, 1 month, 10 days

The night of Layla's Halloween school disco, she sits on a bar stool in the kitchen while Dalia paints her skin a sickly shade of teal. I stand ready with the fake sores and scars. Dalia paints Layla's arms with a white sponge, she paints her belly, her neck, her face, her ears. Layla smiles the whole time. Patch by patch, her face becomes dead, almost unrecognizable.

— Okay, start sticking those things on her arms.

I peel one off the cardboard packaging – a cartoonish gash that I stick on Layla's forearm. Dalia brushes some paint over the edges until it's seamless, and then I stick one on her shin – this one has black stitches. I stick a long thin one on her cheek.

Layla swings her legs beneath the stool, grinning.

— Anyone would think you're enjoying all the attention, Lay.

I dab some fake blood beneath the cuts, let it drip down her skin.

Dalia watches me. She's cherishing this moment – the three of us, so natural, like a family. She thinks it's the beginning of something. But all I hear is the nagging voice inside my head – I shouldn't be here, I cannot allow it, this isn't fair.

I ignore the voice, and I ignore Dalia's gaze, concentrating only on Layla's wounds – making them as disgusting as possible. A trail of blood from her lip, a drizzle from each ear. And for a few precious moments, I lose myself in this fantasy. Yes, we are a family, and this is one Halloween of many. I am Dalia's husband, Layla and Neda are our girls. We are a happy family, doing happy family things. And it aches.

— We'll give that a few minutes to dry, then you can put your dress on.

— Does it look good?

— You look amazing. The prettiest zombie princess in the land.

— I don't want to look pretty, I want to be *scary*.

— Oh, you are. Go and look in the mirror.

Layla hops off the stool and runs to her mother's bedroom. Dalia washes her hands in the sink. She's smiling with the same smile as her daughter.

— It means so much to her that you came here tonight.

— Does it?

— She kept asking when you were coming.

While she washes the sponge and the brushes, I tidy the paints and throw away the packaging from the scars. Layla comes back, but she looks different from when she left. She's fluffed up her hair – big and spidery, like a corpse freshly crawled from the grave.

— Whoa! Now we're talking.

— Do you like it?

— Absolutely. Now you look really scary.

— Travis, do you think I look scary?

— I don't know, I can't look! Make her go away.

I cover my eyes with my fingers. She looks at me like I'm stupid, then runs over and tickles me. I squirm – make her go away, make her go away – until I sling her over my shoulder and carry her into her bedroom.

— Where's your dress?

— On the bed.

— Get it on so we can get rid of you. We don't want any zombies here.

— Silly. You're not really scared, are you?

— I am a little bit.

The dress is nylon, all pink and purple and black and white, all ripped and hanging with tatty ribbons. Layla slips it over her head, then messes her hair up again. She's wearing black and white striped leggings, and she perches a silver plastic tiara amongst all the hair.

She opens her arms and says, *ta-dah!*

— It's almost perfect.

— Almost? What's wrong with it?

— Come here.

She folds her arms, sceptical, but she follows me back into the kitchen.

I pass her a carrier bag from the worktop.

— What is it?

— Have a look.

Layla plunges her hand into the bag and pulls out a big package wrapped in white crepe paper. When she tears the paper away, her zombie face comes alive.

— Fairy wings!

— Wow, look at those. What do you say to Travis?

— Thank you, thank you, thank you, thank you.

— You'd better go and get your shoes on or we're gonna be late. Your fancy ones are in the wardrobe.

Layla skips off to her room. Dalia turns to me.

I'm expecting to see a smile, but there's no smile, it's something else. She rests her hands on my chest and kisses me.

And when Layla comes back, she's wearing her fairy wings and her sparkly silver slippers and a camera around her neck, and she's never looked happier. They both pull on their coats, I pull on my shoes. Dalia asks me where the hell I think I'm going. She says she'll be ten minutes, and she expects a cup of tea to be waiting when she gets back.

She's late, but a cup of tea waits for her on the coffee table.

Without a word she closes the door and walks over and sits beside me on the sofa. She drapes her legs over mine, rests her head on my shoulder and kisses my jaw.

We sit like that for a while, and I think about Layla.

— I hope she has a good time tonight.

— Oh Travis, you should've seen her. She was so proud walking into that disco hall. Most of the other kids are wearing little masks or whatever, but she's gone all-out.

— You did a great job with the make-up.

— Well, I practised on my brother a lot when we were kids. We'd raid my mum's dressing table and see what we could find. Layla will be raiding mine soon. Do you mind if I wear your jumper?

She points to my jumper draped over the arm of the chair. I pass it to her, and she slips into it and rests her head on my chest, fiddling with my shirt buttons. We stare at the switched-off television, our tiny reflection in its surface.

— You never talk about your childhood.

— I know.

She fidgets a little, and I know it's from all the questions she's deciding whether or not to ask. She asks a few — some she's asked before. Where I grew up, if I went to university, how long I've lived in this town. I invent stories that seem to satisfy her, or I give one-word answers when I can't think of a suitable lie. Sometimes she tries to tease information from me by talking about herself.

— Layla's dad is a bit useless. I mean he's not that bad — I feel for him. But he hasn't seen her in a while. She used to care, but I think she's grown out of it. On the rare times when he did see her, he'd ring me after a few hours saying, she's bored, can you come and get her? And I'm like, kids get bored. How about you be a dad and do something with her?

Dalia pulls off her socks and rests her feet in my lap. She sighs, and I'm not sure if it's frustration at my lack of conversation, or at Layla's dad, or if she's feeling relaxed, or some combination of the three. She switches on the television and cradles her cup of tea in both hands.

— I like you being here.

— That's good. I like being here.

— You make me feel calm.

And we watch the television, wordless, for an hour or so. Watching the gardeners transform a rundown patch of grass into a Japanese-inspired landscape complete with koi pond, miniature bridge, sand area. Little wooden statues of fishermen. Wind chimes hanging from the gutter of the summer house.

Dalia tells me she's been thinking. Thinking about time, and how quickly it goes.

— The other day I was looking at a photo of Layla. I could have sworn the photo was taken a few months ago, and I realized it's been three years. Three years! And it hit me – since that photo was taken, she's grown lankier, and she's got all her adult teeth, and she doesn't muddle up her words. And every day – every single day – is one less day of her childhood.

She glances over at her bedroom, where the toddler is napping.

— Neda, too. It feels like yesterday since I was pushing her out of me – now she's walking and babbling, she's starting to become an actual person — and how much time, how long do I *actually* spend looking at her each day? Savouring her? Taking it all in? One hour? That seems generous. We're always too busy getting ready for school or cooking or washing or sleeping. It's crazy — sometimes I do the maths in my head. I had Layla when I was twenty-six. I'm thirty-four now. And it feels like it's flown by, but in that same stretch of time, I'll be forty-two. Then fifty. She'll be twenty-four. Just like that, she'll almost be the age I was when I had her.

— How long does it seem since you were Layla's age?

— It feels forever ago. Those first years are a lifetime in themselves. But the ten after that were quicker, and my twenties were quicker still. Each year just gets faster and faster — so although I'm thirty-four now, it won't feel like another thirty-four years before I reach sixty-eight. And sixty-eight sounds like the beginning of the end, doesn't it? That's basically seventy. What can you do at seventy? Nothing. I get obsessed with it sometimes. I torture myself with it. I know it's stupid, I can't help it.

— It's not stupid.

On the television, the gardeners reveal the new garden to the homeowners. The husband laughs and the wife cries, and they walk around their new garden, not quite able to believe it belongs to them. Dalia sits up.

— You know, sometimes I look at her. At Layla. I look at her face, but I'm not *seeing* it. I want to appreciate every moment, I really do. But it's hard. It's like trying to taste your own tongue — you're too used to it. Do I sound like an idiot? Does any of this make any sense?

I glance at a photograph of Layla in a silver frame beside the television. It's from last Halloween – she's a fairy witch, carrying a plastic cauldron.

— Yes, it makes sense.

She moves her head towards me again, sleepy eyes. She kisses my shoulder.

And it sneaks up on me – this sensation. A sensation of deepest comfort. Here we are, doing small things, nothing really, just talking, watching television. And yet in the nothingness there is a life more real than any wedding or christening or birthday party. In these tiny moments, when the spectacle is stripped away, when there is no reason for the day, what's left appears to be something true, something fundamental to being a person.

I breathe all of it in. Dalia resting on me, the soft scratch of my own jumper pressed against my skin – the way the sleeves are too long, only her fingertips peeking through. Her hair, with its smell like blood oranges and fir trees. Her breath on my hand. Her legs curled on me, her toes clutching softly at nothing. We're little more than strangers, but in these quiet moments we're just two people sharing a life, and we might have done this every night for twenty years.

— Travis?

— Yes?

— You need new socks.

— They're okay.

— Okay? There are more toes out than in.

— They're okay. I like them.

— I'll get you some new ones when I'm in town tomorrow.

I stare at my feet for a while. Grey nylon socks with a few holes. I pinch one of the holes closed to see how my toe might look if the socks were fixed.

Dalia's phone rings. She sits up.

— Fuck's sake, not again. I bet it's the hospital. I bet it's the bloody – nope – hello? Yes, I'm her mum – what's wrong?

She looks at me. She sits up straighter.

— Right. Oh no, she was fine when I dropped her off. Okay. Well, it's completely up to her, if she – would she – yes. Okay. No worries, I'll pick her up. I'll be there in ten minutes or so. Okay. Thank you. Bye.

— Everything alright?

— Layla's come over a bit funny. Says she feels sick. Bless her – that is typical, she's been looking forward to this since forever. I'm sorry, Travis.

She stands up, glances around for her keys, realizes they're in her pocket.

— I won't be long.

— Actually, I should leave you to it. Sounds like she needs her mum.

— Oh. Okay, well maybe I'll see you tomorrow?

She switches off the television and picks up Neda. She searches for her keys again, remembers they're in her pocket again. I pull my shoes on, and I tell her I hope Layla is okay, but I know this is the beginning. And all I can do is watch.

Dalia pulls up outside the school and carries Neda to the office where Layla waits with Miss Hemsworth. Layla's head is in her hands. A faint pulse of 'Ghostbusters' from the hall.

— I'm sorry, Mum.

— Don't be silly, baby, it's not your fault.

— I feel hot.

— Probably all that running around.

— She seemed to be having a good time, but one of the boys knocked into her – an accident – and she told me her neck was hurting.

— Come on, we'll get you home. Thank you, Miss Hemsworth.

— That's alright. See you on Monday, Layla.

Layla, the fairy zombie princess, takes her mother's hand. She's too tired and dazed to say much, and the two of them walk out of the school, back up the path towards the car.

— He knocked into me on purpose.

— Who did?

— Bailey. He knocked into me on purpose.

— I'm sure he didn't mean it.

— He did, and now he's broken my neck.

— He hasn't broken your neck, baby, you'd be in a lot more pain than that.

— Well, that's just because I'm brave.

Dalia helps the zombie into the car, straps her in.

When they arrive back home, Dalia thinks about
bathing her — she really should get the make-up off — but
Layla can barely keep her eyes open. She slumps towards
her bedroom, groaning.

— Alright, little Miss Dramatic. Don't worry about
your teeth, you can do them in the morning. Just get that
dress off, yeah? Sleep naked if you think you'll be too hot.

Dalia helps with the wings and the dress. She takes the
camera from around her neck and rests it on the drawers.
She gives her some Calpol. And Layla climbs into bed, the
teal girl, smudged, her fake scabs peeling. Hair somehow
messier than when she left. Dalia kisses her head, and it's
warm. She tells her to get some rest.

In the morning she strips Layla's bed sheets, all smeared
in zombie blood and glitter. She runs a bath, and Layla
staggers towards it, sleepy, moaning like the undead.

— A bath will sort you out.

— Hnurgh.

And while Layla stews in the water, Dalia sits on the
arm of the sofa with a cup of tea, watching the microdrama
of the city below — bins wheeling about, lamp posts
switching themselves off, two gulls squabbling over a dried
puddle of sicky chips. A car stops and someone gets out
and says, see you next week. A crisp packet skips across
the car park. Dalia rehearses the upcoming day in her
head — feeding Neda, putting the washing away, cooking
dinner — maybe pasta, something easy — yeah — pasta,
cheese and beans.

She sips her tea and pokes her head into the bathroom.
— You alright, Stinks?
— Just sleepy.
— We'll have a lazy-day today.
— Okay.
Layla sits in the greenish soup up to her neck. Her face still zombified.
She can barely keep her eyes open.
— Make sure you wash everywhere, alright?
— Okay.
— Do you want some toast?
— Okay. Mum?
— Yeah?
— Will you wash my face please?
— Course I will.
Dalia rests her mug on the sink and kneels beside the poorly girl.
— You're really not feeling good, are you?
Layla shakes her head.
The little room is humid and smells sickly sweet, like lychees, and Dalia wets a flannel under the tap. Layla sits in the bubbles, eyes closed, shoulders hunched, swaying. Dalia dabs the paint with the flannel.
— Hmm.
— What?
— Nothing, you've got a little rash on your cheeks.
— A rash?
— It's just a bit blotchy. Does it hurt? Maybe your skin didn't like the paint.

— Get the rash off.

— I can't, baby, we'll have to put some cream on it.
I shouldn't have let you sleep in the paint. Silly Mummy.

— Do I have to go to hospital?

— No. We'll just have a lazy-day.

Dalia washes Layla's hair, her shoulders. She talks to
Layla about her work, like the baby born with a full head
of hair, or the boy who weed all over his dad. It doesn't
make Layla laugh. She nods. She keeps her eyes shut.

The sun rises through the little window, impossibly
bright, a blazing rectangle on the opposite wall. The room
sweats around the mother and daughter. Quiet, but for the
trickles and plops of bathwater.

Dalia lathers Layla's arm. She washes the paint and
soap away, revealing the rash beneath. This one is coarser,
redder. She washes the other arm – another rash, from
wrist to shoulder. Dalia dunks the flannel and washes Layla
more quickly now, frantic. Her tummy, her back. Rashes
everywhere the paint touched.

— Layla, stand up.

She stands up, groaning.

Her legs are dark red, scaled like leather.

— Can I lie on the sofa?

— We didn't paint your legs.

I'm restoring photos at my table, but I feel you, Dalia,
rushing about your flat. I feel the tightness in your chest.
Your dry tongue sitting in your mouth. I feel the prickling
in your stomach, rising, rising, as you grab your shoes

and Layla's. You glance around – the place is a mess, the television is on. Neda is tearing pages from a magazine. It all looks so normal.

And you knock at my door with Layla in your arms. She's wearing a nightie and pink trainers. Damp hair, head lolling. You ask if I can look after Neda, and I don't ask what's wrong, but you tell me anyway – Layla's got a rash. You lift her sleeves and show me. Maybe she's got an allergy, you say. You're taking her to the hospital.

    — Do you want me to come with you?

    — No, we'll manage. Actually yeah, do you mind?

At the walk-in centre you start telling the receptionist what's wrong but she interrupts and asks for your surname, date of birth, postcode. You tell her everything. You tell her you work here. She tells you to take a seat.

The rubbery blue chairs of the waiting area are arranged in rows like at the cinema, except we're all facing a white wall full of posters of people sneezing, people with sagging faces, checklists, acronyms, a foetus choking from cigarette smoke. Layla sleeps on your lap while Neda sits on mine, fiddling with a thread of wool on my jumper. Neda is as unaware of Layla's condition as everyone else in this room. The old man reading the magazine. The woman with her teenage daughter. No one looks ill or injured, but they are.

I want to hold your hand. You look at me.

Your smile is forced yet somehow real, and I put my arm around you. We sit in the waiting area, this cinema, waiting for the film to start. It starts with a name. Layla Preston?

The doctor suspects it's meningitis – meningitis – and the word is sharp and absurd and you knew it – you knew it would be meningitis – and he asks if there's any reason you didn't bring Layla in sooner. You mention something about

Halloween, and you stumble over your words. I want to help you. I want to finish your sentences, explain it all away, but I don't. She was wearing make-up – you didn't see the rash. Has she complained about an aching neck? Bright lights? They check Layla's temperature, her blood pressure, they take some blood and rush her to the paediatric ICU. They tell you to wait in the corridor. You argue. You can see her when she's in a more stable condition.

We sit on a couple of those same rubbery chairs in a nook in the corridor, and there's a boy on a bed outside a ward. He's attached to a drip. He's asleep.

You're shaking. Your knees bounce like the cams of an engine, your whole body is rattling, rumbling, you're ready to bolt to your car and lock yourself inside. Neda is restless. Grumbling, wriggling in my arms. You pinch your eyelids and whisper for her to shut up, please shut up – and I want to help, say something of comfort – but there is nothing but clichés.

— She's going to be okay.

— You don't know that. Travis, you don't know. Oh god. If anything happens to her, that's it. I mean it. I will run in front of fucking traffic, I swear. I'll be done. It's my fault.

— You didn't know.

— Shut up, I should've known. I'm her mother. Meningitis, you've got to act fast. I shouldn't have let her sleep in that make-up.

Your head is full of the baby's whingeing, with a deep hum from pipes somewhere and a beep of a monitor. You

can hear the slapping of footsteps, the rolling squeak of a
lift, the bleating of a phone. There's murmuring from two
nurses, a shiff-shiff of swinging doors, the heaving waves of
your own blood in your ears. You stand up. You need air.

For half an hour, Dalia leaves me with Neda and locks
herself in her car, as she's done on so many lunchtimes.
She rests her head against the steering wheel, eyes closed,
listening to her breath, smelling the cold plasticky scents of
the car, listening to the rumble of other cars parking and
leaving, parking and leaving, the thud of doors, garbled
voices. The cool steering wheel against her forehead,
warming up. Her close breath. The firm seat, her feet on the
plastic mat, some grit beneath her soles. Pay attention to it.
An itch on the side of her hand, a bird singing an unfamiliar
hoo-coo-caw, a gurgle in her stomach. So much to pay
attention to. So much. There's really no need to ever leave
this car, to ever open her eyes again. Someone outside says,
which entrance is it? Another one says, how should I know?

The worst part, she finds, is the waiting. The hours pass
like a dizzy tide, and sometimes a doctor will update her.
It's bacterial meningitis, not viral meningitis. What does
that mean? Well, it means a few things. We've put her on
antibiotics. She's resting, but you're welcome to see her.

And when Dalia sees her in the hospital bed, she doesn't
move. She was expecting tubes and wires, maybe an
oxygen mask, but there's none of that – just a girl in a

bed – and somehow this is worse. The girl is unconscious, arms at her sides on the white sheets.

Dalia approaches. Tentative, as if she's frightened of waking her or breaking her. She sits on the chair beside the bed and I stand with Neda in my arms, but Dalia grabs my cuff and gives it a gentle tug, and I sit on the chair beside her, and the three of us watch the girl's chest inflate and deflate. Disinfectant and cigarettes. Blue curtained booth. Pale yellow light.

She watches her all night, even though I tell her to go home. Go home and rest. If anything happens, if she wakes, I'll let you know. I can't leave her, she says. And she doesn't – she sits at the bedside, bloodshot eyes, cheeks sagging with exhaustion and the tears that won't come. Go, I tell her. She doesn't answer.

Neda's dad picked her up an hour ago, and everything is quieter. The soft shuffle of the ward – beeps and murmurs, beeps and murmurs – she tries ringing Layla's dad again, but he won't answer. And as she watches Layla's little body, she's counting the breaths, waiting for the last one. Her mind is only noise – it's all past and future, for all the things she should have done, and all the things that will happen because she didn't do them – sometimes she mutters words, but they're fragments. Wishes for the girl and curses for herself. Why didn't I, and please, she's got to. I ask if she wants me to leave, and she answers before I've finished the sentence.

I look at Layla. I want to feel what her mother feels.

*

Doctors come and go. Dalia knows most of them. Some are sympathetic, others are coldly professional. Dalia tries to listen to their words, but all she hears is the tone – is she going to die? When will she wake up? Spinal cord and vital organs. Nasogastric tubes. Little blue wristband. Now the girl looks like a patient.

Dalia stares at her daughter. In many ways, she still looks like the baby who would toddle from sofa to table, who would muddle her words, would say *wunf* instead of *first* – she still has those small pink lips and round cheeks, she still has a big baby forehead and fingernails the size of chocolate chips. The years are weeks. Weeks since she wore her last nappy, wore her first school uniform. Now she's here, a story cut short like a book dropped in the bath, the pages soggy and blurred but not unreadable, what happens next, please, please let the pages dry.

Sometimes we look at the sleeping girl, but most of the time we look at our hands, at the walls, at the ceiling. Dalia draws a long breath and says, thank you, Travis. I say, for what? She says, just for being here. You didn't have to be here, but I appreciate it. Layla appreciates it. I don't know what I'd have done.

She rests her head on my shoulder. I rest my head on hers.

And when Layla's dad finally arrives, he stands at the curtains. He can't move. He turns away, then turns towards her again. But where Dalia was silent, he cries, red puckered face, fingers to his mouth. His crying is all teeth and spit. He sits on the bed and kisses his daughter's hand fifty-one times while Dalia weeps without a sound. She didn't know he'd cry. Seeing him cry, she knows it's real. She stands and strokes his back, but she doesn't take her eyes off the girl.

I leave the parents alone.

She tells him about Layla's condition and what the doctors have said. He nods and almost cries again, but he holds it together. She tells him about the Halloween disco and the make-up. She says she'll never forgive herself. He tells her it's not her fault, but they're just words. After that, they don't speak for an hour.

She watches Nick out of the corner of her eye. He scratches the dry spot on his arm. He raps his fingers on his knees. He checks the time every five and a half minutes.

— Nick, I just feel so fucking useless. Our daughter is falling apart, and I'm supposed to just sit here and watch. Why aren't they doing anything?

— I'm sure they are.

— I can't stand it. I can't stand the quiet.

She pulls her phone from her pocket and plays a song, but it's too depressing, so she chooses a more upbeat folk-rock track called 'Glory Hallelujah' and this doesn't feel appropriate either, but it's better than the silence.

In the early hours, Nick and Dalia sit alone in the curtained booth, watching their daughter fight for her life. She's still unconscious – her hair damp with sweat, her skin blotchier. Nick tells Dalia to get some rest. He'll stay. She rejects it, then asks if he's sure, and when he says yes, she looks at Layla again.

— You'll ring me if anything happens?

— Of course I will.

— I mean it, Nick.

— I will.

She stands up. She brushes some hair away from Layla's face.

Outside, it's bitter and the sky is black. Dalia smokes two cigarettes outside the brightness of the entrance, then she goes home.

She stands in the dark of the flat. For ten minutes, she stands. It's quiet enough to hear the radiators, and she stands in Layla's doorway. She considers crawling into Layla's bed, but she doesn't because it would feel like defeat. Instead, she sits on the kitchen floor with her back against the cupboards and she falls asleep with her phone in her hands.

Starlings roost in the hospital roof, and the sun rises orange over the car park. The air is wet, though it's not raining, and it hasn't rained, and it won't rain for days. A nurse cries in her car. A man on a ladder washes the windows at the entrance. A baby girl is born. An old man pisses into a cup, while another old man dies, his organs yielding to the cancer, and his last thoughts are of steak and kidney pie, school mashed potatoes and apple crumble with custard. A cleaner finds a coin on the floor and pockets it.

A husband brings his wife flowers, but he's told he can't take them into the ward. A doctor can't find her wedding ring. And an eight-year-old girl fights, unconscious, against the bacteria taking hold of her body. To the outside world she's silent, still. She burns inside, this restless soul, this zombie fairy princess, battling the evil presence. It works its gnarly fingers up her spine and over her brain, clutching it, squeezing it, wringing the life away. But the restless soul battles, silent, still. She's not ready to surrender.

When I go back to the ward, Nick's eyes are closed, head hanging. He hears me come in, and I sit beside him. He shakes my hand, introduces himself. And we watch the girl in the bed, like two dads. He makes small talk – asks how long I've known Dalia, where I live, where I work. For every question, he gives his own answers, and when he's out of questions, he looks at me.

— This might sound weird.

— Go on.

— She's going to die, isn't she?

I glance back at Layla. The skin around her eyes is dark. Her lips are violet.

Nick takes my silence as a yes, and his lip wobbles, and he releases a shaky breath into his fist. He's younger than Dalia. Almost five years. A frightened boy, too young to understand being a father, too young to understand how to stop being one.

— Is there nothing you can do for her?

— No, I don't think so.

— You could take me. I'm a useless bag of shit. Layla is good. She's so good. She'll do good things – she's cleverer than me already. She doesn't deserve to be here, mate. Please, there must be something. Please.

— I'm sorry, Nick.

— Fuck, man.

He hugs himself in his hoodie, hanging his head and huffing dry tears into his chest. When the tears won't come, he screws up his face to squeeze them out, but it doesn't help.

— Dalia's gonna be devastated.

— I know.

— I was never there for her. Not once. Not during the pregnancy, not after. I was scared shitless. But not as scared as I am now. Not as scared as I am now.

I nod, and a nurse pokes his head through the curtains but doesn't say anything, and he's gone again. Nick stares at the flap of curtain where the nurse had been, then wipes his face with his sleeve. Sniffs.

— I'm gonna get a coffee. Do you want a coffee?

— Okay.

— Won't be long.

He stands up without looking at Layla, and disappears through the curtains.

The moment Nick leaves, Layla begins to stir.

I wait for it to happen, the eyelid flutter, the soft groan, the clutching fingers. She opens her eyes. Her eyes scan the

small room. She doesn't sit up, not yet. When she sees me,
she winces and closes her eyes again.

— Where's my mum?

— At home. She'll be here soon.

Layla nods, then coughs and squeaks in pain.

She rubs the back of her neck, holding in the tears.

— I'm not stupid, by the way. I know who you are.

— I know.

She looks at me from where she lies. Her eyes are dark,
and not just from the bacteria coursing through her blood.

— Did you ever care about us, or were you just there to
kill me?

— I'm not killing you, Layla. The meningitis is.

— But did you care?

— Yes, I care. Perhaps not in the way you'd expect. But
I do care.

— That's a no then.

She coughs again. Winces again.

— This is so stupid. I'm only eight, I didn't get a chance
to do anything. What was even the point? What was the
point in any of it?

I look at my hands. I wish they wouldn't ask questions.
The questions are the worst part, especially those of
children. They ask the hardest ones.

I release a breath and shake my head.

— It's not for me to say.

— You're rubbish. You don't say anything. You talk,
but you don't say anything.

— Layla.

— Just leave me alone. I'll wait for my mum.

She closes her eyes and rests her arms by her sides, pretending to be unconscious. But when she feels my hand on hers, she looks at me again.

— Layla, I have a very complicated job.

— Oh, poor you. Poor old Travis.

— I think you're a fascinating little girl.

— Don't do this then. Say no, you're not doing it.

— I can't.

— Why? Who says?

She sits up and folds her arms, waiting for an answer, as if it's the simplest thing in the world. I let go of her hand.

— I know it's not easy to understand.

— Don't talk to me like I'm a baby. I'm eight years old. Either talk to me properly or leave me alone. Let me see my mum and my dad and my sister, and then you can do whatever you need to do. But I hope you know I hate you. You're disgusting. You'll never have anyone.

Nick comes in with two coffees. When he sees Layla awake, he thrusts the drinks at me and rushes to her side, crushing her against his chest.

— Ow, Dad! I'm poorly here.

— Sorry. You're awake.

— Surprise.

— I can't believe you're awake.

Nick scampers into the corridor, calling for doctors and nurses. And he comes back, holding and kissing her hand. She laughs.

— I'm gonna ring your mum.

— Tell her to bring Spike.

— Who's Spike?

— My narwhal.

— Okay. Hello? Yeah, it's me. She's – yep. She seems alright – she's talking. Sure, here she is.

— Hello? Mum, don't cry. I'm okay. Yeah, Dad and Travis. Yeah. Okay, but can you bring Spike? Okay. Yeah. Okay, see you soon. Love you too. Bye. Bye.

Layla passes her dad his phone, and I pass him his coffee. He clutches it, trembling. Layla rests a hand on his knee.

— You can go now, Travis. My dad's here.

— Travis can stay, can't he?

— No, it's fine. I have some things to do.

— Okay, well. Thanks for being here, mate.

Nurses arrive. I stand up and watch the father and daughter holding hands. Neither of them sees me. I am witnessing this silent scene as if through a window. And despite all the pain he's enduring, I wonder if I'd like to feel it.

Dalia rushes to Layla, bundling her up in her arms. She cries and says, you're awake, you're awake. I'm so sorry, Layla. I'm so sorry – I should have brought you here sooner. I didn't know you were ill. I'm so stupid.

Layla says, no Mum, you didn't know. I'm okay. She lies, I'm okay. I'll be okay.

They sit on the bed – Dalia to her left, Nick to her right. They stroke her hands and her hair like it's the first time they've noticed they have a daughter. Layla smiles, brave. She thinks they're both a bit crazy.

— Where's Neda?

— She's with her dad, baby.

— Oh.

Now Layla's bravery falters, and she almost cries.

— What's wrong?

— I wanted you to bring Neda.

— You'll see her soon. This isn't really a place for babies – she'd be bored and make lots of noise.

— But what if I never see her again?

— Of course you'll see her again.

— But what if I don't? What if I die?

— Now, look at me. You're not going to die. They've got you on antibiotics. You're awake. You're getting better, baby, I promise.

Dalia pulls Spike the narwhal from her bag and passes it to her. Layla nods and wipes her eyes on the back of her hand. She stares at the turquoise stuffed toy.

— I'm always so mean to Neda.

— Come on, no you're not.

— I am. Always telling her to shut up, always calling her annoying and stuff. But she's not. She's not annoying. She's the best sister in the world. I'm so sorry, Mum. Tell her I'm sorry.

There's a panic in her voice now. As though she can see her little life slipping away, and she needs to tie up the loose ends.

— I'm a bad sister.

— No, Layla. You're not.

— One time I pushed her over on purpose.

— We all do things we're not proud of.

— No, this was different. I was proud of it. I wanted to see her fall over. This is why I've got ill. Because I was a bad person. If I could take it back, I would. Even if it meant I'd still be here in hospital. I'd take it back. She's a good sister. She didn't do anything wrong. I want her to have Spike.

— Now that's enough. I don't want to hear any more talk like that, okay? In a few days you'll be out of here, and everything will be back to normal.

Dalia's mind flickers with images of Layla's future. Perhaps she'll be a botanist. Or a forensic scientist. Maybe she'll have some boring job in an office, but she'll practise art in her spare time, and her husband will be an artist too. Dalia sees weddings and Christmases and a twenty-first birthday. Driving lessons, college, pregnancy. The images flicker and flutter, blinding, until they stop.

What, she wonders, would it be like to lose a child? How could a mother live with that? A mother has one job – to protect her child – and I'm failing. If she dies, it's over. I'm done.

She's been in hospital for two days when the doctor asks Dalia and Nick for another word, in his office this time. He explains that, although Layla seems better, he's still very concerned about her condition. These moments of lucidity are a symptom of the bacteria, he says. Although she's awake, she's suffering from severe inflammation around the brain and spinal cord. They will continue with the antibiotics and introduce steroids to reduce the inflammation. If she doesn't show signs of recovery within a day or two, she's in danger of hearing loss, even brain damage. Nick says, can she die? There is a possibility that if she doesn't respond to the medication, the infection could lead to death. But we're doing everything we can to prevent things getting that far. Dalia asks when Layla will be discharged. Not just yet, the doctor says.

While the doctor recites statistics and strategies to the worried parents, I visit Layla again. Her skin is still blotchy, but she looks more alert. I sit on the chair beside her, and she pretends she can't see me. She flicks the horn of her narwhal, she traces her fingers around its eyeballs.

— I've brought you something.

— Whatever it is, I don't want it.

I lay a shoebox on her lap, and she stares at it. She'd love to resist, but curiosity gets the better of her. And when she lifts the lid, she smiles, then cries. She grabs a handful of photographs from the box – some printed on cheap paper, others on full-colour film – but all of them taken by her. All the ones she didn't snip to pieces.

— I didn't look at them, I promise.

— I'd forgotten about most of these.

— I'll leave you to look at them.

— No. Look at them with me.

She pats the space beside her on the bed, and I sit. She tips the box upside down so they all fall on her lap, and she studies some colour ones first. An orange peel at the side of the road. A ladybird on her palm. A bowl of cornflakes.

She picks up a photo of Neda gnawing on a chicken nugget. This one, she studies for some time. The stark white light, Neda's shiny eyes, her shadow on the wall. It was the last photo Layla took with her colour camera. She looks at it until her hand starts to shake.

— Travis, I don't want to die.

— I know.

She puts the photo to one side and picks up another. Moment by moment, she rewinds her short life, until she reaches the first photograph she ever took. Two years ago, the Christmas she got the camera. It's a picture of Dalia, heavily pregnant. A glare of fairy lights in the background.

— I don't even remember it.

— Well, that's what photos are for.

— Thank you for bringing them.

She scoops up all the pictures and drops them back into the box. She places the lid on top, passes the box back to me. She doesn't look angry any more.

— Travis, tell me what happens when I die.

— What do you think happens?

— I don't know. They taught us about Heaven in school, and I always thought it was stupid. But now I'm in hospital, Heaven seems like a pretty good idea.

— And what does that mean to you? Heaven?

— Everybody being happy. Somewhere nice. That'd be good. I bet it's warm and everyone's friendly all the time.

But I don't think I'll get in. I was always nasty to my sister.
They don't let nasty people in.

She picks up her narwhal and flips his flippers up and
down. She makes some whooshing noises, like waves.
I reach out and touch the narwhal's soft back. Flannel
texture.

— Layla, do you remember where you got him?

— Where I got Spike? The fair. Hook-a-duck.

— That's right. You were allowed to choose anything
with a red tag, do you remember? You were so happy
when you saw him. Then you lost him.

— I didn't lose him.

— You were walking back to the car with your mum.
And you shouted, wait, I haven't got my narwhal!

— That didn't happen. I would never leave him.

— You walked back to the fairground. Back into the
crowd. Your mum told you to retrace your steps. And
that's when you realized you'd left him on the Ferris wheel.
The man gave him back to you, and he said—

— He said, don't worry, narwhals ride free.

— That's right. Narwhals ride free.

I brush some hair behind her ear. Her lobe is pocked
with a tiny hole where her ears were pierced, but she kept
losing the studs. She lays the narwhal beside her.

— Everyone seemed happy there. Just having fun and
eating candyfloss and going on rides. I think when Neda is
bigger, I would've liked to take her on a big ride. Because
she'd be scared, but then I could make her feel better,
because I like the big rides. Even the upside-downy ones.

Is that what Heaven is like? Do you even know? I bet you
don't even know.

— A fairground sounds good. It could be like that.

Layla leans back against her pillow and stares at the
ceiling tiles.

She releases a long, slow breath.

— Travis?

— Yes?

— Do you keep a souvenir from each person you take?

— Absolutely. They're just not things you can see.

— I'd take something. Just something small.

— You'd have a lot of souvenirs.

— Well, that's alright because I'd have a big house to
put them all in. I'd be rich, I think. Because I'd take loads
of photos and people would buy them for loads of money
because they'd be such good pictures. They'd put them
on the front of magazines and stuff. They'd put them in
galleries, and they'd say, how could someone take such
a good picture like that? But the best pictures, I'd throw
away. They'd be a secret. Maybe I'd show my best friends
first.

She reaches beneath the covers and pulls out a photo.
She must have taken it from the box – I hadn't even
noticed. She looks at it now, this photo, stroking her
fingers over it.

— Travis?

— Yes?

— Please look after my mum.

*

They move her to a bigger ward around the back of the hospital, overlooking the marshlands and the developing housing estates beyond. There are two other beds in the ward – one empty, one occupied by a forty-year-old woman named Nelly, with her crossword books.

While the nurses settle Layla in, Dalia and Nick stand in the doorway and watch them fussing her, asking if she's comfortable, asking if she needs anything. She says something, and the nurses laugh.

— God, Nick.

— She's getting better.

— That's not what they're saying.

— I don't care what they're saying. Look at her. She's a strong kid. She's full of life. It'll take a lot more than this to bring her down.

Dalia smiles at that. You're right, she says.

She holds him close, this scruffy young father smelling of unwashed clothes and stale chewing gum. They watch their daughter crack silly jokes, showing off to the nurses. Even crossword Nelly watches with a smile.

Dalia hasn't prayed since the school assemblies where they'd sing hymns and recite the Lord's Prayer. She hasn't prayed since she developed her first crush on a boy and asked God to make him love her back. She's never truly believed or disbelieved – she's never had a reason to dwell on it. But she has a reason now. And belief or not, she prays in the hospital faith centre. A white room with laminate flooring and rows of uncomfortable chairs. She sits up straight, respectful. Head bowed, eyes closed, she prays, and she says sorry, and she says please. She makes promises. She tries to bargain. She'd like to cry, for sympathy. She says amen.

Layla sleeps. She dreams of the day she forgot her lines in the school play but made up new ones instead. There was a day she watched green caterpillars crawl along the top of the fence. There was a day she stepped out of the back door to see the puddle of maggots where the cat was sick. There was a day she blew bubbles in the sink through a straw. There was a day she built sandcastles in the sandpit at the park. There was a day she opened tins of paint, the chalky smell, and she painted nonsense on the paper on her easel. There was a day she ate microwave chips from the box, with a blob of ketchup on the side. There was a day she kissed the blond boy in the playground and his hands were cold. There was a day she stole a plastic diamond ring from her friend's house. There was a day she acted out every scene of *Beauty and the Beast* while watching it on the television. There was a day she fell asleep in her mother's arms on the train to London. There was a day she got told off for doodling on the wall. There was a day she made burgers from Play-Doh and her dad pretended to eat them. There was a day she wet herself at school because she didn't ask to go. There was a day she saw the sex education book in the library. There was a day she played the keyboard but spent most of the time choosing different sound effects. There was a day she fell over in the car park and her mum put a zebra plaster on it. There was a day she got meningitis and had to go to hospital. There was a day she got better, and a day she got worse. That was the day her parents cried.

Her mother sleeps beside her.

Nick left to get coffee, but he's been gone for three hours.

It's dark, and the ward is quiet. There's nothing left to do or say, she's run out of moments, and there is no way of dragging this out any longer.

I lean forward in my seat and allow my eyes to wander the child, this pretty thing. She doesn't look much like either of her parents – she's some third mysterious spirit who came for a while and had to leave.

I hold her hand. It's warm.

I whisper some things.

She releases a soft breath. Peaceful. Dreaming, not of fantasies, but of normal days. Shopping and school and baths and dinners. Simple perfect days. Her fingers loosen in mine. She fades away to somewhere else.

And I stand up with the shoebox of photographs, leaving her and her mother to what follows.

When she sees Layla dead, she cries out the words oh no. Nothing-words. Just like that – *oh no!* Such pathetic words they might have been comical under any other circumstance. She knows, the moment she lays eyes on the child, what she sees.

*

Outside, the world carries on like usual. Cars leave and arrive, leave and arrive. A man checks the time on his phone. The moon is full and white.

Nick sees me at the hospital entrance, he's swaying, stinking of drink. He staggers, rests his hands on my chest.

— Take my car keys. They're in my pocket.

His face is stretched and grey, his mouth, the folds beneath his eyes. I reach into his jeans pocket and pull out the keys. He squints up at the bright hospital sign above the doors.

— Are they inside?

— Yes.

— How is she?

— I think you'd better go in.

He nods vigorously. He pats my chest and lurches through the automatic doors. I don't follow him in, but I see him anyway, as he goes through the foyer, into the lift, presses the button, leans against the mirrored wall. He looks like he might fall asleep.

The lift doors open, and he makes it to Layla's ward and Dalia is there, turning to him, turning on him, you useless dick, where were you? Where were you? – pushing him with both hands and— I tried to ring you about fifty times, you useless dick – where were you? She's dead. You missed it. She's dead and you weren't even there. I tried to ring you.

You weren't even there.

I leave them alone.

I leave them in the square yellow frame of the ward.
I walk away from it all, away from the entrance, out
into the dark of the car park. Spitting rain, cold needles.
I glance around for a thing to do, but there's nothing,
so I walk five miles to the flat. Before I unlock my door,
I stand in the hall and listen to the quiet of no one. The
place feels different.

I step inside. Quiet again, except for the cat who
lands on her paws somewhere and slinks towards me
with an inquisitive mew. I crouch and look at her. She
snakes around my legs. As I watch her, I'm aware of a
great weight, a tension — as if there's something heavy
suspended inside me, and I don't know where or how or
what will happen if the suspension should break and the
weight should fall. Maybe it never will, maybe it's always
been there and I can only feel it now by the slightness of
its swinging, and I hold the cat in my arms, and I stroke
her for a minute or two, then I stand up and carry her to
the bedroom. I drop her through the window, she lands
on the ledge. I shut the window, close the curtains. I walk
to my desk and sit with a photo album. I will restore
photos now.

In the ward, you're delirious. Your head is so full you're
too weak to stand, so you sit in the corridor while Nick
mutters nothings beside you — I can't believe it, what are
we gonna do — and his legs are bouncing, he's bitten his

nails to the size of babies' teeth. You hold your head in your hands trying to contain it, like your head is filling with water, building in pressure until it bursts and leaks from every hole and crack in your skull, and it's taking all your strength not to let it — not to roll on the floor and scream and punch people and jump out of the window. Nick rests his hand on your arm and you flinch.

I'm holding a photo of twin boys on quad bikes. The sky is red and yellow behind them. They're Layla's age, riding through a cornfield with pylons in the background. I can smell the dust of the corn. I can smell the two-stroke exhaust. These boys are still alive. They'll die when they're very old men, three years apart.

A doctor tells you some things, but none of it sinks in, it's like reading a book while listening to music and watching a film — jumbling, nonsense, but Nick nods and keeps glancing at you. He listens to all of it. He answers the questions he knows the answers to and helps you with the ones he doesn't. He's stopped crying for now, but his face is sticky and bloated.

There's a photo of an old black dog. A Belgian Shepherd named Maxi. A little boy would love her for the first three years of his life, and then she'd die, and he'd forget. These photographs would be his only reminder. He'd stare at them so much, he could almost trick himself into remembering. You used to poke her in the eye, his dad said.

152

Starlings roost in the hospital roof. The sun rises over the car park.

Layla Preston – 8 years, 6 months, 13 days

A HEAVY BOX

On the morning of her mother's funeral, Lucy stands at her bedroom mirror, fastening her bow tie. Her mother always preferred to see Lucy in dresses, but today she wears a black blazer, black trousers, white shirt. She's twenty-two. Her mother, Sandra, died at sixty-three from all the cigarettes and greasy chips clogging the tubes. She died bed-bound and naked, her skin brown and scaly with sores. At least stop smoking, Lucy told her. Give yourself a fighting chance.

At a quarter to eight, Lucy rides the bus to the crematorium. The morning is wet and cold but sunny, and steam wafts from the pavement between the car park and the building. Her three older brothers wait outside in their suits. They're smoking, chatting about football. Her sister, Alice, wears a black dress and a pink swollen face. When she sees Lucy coming up the path, she jogs towards her and holds her tight. Alice sobs into Lucy's shoulder.

— She's gone. She's actually gone.

— I know.

— Are you alright?

— I'm fine, just tired.

— You know you can cry. I'm here.

— I'm alright.

Together they walk to their brothers, and the eldest, Ricky, puts an arm around Lucy. He offers her a cigarette, but she shakes her head. None of these siblings will die today, but they will say goodbye to their mother.

The hearse pulls into the long driveway through the iron gates, arcing around the shrub-lined courtyard, to the entrance. The driver steps out, tall and solemn.

— Bloody hell, look at him. Lurch.

— You raaaaang?

— Do you think it's a job requirement to look like that?

— Ha. Yeah, you can't be a jolly little cherub.

The five of them watch as the man stoops to the back of the hearse. He opens the door with white-gloved hands. The boys jump as a woman speaks from behind them.

— Are you Sandra's children?

— Yeah, that's us.

This woman is the jolly cherub. Sixty years old, squat, with curly brown hair and a sympathetic smile.

— Has anyone told you about the coffin situation?

— Coffin situation?

— Well, usually at this stage we'd select six pallbearers, usually the grown-up children, friends, a spouse. But because there are only five of you, and because your mother was quite a bit larger than most people, we have a special trolley we'd like to wheel her in on.

— Nah, fuck that. We're not wheeling her in. Come on Ad, take that side. We'll lift her on our own.

— Yes, but I don't think—

The three boys stand at the back of the hearse. Adam rubs his hands together. Ricky limbers up against the side of the car.

— Right, how the hell do we get it out?

— It's on rollers.

— What is?

— The coffin. The floor underneath has rollers.

— Right.

The driver stands aside while the cherub woman fusses, muttering, this isn't a good idea, we have a trolley, this isn't a good idea, you'll hurt yourselves.

— It's alright, love, we've got it.

Adam places his hands on one side of the coffin.

— Right, Rick, you grab the pall on the other side.

— It's not called a pall.

— What is it then?

— Just a handle, I think.

— What's a pall then?

— Like a cloth.

— Just grab the bloody thing, for Christ's sake. Tom, you hold the back. It's alright love, mind out the way, we've got it.

When it's clear they haven't got it, and they'll never be able to lift it with three people alone, Lucy approaches.

— How about me and Tom take this side? You and Rick take that side.

— Alright.

With two each side, they slide the coffin over the rollers, then kneel down to rest it on their shoulders. Ricky groans.

— Fucking hell, Mum. I thought you were supposed to lose weight when you die.

— Don't make me laugh, I'll drop it.

— Fuck's sake.

— I can't stand up!

The four of them laugh while Alice stands aside weeping, chewing the loose skin of her knuckles. The cherub woman asks if Alice would like to help lift it. Alice nods, and the driver takes the other side.

— That's it, come on, Lurch. Cheers, mate. We've got this.

Together, the six bearers rise. They lift the dead woman, and she's heavy, but not unbearable.

— Right, quick, love, where are we putting her?

— In there. On the table.

The cherub scurries indoors, presses play on the music, stands at the table all flustered and red – this isn't how it's supposed to happen.

The pallbearers walk slowly, as dignified as they can. Lucy hears Alice weeping on the other side and wishes she'd shut up. She was the one who'd always give in to Mum's indulgences. A Chinese takeaway here, a pack of cigarettes there, a pint of ice cream. Lucy doesn't blame her for their mother's death, but she can't stand the weeping. She always preferred the company of her brothers. Still, the five of them carry their mother down the aisle.

The crematorium is all magnolia and pine. Their mother's favourite song, 'Every Breath You Take'. The lyrics couldn't be less relevant, but somehow the clock-like pluck of the guitar almost teases the tears from Lucy's eyes.

They rest their mother on the white-draped table. The five of them sit in the front row, while the driver walks back down the aisle and closes the doors. The cherub presses stop on the music, and it cuts out with an echoey click. We're here today to celebrate the life of Ms Sandra Elaine Burke.

Alice stands at the lectern and gives a speech, all love and kisses, and a poem she wrote herself. After each line, she glances at Lucy to see if it's making her cry. She uses words like embrace and cherish. She uses the word bosom, and Ricky snorts. He holds his nose, trying not to laugh, then holds up an apologetic hand. Alice shakes her head and tries again.

— And when she held us in her bosom…

Now Ricky bursts, and this makes Adam laugh, then Tom and Lucy.

— Guys, for god's sake. You're really upsetting me. I wrote this specially for Mum.

Ricky tries to calm himself. He looks at his knees, sighing a big wobbly sigh, and he wipes his tears on the back of his hand.

— I'm really sorry, Alice. Go on, love. Maybe just skip that bosom part because, fuck me, I don't think I can handle it. It's a very emotional poem.

Alice composes herself. She clears her throat, dabs a finger at the corner of her eye and checks it for mascara. She scans down the page. When everyone's quiet, she continues.

— And when she held us in her *heart*, and pressed us to those rosy cheeks—

Ricky howls with laughter into the crook of his elbow, and soon they're all in hysterics – all but the cherub and Alice, who folds her paper and gives up.

— I can't believe you lot.

— Alice, I'm sorry, love. It's a weird day. I'm all over the place.

— How can you laugh on the day of your mum's funeral?

— Because crying won't bring her back, will it? She wouldn't want us all to be sad, would she?

— Yeah, well, you've made me sad.

Alice leaves the lectern and sits back down beside Lucy. She folds her arms.

The cherub stands beside the coffin.

— Do I dare ask if anyone else would like to say a few words?

The hall is silent. Then Ricky raises a hand. He says, yep, I will, then stands at the lectern.

— I haven't written anything. I wasn't gonna say anything. I don't have a way with words like Alice. I mean, what is there to say? Mum, god love her. She had a funny old life. She was athletic once – a bloody good swimmer. But then she had us lot. Three kids by twenty-five. Divorced at twenty-eight. And she always tried her best. Always. Even in the hardest times. I reckon that's true, isn't it?

Alice smiles. She squeezes Lucy's hand. Ricky continues.

— In a few moments she'll be doing what she loved most. Smoking up a storm.

Now Alice lets go of Lucy's hand and buries her face in her palms.

Lucy and the boys try not to laugh.

— My favourite memory of Mum is when she shat herself at Skegness beach. Alice, this was before your time, love. But the four of us, do you remember – we had to stand all around her, holding up beach towels like four little walls while she changed her clothes. Think she'd had some dodgy scampi or something. But she wasn't embarrassed or angry, she laughed about it. I remember thinking she was so strong, then. I'd have been mortified if I'd shat myself, I couldn't have lived it down. But she just carried on like normal. She joked about it to all her pals from the cafe. And I think that's the one thing I'll always take from her.

He turns towards the coffin.

— Mum, we love you. Hope you're doing alright up there, darling. Thanks for everything.

When he sits back down, he sits beside Alice. She hugs him. She cries into his neck. And this moment – seeing the two of them, so different, so alike – her eldest brother, her younger sister – this is how Lucy's tears finally break.

❧

Curl up on your bedroom floor, bury your head with your arms. Tinnitus screams in your ears. Everything is too heavy, too loud. Everything crushes and grips. Whine, drip with snot, rip clumps of hair from your head, circle around in your hole like a dog – you are outside yourself, this is dull and sharp and it boom-boom-booms inside your sloshy head, your chest swells to the size of an oak tree, disgusting creature, sick fuck, it's over, it's over, there can't be a day beyond this day, nose on the carpet, teeth chomping through salty lips with the iron flow and fuck fuck fuck. Dig your nails in your cheeks, thump that forehead on the boards, wail like a banshee in the night, all contorted and ugly, unnatural and diseased, grit those gnashers, girl, until your brain pulses, when's it gonna, it's just you in this hole forever, just you in the dark and nothing will pull you out, it deepens, it closes as the mouth of some great earth whale, swallowing, tightening, and the vertigo rush of falling in your ears and toes, of spinning and the air knocked out of your body and your bones bending brittle for a snap of some release that never comes, and in all your contractions you accelerate back to where you saw her but she didn't see you and that was the last time and you are nothing, you are nothing, you are nothing, you are nothing, you stupid sack of shit, you are nothing.

In the place where no one goes, in this spot beyond time, the hole inverts, becomes an open mountain spewing its angry innards at the sky, a choking smoking dust that curls black. It flegs the fiery phlegm while red veins eat channels through the earth, bubbling and

burping, overflowing from hollows of hell, this sim-
mering soup, these burnt rolling folds slipping out and
smoothing over the gnarly cracks of the before-world,
and no one sees it. Loudest forever, but no one hears it.
A glory, a proclamation, a changing shifting breaking
sea, a steaming heap, a boiling roiling open crater for a
hundred million years. For nothing, for no one.

The woman with no name and no face stands at the
kitchen sink with a glass of water in hands that tremble.
She sips it, gags, vomits white in the stainless-steel
plughole. Never seen a world so sharp, so blurry. Every
speck, every sliver of light, every line, but there's nothing
beyond any of it, it's all just a blade on almost-numb skin,
it's the sticky wet wood beneath the bark, it's scratching
fingernails over bumpy brick, it's burning guts and dry
heaves, it's this it's that, it's not that, it's shopping trolley
static and cuff caught on the drawer handle and the public
toilet and the ghosts wandering, gawping, wonder why
she cries, who walks and cries? It's cold windows and
papercuts. It's stop hitting yourself, stop hitting yourself
and falling belly-first on the cathedral spire, wandered in
because where else to go, it's an organ playing gay and
disrespectful, pews, children's drawings on stone walls,
free guided tour, mausoleum, help me someone help
me oh god, it's giving birth with the stretch and empty
and seeing black hair and a bag of sugar with arms and
legs and hating her because how can you do it alone, it's
prayer cushion dust, it's history brass plaques, it's gift shop

tat, it's toilet again and disinfectant and head deep in the
ceramic bowl, choking, faint reflection in the white bowl
all warped, reflection in the rounded square of water, spit,
spit, spit, bile and water, spit. It's closing your eyes and
seeing more than when they're open. It's home, it's a blue
elastic band on fingers until the blood stops, it's tiny plastic
buttons and suffocating in the sealed duvet cover cave,
it's a soft shroud over the body of giving up and being
no one.

And the lava cools, solidifies, becomes something else.
Black rock, baked flesh, molten rivers just below, rushing
fire, but for now it's a rock, a rock, a rock, and the rock is
fixed on the barren mountain slope.

When you left here, you left with a child – you've
returned with nothing – where is she then? Where's Layla?
Failure. You are a failure. You had a job, and you failed.
There's her breakfast bowl beside the sink, still spackled
with Weetabix like cement, and there's a pink sock on
the sofa – where's the other one? Where's the girl? You
promised you'd look after her. You left her in that place.
And her bedroom door looms like a vacuum, sucking you
in, but you pull away. Her door breathes cold air, framed
with smoky tendrils, while the door beside it is normal and
dull. There's the other sock. You mucky pup. You messy
little tyke, pick it up. There's nothing to do. You left her
in that place. There's nothing to do. There has never been
less to do.

She switches on the television but everyone's having a
normal life, so she switches it off again. She blinks. Glances
about the flat, and it's a strange place. She tells herself to
move. Move your legs, plant your feet flat on that floor
down there. Her body obeys with ten-minute delays, but
it obeys, and she's standing. Her next instruction is to give
herself the next instruction. Go to the bathroom. Go to the
bathroom. She doesn't encourage, she doesn't urge – she
orders – go to the bathroom. Ten minutes, and she's there.
There's a woman in the mirror. The water tap is heavy.
The toothpaste tastes of mint and chemicals. She can't do
the bath. She can't brush her hair. Go to the bedroom.
Take off your clothes. The warmth comes off with them,
the comforting reek is gone, exposed gooseflesh. Stand
naked in the not-quite-middle. Her hands look big. Pull
on some underwear. Pull on those jeans, a T-shirt. Cold,
scentless, like metal. Standing there in clean clothes, there's
a weight of real life. Of being ready. Of responsibility. Of
outside. Of forward. Of normal. Her shoes feel too dry,
like moccasins made of baked clay and straw. The front
door is impossible. There's a world out there. There's a
hallway, and stairs, and streets, and humans. Forward feels
like backward – that's the world she came from, before
it all changed, but no one knows it's changed, so while
everyone else bobs about in their normal world, she's
slipped between, she's before the beginning, and it starts
with this door. This stupid ugly pine-laminate door with

brushed silver fittings, a twist-lock, a peep hole, a chain. This doesn't feel like going out, it feels like going in. If anyone speaks to her, she's coming straight back. That's the deal. That's the only way she can bring herself to place her fingers on the handle. She thought the handle would feel cold, but it feels like nothing. The brush of the door along the carpet. Hallway smell, dim light from the window at the end. She steps into the light. She closes the door behind her but doesn't lock it. She's out.

I am waiting in the corridor. When she sees me, she offers a weak smile.

Black suits you, she says.

It's a small funeral, quiet. Wouldn't be right for her school friends to come. There are no speeches, no anecdotes. It was a life too brief for long stories, or old friends – but you did have a favourite song, and they play all three minutes of it. Too upbeat, too tinny.

No one sitting here thought they'd be here. They thought they'd be long gone. A little chapel. The priest says some things – he speaks of tragedy and loss, he speaks about lives cut short, he mentions narwhals and photography and he hardly speaks of his god. We sit on the pews that are cold and never grow warmer.

Dalia is surrounded by friends – two of them clutch her, while others stare and some look away. Nick has only his dad. And I sit behind them all, watching.

I watch Dalia, who doesn't cry – she's trying to listen to the words of the priest, but they're jumbled and far away, so she just stares at the cracks in the stone floor. And I watch Nick, who doesn't take his eyes from the white coffin. He can't believe he's looking at this white coffin. There's a hymn, a couple of prayers, but Dalia can't bring herself to sing or say amen. She's waiting for the priest to say, it's a miracle, praise the lord, she's alive.

We walk behind the hearse from chapel to cemetery. It's a short walk, so the driver makes it longer by driving down the adjacent road – a shallow bend lined with conker trees. The procession drifts, a few onlookers. Dalia can feel everyone's eyes. She wants it to be over. At the grave, the priest says some final words, and the sky should be drizzly. The world should be sapped of colour, but it's not. Cartoon blue sky. Doodle trees. The scaled-down coffin looks almost comical – a Halloween decoration to prop against the front door. As they lower it, Layla's dad opens his jacket and buries his face in it, and he sobs with heaving shoulders, and Dalia rests a hand on his back, but she doesn't cry – she's barely here, she's watching this through a pinhole in a black box, like someone waking from a dream without remembering ever falling asleep, and the man asks if anyone would like to toss any flowers or soil into the hole, but she doesn't. She walks away and leaves them all to their ceremony.

❧

You sit on the sofa, knees to your chest, bare feet, and you
stare across at a single grey spider's thread dangling from
the ceiling, furred with dust and fluff, its identical shadow
on the white wall, drifting gently in imperceptible breezes.
A fizzled form of a woman in the matt black of the television screen. It's daytime, some time. Neda is at her dad's
for the weekend – he said he'll take her for as long as you
need.

All is silent, all is still. You hold your toes. Cold. Your
face hangs, dark wet eyes, pink hanging lips, tangled hair,
armpit stink, empty stomach, no tears, nothing.

Now I'm at your door with a bag of groceries. When
you see me, your face is vacant – I'm a relic from a time
that no longer exists, I'm a vague reminder – but you let
me in. We sit on the sofa in the nauseating quiet, a cushion
between us, the shopping bag on my lap. I've brought baby
formula and nappies. I've brought you fruit, vegetables,
dry crackers, sugary drinks, fresh cream cakes.

— You should eat something.

— Why?

— You're hungry.

— I'm nothing.

I take out the bag of apples, the carrots, the celery,
the cans of drink, the box of cakes, and I set them
on the cushion. You don't look at any of it. You sit
up straight, hands on your knees like you're waiting.
Without your make-up, the acne on your cheeks is
exposed and sore.

— Have a cake.

— I don't want a cake. Why are you here?

— I don't know. I want to help.

— With a bag of apples?

There's no venom in your voice, just a tiredness. You grab the bag of carrots, pierce the plastic with your finger, pull out a carrot, start munching on it. I open a can of purple grape juice. The crack, hiss, fizz, it's all too loud.

— Dalia, is there anything I can do?

You raise your eyebrows and shake your head, casual, as if to say, nope, not that I can think of, I'm fine, you can leave me alone now. I sip the fizzy grape. It tastes like no grape that has ever existed. I sit with you for thirty-three minutes, and when I'm sure I'm not helping, I stand up. You clutch my sleeve.

— Just talk to me.

— About what?

— Anything. Random things. Boring things.

— I saw a heron yesterday. It was carrying a fish in its beak, but then it dropped the fish into a bush and couldn't find it.

— What else?

— I travel a lot. I know it might not seem like it, but it's true. All over the place, all the time. I've seen some strange things.

You lean back on the sofa, close your eyes.

— Mmm? What things?

— I once saw a man who could roll grit in his mouth and make pearls like an oyster.

— Did you? That's nice. Keep talking.

— I saw a boy with no arms or legs who could pluck the strings of a harp with his nose and eyebrows, masterful as any virtuoso.

— That sounds good.

— People are extraordinary.

— I bet. What else?

You drop the carrot stump into your lap. I brush the groceries aside and sit near you, and you rest your head on my chest. You breathe like someone who fell into a cold pond and is now resting in a blanket beside the fire. You ask me what else, what else, your voice fading with each answer. I tell you stories and truths and half-truths and forgotten things. In your faraway state, I whisper secrets and impossible verses. I speak of every person and all histories, the tragedies unseen, unwritten, the tree that spreads its fingers to fasten it all together, and me.

You stir on my chest. That's nice, you say. What else?

This is the weekend we wallow, and it's the most curious sting I've ever known. To wallow, to surrender. To release any notions of grace or progress, to embark together in this freedom. Somehow in this squalor, with our bodies knotted like roots, our hot close shared breaths, there is a connection so acute and turbulent it feels like love. And when I think about the little girl who was here one day and gone the next, there is an absence inside me, and it's not entirely unpleasant. Do I truly feel it, this absence, or am I only sensing it vicariously through the mother whose body is tangled with mine?

Are you my parasite, or am I yours? It's confusing, isn't it, all this grief?

Sometimes we lie in the dark. We don't speak. I rest my head on your chest and we stay like that, two birds in a nest, two stranger-birds who found each other and decided to keep each other warm. Hold me in the stark awareness. Hold me until I'm cramped and sore, weep into my shoulder until your breath smells stale, claw your cold toes between mine, bite the skin where my cheek meets jaw, tug the hair at my nape, you whisper, I want to forget, I want to forget, I want to forget. Your messy bed, loose sheet stripped back from corners of mattress, sweat and linen, lumpy pillows, old underwear elastic. Forty seconds, desperate, gross relief, quiet shame, side by side.

I sit on the edge of the bed and pull my clothes back on. Neda's dad calls again and you ignore it again. He's calling to see if you're okay. He's calling to ask if you want to see Neda, and you know that's why he's calling, but it makes you dizzy, the thought of speaking about real things.

— When do you think you'll answer it?

— When I'm ready.

He calls again, your phone lighting up with a picture of Neda in her pushchair, and Layla feeding a goat through a wire fence, and you bury the phone under your pillow. You sit against the headboard and pick the last few flakes of black polish from your fingernails. I say your name, but you don't answer. I ask if there's anything I can do.

— Stop asking that. That's what you can do.

In the light of the morning sun from the window, the shadows cut deep into your face, and you look older, and younger – too old for your age, too young to pine for a daughter – and even with your eyes open, I know you're dreaming, you barely see a thing.

— Travis?

— Yes?

— Would you make me a coffee, please?

I go to the kitchen and fill the kettle and fetch two cups from the cupboard, and I make us each a black coffee. We stand in the kitchen, and I wait for mine to cool, but you sip yours right away.

— Travis, there's something I need to do. I've been putting it off.

Your voice is all breath. You speak to the centre of the floor.

— What is it?

— Layla's room. It's starting to smell. There are dirty clothes in there, an old hamster cage. I need to clean it.

— Okay.

You look at me.

— Will you help me?

— Of course I will.

You step inside as if by accident. The room looks just as she left it. A messy bed, lived-in. Drawers open. School clothes on the carpet. Curtains neither open nor closed.

And as you stand there, you try to imagine it's just another day – you'll pick up the clothes, you'll open the curtains, close the drawers, make the bed – and you savour it, this silly story, because if you make this bed now, it'll never be unmade.

I start clearing out the plastic hamster cage. You pick some books off the floor. You start tidying the wardrobe.

You can hear her voice. Mum, where's this, Mum, where's that? Mum, we're out of toothpaste. Mum, I've done my homework. Mum, is it a Dad weekend? Mum, are you okay, you look sad. You can hear her, and she doesn't feel dead. You're just in the wrong reality. You've slipped, fallen between the cracks, and she's disappeared, or you've disappeared, and you just need to find your way back.

In the wardrobe, you find a lump of furry green matter, and you cough.

— Oh Layla, what is this?

— It looks like bread.

— Bread?

— It looks like mouldy bread.

You look at it, this unrecognizable thing, and you smile.

I fetch a bin bag from the kitchen, and you drop the bread in with a puff of blue dust. I think of old John Lamb's poem – the one with the bread.

Now the room smells of chalk and rubber. You wash your hands in the sink, and when you come back you open the curtains and the window. You make her bed. You pick up the clothes and you sit on the bed with a grey pinafore in your hands, and you can smell the day of her – you can smell pencils and exercise books and grass and buttercups.

It's an impossible smell, all swirling and wafting to conjure
something so familiar, so present.

The leggings are inside-out, so you reach inside, and
find some scraps of paper. Black and white photographs of
disco lights and dancing skeletons, a vampire girl, a devil
boy, a pumpkin. You feel she's here. She's actually here.

I sit beside you on the bed. We gaze at the pinafore and
the photos.

I'm sorry, you tell her. God, I'm so sorry. It was my
job to look after you, but I didn't, and you deserved more.
I don't know what to do. I'm so sorry. I don't know what
to do.

My eyes scan the bedroom. It's tidy. Ready for a little
girl to move in and mess it all up again. This room has been
looming over you, and now it's done.

— At least now, maybe it'll be easier to move on.

— Move on?

— From all this, I mean.

You look at me, blank-faced.

— Travis, move on? What do you mean?

You hold out a hand, waiting for an answer, as if there
must be something very important you've missed about
this whole situation.

— Seriously, Travis, what does that mean? Moving on?
What does that look like, exactly? What would you like me
to do?

— Everything you're doing is fine. I don't know what
I meant. It's just, surely you don't want to stay like this
forever?

You release a scratchy kind of laugh and shake your head.

You stare at the tidy carpet, fingers at your lips.

We're quiet for a minute.

— Dalia, if there's anything I can do—

— Yes, there is. I need you to leave me alone.

— I've upset you.

— I'm not angry. Alright? I know you didn't mean it. You've done all you can do, and I appreciate it, but now I need you to leave me alone. Even just having you here, it's like a different life, and it's finished, and it's making me feel sick how it's clinging on. Let's go back to how things were a year ago, okay? I just want to be alone.

You don't look angry, but you're shaking. Your left leg bounces as you stare at the ceiling, hugging yourself, waiting for me to leave. I stand up. I want to say some things, but the words won't come. For the first time in days, I see tears in your eyes.

∾

A PICTURE MAKER

Mansoor spent the next ten years nurturing his deceased wife's humble printing business from a market stall into an eight-figure multinational company, but still he refused to buy a widescreen digital television. His much-too-old

Panasonic CRT sat in its little corner in the same old kitchen, and that was how he liked it.

His wife had begun with posters, T-shirts, hats, key rings, mouse mats and mugs. From there, Mansoor expanded into leaflets and business cards. Instead of selling cheap merchandise to Joe Bloggs off the street, he wanted to capture the B2B market, he told his boys. Now eight, ten and twelve, they flitted between feigning interest, staying quiet, or downright assuring their dad they didn't care. Business cards are boring, Dad. Leaflets are for chucking in the bin. But the youngest, Krish, remained supportive. Every week he'd ask for a new poster for his bedroom.

Within three years of printing his first business card, Mansoor had earned enough money to buy his first major printing press. A quarter-of-a-million-pound investment, the size of a tank. He leased a warehouse, bought a binder, a trimmer and a shrink wrapper, and he hired five men for his production floor. Now he could print in high volumes and bind the loose leaves into books and booklets and ship them all over the world. And when he walked through that warehouse for the first time, listening to the press hissing and whirring, watching his employees pushing palettes of paper from machine to machine, seeing the finished books being wrapped and boxed, Mansoor felt absolutely nothing.

Before long, the books and booklets were so lucrative, he stopped selling the business cards. He stopped selling the key rings and hats and the other bits of crap – the return was too small, they weren't worth the effort. But the books – the softbacks, the hardbacks, the coiled, the stitched – these were enough to secure him two more presses over the next two years. By the time he was fifty-five, Mansoor's company had become the largest digital printer in the country. He accepted his national print award with a smile and some humble thanks, and when he returned home that night he sat at the kitchen table with a picture of his wife and a bottle of white rum and he cried for three hours.

The little television watched. It watched the boys become men – men with shirts and briefcases, men with impossibly deep voices that seemed to have broken overnight, men with lovers and cars and phones and opinions. The little television watched Mansoor's hair turn grey, his beard grow long. Deep lines from the bridge of his nose to the corners of his mouth. Thick grey sacks beneath his eyes. Stubbled jowls. Yellow teeth. Mansoor spent less time at the warehouse these days, and his boys would visit him once a fortnight or less, even Krish, who had moved to London with his boyfriend Callum. Mansoor would wake up around eleven in the morning, and he'd sit in the kitchen and watch his daytime programmes – the quizzes, the endless talking – and he'd drink coffee. With the boys gone, with the business taking care of itself, these mindless programmes, the idiot adverts, became his only distraction. His next distraction would arrive in the form of a brain tumour.

Mansoor wasn't scared. Nor was he pleased. But he was surprised to feel a cool wash of relief fall over him – he'd dreamt of death a thousand times since Meera, but he could never leave the boys. Not on purpose. Now, if he died, it wouldn't be his fault. Maybe he'd live. It was win-win. And over the next few weeks, he met with the solicitor, Mr Smith, to set his affairs in order.

When it came time to tell the boys about the tumour, Mansoor planned on telling them all at the same time, but their schedules were too hectic. He told Ravi in a cafe. He told Aryan in the kitchen. He told Krish on the phone, and Krish rode the first train home.

Krish and Mansoor drink coffee in the kitchen, and the television watches. Mansoor was expecting tears, but Krish is calm – he's been through all this before, and he's become a man since then. They speak, these two men, about the future. About Meera, about the business. About cancer, and how it's a bloody pain in the arse, and when will they find a cure? Mansoor is peaceful, and Krish understands. If Meera were still alive, the tumour would mean something different.

— Krish, I'd like you to take over when I'm gone.

— Take over your printing company?

— It's not mine. It's your mother's. She started it, I just took care of it for her. Now I need you to do the same.

— Dad. We've spoken about this.

— It's different now. Someone needs to take over. It's a lucrative business – no debts, plenty of assets. People will always need print, even with the internet.

— I'm not worried about that, Dad. But I've already got a job in London. I've got a life there.

— I know, I know, it'd be an adjustment. But you'd enjoy it, I promise. You'd be your own boss. It's not difficult. The place takes care of itself these days.

— Have you asked Ravi or Aryan?

— Yes. They're not interested.

— I just don't think—

— Don't answer now. Think about it. Everything I've built, I built for your mother. I want to know it's in safe hands when I'm gone.

— I'm sorry, Dad.

Mansoor's peaceful foundations begin to quake and break apart. He's been ready to die for so long, but he can't leave Meera's business to a bunch of soulless investors. He stares into his hands now, and Krish stands up and kisses his father's head. He leaves him in the kitchen, alone, but not quite alone.

The television watches Mansoor reach his sixty-fourth birthday. To his surprise, all three boys come to visit. It's the first time they've all been in a room together since Ravi left home. They set a giant parcel on the kitchen table – a present wrapped in glittery red paper. Mansoor shakes his head, but he's smiling. When he rips away the paper, he sees a cardboard box with a black image of a widescreen television.

— I already have a television.

— It's about time you had a new one.

— That bloody old thing has run itself into the ground.

— This new one's got all the channels on it.

Mansoor considers arguing. But he nods. He tells them thank you.

They take the old television away, leaving a bright
square of worktop where it sat, and they mount the
widescreen on the living room wall. That night, Mansoor
sits on the sofa and flicks through the channels. There are
so many, he doesn't know what to watch.

I sit beside him. We don't speak.

The boys load the old television into a trailer along with
a bike, a wardrobe, a record player, a teddy, three large
candlesticks, a lava lamp, a sack of coat hangers, and a
colourful mass of other shapes and textures. It's all dumped
at the tip, onto the mountain of discarded objects –
discarded, once loved. The television watches the blue
sky obscured slightly by the handlebars of the bike. The
television watches for years and years, its view of the world
shrinking, shrinking, beneath layers upon layers of rubbish,
until everything turns black, and then the television listens
to the muffled machinery and voices, and forever dreams of
a little family in a quiet street, a mum and a dad and three
bright boys.

Mansoor Gupta – 65 years, 6 months, 19 days

Dalia drives to Neda's dad's house and barely remembers
the journey. She's on autopilot, simple instructions. Open
car door. Get out. Walk up driveway. Knock on door.

Solomon answers, his face skewed with pity. He looks at her, and she looks like a mother who has just lost a child.

— Dalia, I am so sorry. Come in.

She walks in, he closes the door behind her. He opens his arms for a hug, but she just looks around. A beautiful hallway. Big silver-framed mirror, pine flooring, clean white walls. The place smells of vanilla and polish.

— Where's Neda?

— She's just having her dinner. She's fine. Dalia, god. I don't know what to say. I've been trying to call. I'm so sorry. Can I get you a cup of tea or anything?

— No. Okay then.

She follows him into the kitchen and he sticks the kettle on. It's a perfect kitchen – spacious, a big island, lots of frivolous utensils like the giant pepper grinder and a pestle and mortar. Solomon makes the tea the way she likes it – plenty of milk, half a sugar. He's a handsome man. Darker skin than Neda's, and hair as short as his stubble. He passes her the cup of tea, and she clutches it with both hands, feeling dirty in the pristine home. She can hear Neda babbling somewhere.

— Dalia, I want you to know that if there's anything you need, we're here for you. Day or night. You don't have to do this alone.

— That's nice. Thank you.

Dalia sips her tea. Too hot, but she closes her eyes and savours the scald on her tongue and down her throat into her stomach. When she opens her eyes, Solomon's fiancée is there. Dalia hasn't seen her all year.

— Dalia, I'm so sorry, sweetheart. It's awful.

— You're pregnant.

— I am.

— Eight months?

— That's right.

Carrie rubs her abdomen and smiles at Solomon.

Her smile fades and she looks at Dalia again.

— God, Dalia, I can't even imagine what you must be going through.

— I told her we're here for her. Day or night.

— Definitely. Any time. We've been trying to call.

Dalia knows they're trying their best, but still they grate on her. She rubs her temples and stares at the genuine slate floor.

— Neda's been good as gold. She misses her mummy.

— Can I see her?

— Course you can. She's ready to go home. I'll just go and fetch her.

Carrie disappears again, and Solomon approaches. He holds Dalia in his arms, but it's more for his benefit than hers – he wants to feel like he's doing something. Dalia stands there, arms by her sides, letting it happen. After a few moments, he lets go.

When Carrie comes back, she has a baby bag over one shoulder, and Neda over the other. She looks like a natural mother, fresh and strong, as if a baby is just another feature of a home, like a cushion or a tea towel. Neda chews her giraffe teether, gurgling. She looks perfectly at home in Carrie's arms, in this kitchen, beside her father. Carrie speaks to her in a baby voice.

— Can you see your mummy? Yes? You've missed her, haven't you? Yes, you have. Are you ready to go home? Are you ready to go home and be with your mummy? Yes, you are.

Dalia has never spoken to Neda like that, not once.

The baby barely acknowledges her.

— Look at you, with my daughter. In your perfect home.

— Dalia?

— You've got everything, haven't you? Not a care in the world. You just bumble from one day to the next, and it's all so easy. You wouldn't know a problem if it punched you in the face.

Solomon puts his hand on Dalia's shoulder.

— Dalia, it's okay.

— Get off me. You don't know anything.

— You're going through a lot.

Dalia steps towards Carrie, slips the baby bag off her shoulder.

— Give me my daughter.

— Dalia, I'm really sorry. I wasn't trying to upset you.

— I'm sure you weren't.

Carrie passes the baby to Dalia, and Dalia strides straight out of the kitchen, across the herringbone floor of the hallway, back outside in the block-paved driveway.

— The car seat. Where's the car seat?

— I'll fetch it for you.

Solomon unlocks his top-of-the-range electric car and unfastens the baby's seat. He carries it towards Dalia's car, but she snatches it off him.

— We're here if you need us. I mean that.

— We don't need anyone. Go and play happy families.

He stands in the road looking at her. He's never felt more helpless. There's concern in his eyes, but Dalia knows it's not for her, it's for Neda. Drive carefully, he says.

❧

You sit in the dark on the sofa, your spine perfectly straight, in the blue glow of the television. A shopping channel flogging wooden ducks. I stand in the shadows. You can feel me there, standing in the shadows, but you blot me from your mind. You can feel me, silent and still, watching you. I am there like a mannequin in the corner, always. When you stand up to pour yourself a glass of water, you walk past me. You feel my breath. You're at the sink, drinking the water. You glance in my direction, the figure, the presence, but you can't see my eyes in the gloom. I am here, even if you pretend I'm not. And I will be here, standing in my corner in the dark.

❧

In the autumn the air smells greasy and foul from the sewers that overflow with dead leaves – a stench that ripens as winter arrives and the pipes freeze, and expand, and burst. I wander through the town centre, all festive lights now, a winter market. Powdered sugar scents of pastry and hot chocolate. I pull my collar around my neck and walk. The world is white and grey and black and dark blue, it's yellow in the windows. I stand outside the cathedral and marvel at my own breath. I wander one way, then stop and go back. I buy a hot chocolate and throw it in the bin. There's a woman selling bracelets and notebooks. She smells of incense. There's a coil of dog shit near the ATM. There's nowhere to go.

The avenue is thick with fumes from all the cars in all the driveways, all of them left running for their windscreens to thaw. In the gravel, a crushed cigarette box with saturated photos of scarred lungs and bleeding throats, and Jade bikes to school without a helmet. Niamh walks to school with her rainbow backpack, past the flowers tied to the lamp post. The squeaky crunch of frosty grass. Prickly pancake hedgehog, these bin-smell streets. The lumps and bumps and spikes and humps – all the shapes designed to keep the humans from sleeping. Do not rest here. Rest somewhere else. Where? Somewhere else. Concrete blocks, cast-iron rocks. Send those pesky humans away.

Now I stand in the centre of my living room peering at the table of photographs. I have a lot of work to do. I pull out the chair to sit down, but I sit on the sofa instead and switch on the television – a programme about antiques. The cat jumps on my lap and starts padding my stomach, but eventually she curls up and we watch the antiques – the

medals, the jewellery box, the jug. The corners of my
mouth are wet, and my stomach churns. I wipe my cheeks,
stare at my tacky fingertips. The cat watches me.

When it's dark, I open a beer from the pack I bought.
The can has gothic writing and an image of a skeleton in
a hooded cloak. The skeleton holds a scythe whose blade
underlines the name of the beer. I sip it from the can. It
tastes dirty, like bread and socks, but I drink it anyway in
the light of the news programmes, a bus crash, no fatalities.
The cat is gone. When was I last so aware of my skin, my
fingernails, my eyelids, my tongue? When did I feel the hot
blood running through my arms and legs? I scratch, I pick,
I pull. I remember this. Yes, I remember. By the time I've
finished the can of beer, the taste has grown on me and
I crack open another.

❧

A month after the funeral, you pack everything into cardboard boxes. The flat is making you ill, you can't breathe,
you need to get out. First, the kitchen — every drawer and
cupboard. Every plate and spoon. You dump it all into the
boxes with little care for neatness or bubble wrap. Just get
it packed. You pack up the living room, your bedroom, the
bathroom, until there's only one room left.

Her T-shirts, jeans, her skirts and leggings. School
books, reading books. Felt tip pens, notebooks, a wodge of

185

Blu-Tack, hamster cage. Toys she grew out of but couldn't part with, the mountain of teddies on her bed – things Neda could use but never will. All of it, in the boxes, taped up, marked with the word LAYLA, and it's weird to write it, weird for your hand to form those letters in that order, and you wonder how many more times you'll ever write it. Are you erasing her by stowing these things? Are you silencing her by sealing them away? Or is it protection? Keeping them safe and sacred, unexposed to the world, not binned or sold – these are her things, and they will always be her things. And now the room is shelled and full of echoes. Unfaded rectangles on the walls. Someone else will live here – maybe an old person, or maybe some little girl who will stay alive.

When I see you in the corridor, you're carrying the baby and a big bag. Boxes by the door. I ask if you need any help, but you shake your head. You say you just want to get out. You say it again, I just want to get out. And I help you with the boxes anyway – four trips up and down, Neda waiting in the car. You close the door of your flat for the last time, and you don't even indulge in one final glance around the place. We carry the last of the boxes to the car, load them in. You close the boot. You say thank you, but you don't look at me, you just slide into the driver's seat, and then the two of you are gone.

You can still smell her. Even in the new house, you can smell her – milk and fabric softener – and you wonder, did

she ever really have a smell, or was it the fabric softener
all along? You switch on the ceiling lights even in the
daytime, otherwise the rooms feel dead, but you are calmer
here already. The foreignness of it. Same town, but it all
looks different. You can imagine you're someone else with
a different life. Maybe you won't even unpack – you'll just
buy new things, you'll start from scratch. Change Neda's
name. Change yours. Dye your hair. Find a new job. It's so
seductive you start writing notes on your phone, but soon
find yourself scrolling through photos of the year past –
the trip to the woods, the soft play, the silly sunglasses she
found in the supermarket, the previous Christmas – all
these flat memories on this flat screen – you try to see past
these abstract representations, to see *her*, but it's futile, like
biting into a picture of an apple. Neda explores the new
bungalow, but you sit on the floor of the empty living
room, flicking through the photos. The sun shines from the
window behind you, casting a shadow of your head and
shoulders on the laminate floor in front. You are still. You
are quiet. As long as you stay still and quiet, things cannot
get worse.

I find myself spending fewer nights restoring photos in
the lamp light and more nights wandering the dark of
the town and the warm glow of windows – ground-floor
windows, living rooms that seem bigger on the inside than

out, where the families huddle among cushions and blankets and watch television, the silent motion of characters and words, and the bedroom windows with the wardrobe tops, the silhouettes in pulled curtains. On week nights I find myself wandering the winter market, and on Fridays and Saturdays I follow the booming sounds of music – the club with the sticky floors.

I order a cup of water, and when he asks if that's everything, I say yes, and I turn towards the dance floor to watch the heart attacks, the cancers, the dementias, the pneumonias, a car crash, a suicide, a drowning, an overdose. I watch them writhe in the lights, so overwhelmingly alive, so young and beautiful, so present – and it aches but not enough. It's a dull grinding ache like a blackened tooth begging to be pulled, begging for the hot release of a more intense pain.

The barman looks bored. He's waiting, and they're all waiting, and when I ask the barman for my fourth cup of water, the girl with the pink dreadlocks slumps beside me. Elbows on the bar, each hand fiddling with the bracelets on the opposite wrist, she nudges against me but stares straight ahead, swaying. She orders a triple-vodka-bitter-lemon and asks me why I'm drinking water.

— I like water.

— Are you driving?

— No.

— You should have a 3VB – it's the cheapest drink for the most units and it tastes okay.

— Maybe later.

— Aren't you a bit old to be in here?

— How old do you think I am?

She looks at me. She's short and her eyes are winged with thick black triangles.

— You're a clever one.

— A clever one?

— Yeah, I know people like you. You get bored because you're clever. You don't want to dance or talk because it's too boring.

Her 3VB arrives and she slides it towards me. She says, try that, and I say, no I'm okay, so she takes the drink and holds it near my chin. Her name is Jess and she won't die for a long time. She won't know any of these people in ten years. She won't remember this night or this moment. Her hand smells of cigarettes.

I take the drink and sip it. She takes the drink back and grins. She takes my hand and tells me to come and dance, and I tell her maybe later. She joins her friends. I sip my water to take the taste away. One of the other women takes my hand. She's older than the others. She guides me into the fray, and she holds my waist and makes me move in uncertain ways.

She calls a taxi and takes me to her home on the outskirts of town. It's a quaint house: a bungalow, a front garden with a pond and pebbled path. It's dark outside, but everything shimmers with frost – the window ledges, gutters – and she grabs my hand and leads me to the front door, this woman in the grey dress, this young widow, and she unlocks the door, and it's cold in the hall with the tiled floor. She leads me to the living room where she switches on the light, switches it off again, switches on a lamp instead, and she switches on some festoon lights hanging on the mirror. A blue glow from the fish tank. She asks if I'd like a drink, and I say yes, but she doesn't ask what, and she pours us each a glass of red wine from a decanter near the incense burner. She passes me my drink and says, let's dance some more. She says, I'm not done dancing. And she drops the needle on an old record player – some folk ballad – and she dances with her wine. I stand and watch. She doesn't seem to mind that I'm not dancing. She's in her own place somewhere, eyes closed, writhing and wriggling in her dress, this woman with the stranger in her house.

When she's finished dancing, she tells me to sit down. She sits beside me on the worn floral sofa, wine in one hand, arm over my shoulders. She folds up her legs and rests them on mine.

— Tell me about yourself, Travis.

— One day I will watch you die.

— You have a nice voice – has anyone told you that? Very soothing. I've had a lot of jobs. I travel a lot. Do you get around much, Travis?

— Yes. All the time.

— All the time?

— Every moment of every day.

— And where do you go?

— Everywhere. Everywhere there is.

— Is that so?

— Yes.

— Well, Mister Traveller, I've been a butcher. A baker. A phone operator. I've never been to New Zealand, though. Maybe you could take me.

She nuzzles her face into my neck, and I sip my wine. She smells of lemons and pepper. She unbuttons the top button of my shirt and I can feel her belly and chest against my body, and although she's flirting, she feels motherly to me, and I imagine this is how it must feel to have a mother, and it's comfortable and warm, she's attentive, she holds me like I'm the only thing in the world, and although we'll only see each other one more time after tonight, I allow myself to drift away into this haze of being cherished. She kisses my cheek, and somehow this is more sensual than if it had been my lips. She's taking nothing, only giving.

— You have a hard life, don't you, Travis?

— Sometimes.

— I can tell. Don't worry, I won't pry. I just know these things. It's okay. You don't have to worry about anything tonight.

She whispers, close your eyes. And I close them, and I rest my head back. And I let her do the things she wants to do to me, and when she's done, she says, stay there. She disappears for a few minutes. I finish my drink, and when she comes back she's wearing a thin grey nightdress. She leans in the doorway smiling, this mother, this widow. Before she can walk back to the sofa, my eyes are closed, and I'm asleep.

❧

A ROOMFUL OF LOMS

The line operation managers sit in the coffee room beside the signal box. The windows are steamed up from the cold outside and the little heater hums with its glowing bars. Four of them sit around the square plastic table, three oldies and the new kid, drinking the overbrewed coffee, yawning. The new kid sits with his hands in his lap, wondering what the hell he's gotten himself into. He only took the job to appease his mum and because he couldn't stand one more day of college. Now he's here, plonked between these middle-aged trainline veterans with their newspapers, their sunken eyes, their farts, and the new kid asks himself if this is what they meant by *real life*. Is this it — am I an adult now? Is this how it'll be for the next fifty years? All his friends are at university, scattered across the country. They'll be partying and making new friends, gathering an education for a better life. But he's stuck here, and there's a heaviness in his stomach. The air in the cabin is thin and empty, with a layer of coffee and man-smell. One of the LOMs scratches his belly and rolls his head around on his neck. He asks the new kid if he wants a coffee, and the new kid shakes his head.

The LOM pulls out his phone, taps around, points the screen at the new kid. It's a video of a woman riding a teddy bear with a dildo strapped to it.

— What do you think of that?

— It's okay. It's funny.

— You'd like a woman like that, wouldn't you?

— I don't know. Yes.

— Definitely, you would.

The LOM watches the video a bit longer, then puts the phone back in his pocket. A whistle of wintry air as the door opens and another man comes in wearing a thick coat and gloves. He heads straight for the coffee machine.

— The pointwork wasn't clipped and scotched. Could've ended up with a major incident.

— Useless cunts.

— That's what I told them.

The man slips off his gloves, hangs his coat on the hook, sniffs his cup of coffee, screws his nose up. He sits beside the new kid. The other LOM shows him the teddy bear video.

— Billy, look at this.

— Dirty fucker. Put it away.

— You'd like a woman like that, wouldn't you?

— Put it away. Fuck's sake.

This man is younger. Early thirties. He doesn't look world-weary, he looks normal, and the new kid holds onto this with everything he's got. If the job didn't break this man – if I could become like him – maybe everything will be okay.

They sit in the cold-warm quiet for a few minutes, sipping their coffee.

The younger man looks at the new kid.

— You want a coffee?

— No, I'm alright.

— I don't blame you. Tastes like metal. How are you finding it so far? The job?

— It's good. I like it.

— I bet you do.

The younger man finishes his coffee, then stands up to make another one. He makes one for the new kid as well. He sits down with both coffees, and the new kid sniffs his. It's so black he can see his own grown-up face staring up at him.

— Have these bastards told you anything yet?

— What do you mean?

— About the job. About the stuff you see.

— Not really.

— Right.

They're all looking at the new kid now. One smiles, one looks bored, one is blank, but the younger man looks serious.

— What's the worst thing you've ever seen?

— Umm…

— The worst thing.

— I don't know.

— Well think.

— I'm not sure. I saw a dead duck at the side of the road once. Its guts were all spilling out. I saw a video of a man shooting himself in the head.

— Okay, that's a start.

The younger man folds one leg over the other and leans back with his coffee. He looks at the other LOMs.

— There's a lot of people out there who think the railway is a good way to kill yourself. They see it as their own personal suicide service.

One of the LOMs laughs, but the younger man doesn't.

— We've seen some bloody awful things. Awful. You need to be ready for it, otherwise you're just gonna shit yourself and quit. Paul, what was it you saw last week?

— A cock.

— No, tell him the story.

— We were looking for the body parts. Found pretty much all of it – a foot, an arm. We've got our torches out, and I shine it into the grass on this bank, and I see a thumb. So I go over to it, and fuck me, it's not a thumb, it's a little fucking cock.

— After an incident, we've got to find every little bit, you see. Can't leave any body parts lying around for some family to find on their nature walk. Not allowed to stop until we find every piece. Makes sense, yeah?

The new kid nods and sips his coffee. He's right, it tastes like metal.

— My first day, we were looking for this fucking head. A whole head, mind you. Hours. Absolutely hours it was, looking for this head. We've got the whole body – everything. A barley field. We're searching through it like a bloody hedge maze, waiting to see this head staring at us. He was only about sixteen – being bullied at school, apparently. Still had his uniform on. And we couldn't find his fucking head. You remember what happened, Chris?

— No.

— So it's been five, six hours, right. And I walk back to the headless body. My first day. And I look between the shoulders where the head should be. And there's not much blood. There's a bit, but not as much as you'd think for someone who's had his head ripped off. And I notice there's this stuff coming out from between the shoulders. Looks like hair.

— Oh yeah, I remember now.

— We realize this kid's whole fucking head has been pushed inside the body. Driver said the poor kid stared him down. At the last minute, he put his head down. Pushed it right in.

— They do that. They stare the drivers down. Like they're daring them not to stop.

The new kid puts his coffee down.

— Why don't they stop?

— Who?

— The drivers. Why don't they stop when they see someone on the tracks?

The man with the teddy bear video sits up in his seat.

— You're having a laugh. They can't stop. They're hauling ten thousand tonnes of train. They stop after. Report the incident.

— They get counselling, some of them can't hack it. They quit. Imagine that coming towards you in the headlights. Imagine watching the body hit the screen.

Absolutely obliterated. But some of the drivers don't give a shit, do they? They're used to it.

— Had one the other day ring up. Just said, 'I've killed another one.'

The younger man prods the new kid's shoulder.

— See that's how you've got to be. You can't let it get under your skin, otherwise you'll go crazy. You need to be like a doctor. You gotta laugh at it, really.

— I had one where a bloke was just walking his dog along the tracks. Wasn't even trying to kill himself. Didn't hear it coming. Stupid bastard.

— There's a woman who tries it every week. Jumps out of the way at the last minute.

— My favourite one was last year, this kid tries to jump out the way, the train clips him, pelts him right up into the overhead lines. Electrocuted to death. Wish I'd seen it. Like a bloody cartoon.

The new kid finishes his coffee. And when he goes home that night and his mum serves him a sausage casserole, she asks him if he enjoyed his first day, and he says, yeah, it was okay. But a piece of the boy has died forever.

❧

Icy water trickles through the cracks of black earth, seizing the roots while the ground swells and hardens, the beetles slowing to half-time crawls, the worms digging, their stiff bodies tunnelling down, down, down to curl in slime and wait perhaps forever, and the daffodil bulbs wait, and it all sleeps, shutting down like a factory furnace in the long night.

The big old trees in the market square are tied with blue and white fairy lights. The trunks are lit from circular spotlights in the pavement, gnarly shadows, more spooky than merry. The old man sits in the concrete doorway of the bank, and he'll be dead by morning. He huddles in his vest, his jumper, his coat, his sleeping bag, but it's not enough. Maybe if his belly were full, maybe if he could sleep, he'd have the energy to survive another night. I sit beside him, this old bearded man, and he knows I'm here, but he doesn't say a word. Neither of us says a word. We stare ahead across the square, the closed-up burger van, the bistro pub all lit up and quiet. If someone were to look at me now, they might see a man caught in quiet confusion, reconsidering some things, squinting towards nothing in the bitter air. The old man beside me knows he'll die, and he neither welcomes it nor fears it, but he's glad I'm here. I'll sit beside him all night, while the life drains slowly from his limbs, his face. They'll find him in the morning. Another one. One more. One fewer. And when his body is taken away, there's not a person in the world who notices he's gone.

❧

She can't recall a time when life felt so quiet. Even before Neda was born, when it was just her and Layla, it had never been this quiet. In the new bathroom, she washes Neda — her back, her folds, her tufts of hair, and Neda chatters and splashes, but even these sounds seem isolated, echoing around the sweating tiles. The sounds are miles away, like she and Neda are in the middle of some snowy tundra, and this bath is the hot spring they've found, and there's no civilization for miles in either direction. She rinses Neda's hair with the showerhead, she dries her. Neda stands up, holding the side of the bath for balance, and her legs look too small without her nappy. Dalia dusts her with talc, nappies her, dresses her in the little red pyjamas with the snowflakes.

And for ten minutes she just sits on the bathroom floor with Neda in her lap. She wants to speak to her. About anything. About the future, about Christmas. She wants to say, are you excited? Shall we sit by the window and watch for reindeer in the sky? Shall we leave out some milk and a carrot for Rudolph? Do you think you'll get many presents? But she doesn't say any of these things — there are no presents, and even if there were, she wouldn't have the strength to say those things. All she can do is listen to Neda's tiny noises in all the silence.

Nick sits on the tatty floor of his little house. He's picking the dried patches of carpet with his fingernails — patches where sparks from the fireplace melted it to plastic. It was his mother's house. He remembers how she'd light the fire on Christmas Eve nights, and he remembers the stockings pinned to the mantelpiece. He remembers when he rolled up a sheet of paper and stuck it in the flames to watch it burn, and how his dad caught him and beat him over the head with a dictionary. Now Nick sits watching the empty fireplace – there are no flames, no warmth, just a draught breathing down the chimney and the scent of cold soot.

She tucks Neda into her cot, then changes her mind and tucks her into her own double bed. The little girl looks impossibly small, but cosy. Dalia draws a breath to say goodnight, but she can't, and she smiles, and she kisses the girl's forehead, right beneath her short dark curls.

And now Dalia flicks up and down the television channels, looking for anything unrelated to Christmas. There's an old cowboy film. Some shopping channels. There is a religious channel, and they are talking about Christmas but in a different way, and Dalia rests the remote on the cushion beside her. She's never been religious – her parents were never religious, and she's only ever been to church for weddings and funerals – and she does not feel religious now. But sitting here listening to these hymns, the twinkling lights, the children in the choir singing to something they believe in, the resonance of the stone walls, the primary colours of the hangings and tapestries – she's overcome with something, something wordless, and she smiles, and she watches, and she watches.

There's a noise to her left. A tumbling in the box room. Dalia jumps up and rushes to the door, and when she opens it, Neda is standing there pulling boxes off the bed.

Dalia grabs her, saying, Neda, you stupid kid, you stupid stupid kid – you don't come in here – bad – naughty – this is not your room – not your room, you stupid stupid girl – this is not for Neda – these are your sister's things – you don't come in here ever – do you understand?

Neda's bottom lip sticks out. Dalia holds her firmly under the armpits in the boxed-up room. Neda cries. Her face screws up and her mouth is so wide Dalia can see down her throat, and she cries at what her mother has done, shouting at her, scaring her, making her jump.

And as Dalia watches her daughter, her alive daughter, crying in the hands of her own mother, she weakens. She drops to her knees and stares at the floor.

— God, Neda, I'm sorry. I'm so sorry, baby, come here.

Now she holds the little girl to her chest. Neda has stopped crying, but Dalia cries – the tears are hot and gushing, and she says, I'm sorry, I'm so so sorry, and she squeezes Neda tighter than she ever has, and Neda feels safe now, in these arms, with this woman. I'm so sorry. It's not your fault. Mummy's sorry. I'll never shout at you like that again.

A lukewarm Christmas day. Not the wintry palette like in the films but everyday colours, everyday cars and gardens and roads. On all the televisions, scenes of winter car rides and snow people. Fat white shavings, and families coming together against all odds. On the televisions, every window of every house is lined with perfect fairy lights – red, blue, green – and every roof is a powdered cake. But beyond the televisions, outside the homes, it's metallic sky, mild air. Everyone hibernates with their films about traffic jams and last-minute love, their tinsel and gravy, their electric projected fireplace. Nobody wants to step outside because to step outside would be to break the illusion that this is not just another day, there is no magic in the air, miracles don't happen. A little boy asks his mother, is it really Christmas? Yes, she says. Then where's the snow?

Dalia's Christmas morning feels silly and bare, but they wake at eight, and it's a morning like any another. No presents or decorations, no tree – but Neda doesn't seem to mind. Dalia wraps her up in winter clothes and a snowsuit, and they walk in the world, and it's silent. The roads are silent. The parks and playground are silent like an ended world, but this ended world belongs to them. Dalia points out the lights in the windows, the reindeer made of wire, the inflatable snowman, but Neda is more interested in what her scarf tastes like. Dalia pushes her on the swings. Dalia climbs to the top of the climbing frame and peers over the silent street.

❧

The vicar lights a candle in the vestibule while Louis checks on the turkey that's been cooking all night – his whole house is thick with the savoury smell – and Erin pats the stocking at the end of her bed. It was empty when she went to sleep and now it's full. The crinkly sound of the paper. She unwraps some bracelets, a multicoloured pen, and there's a satsuma that looks suspiciously like the ones downstairs. Later, she'll check her stocking-satsuma against those in the fruit bowl, and she'll learn a hard truth. Two paramedics sit in the parked ambulance at the hospital, pulling crackers and singing along with the radio. In the pub, an old couple drink snowballs, the same as their first date. To their left, a younger couple have come to the pub to clear the air after he kicked the dog. Dorothy wakes up alone. And the babies are born, the Christmas babies, and I sit with Jacek while he has his heart attack on the toilet, and I speak to Anna in her final moments as the Christmas cancer claws into her lungs, and her husband will tell the kids an angel took her to Heaven, but he doesn't believe it. At the precise moment Anna dies, Kyle unwraps his best present ever – a new console with two controllers and four games – and he'll remember this moment forever. It was a bonus present, hidden behind the sofa.

The sky falls dark around four o'clock, and she cooks tomato soup in the microwave, and she eats it by candle-light with her daughter. Neda's mouth is smeared with the luminous orange gloop. And at six, her dad comes to pick her up. He stands in the doorway with Neda in his arms and a pitying expression that makes Dalia queasy, and he glances around at the lack of decorations, but he doesn't mention it.

— How have you been doing?

— We've been okay.

Neda reaches for her mum, but Dalia doesn't move. Solomon hangs about on the doorstep, trying to think of anything else to say. She knows he wants to help.

— I'm okay, Solomon. I promise. I've got a box of chocolates and a nice glass of wine to keep me company. Just have a really nice couple of days, okay? I hope you've got her lots of presents. She deserves to be spoiled. And I'll see you on the twenty-seventh, yeah?

— Why don't you join us?

— No. Thanks, but really, I'm fine.

— Alright. Well, I'll see you in a couple of days. Say goodbye to Mummy.

He takes Neda's tiny hand and makes her wave. Dalia kisses the hand and watches as her father carries her up the little path and straps her into the car. He offers one final sympathetic glance, then he drives away. Across the street, a man drops a heap of discarded wrapping paper into his recycling bin.

The little bathroom, a humid fog. No bubbles, salts or soaps. Just the steaming, clear bath, and a naked Dalia standing beside it, gripping the curved shard of a plate she just smashed.

She steps into the water and it's so hot it feels cold, and her shins flush. She lowers herself in. Her backside, her forearms. She places the shard on the side of the bath, then trickles water over her shoulders with cupped hands. I'm right beside her.

I sit on the cool tiles, one elbow on the edge of the bath, and we don't look at each other. She leans back in the scorching water until her hair is wet. She closes her eyes and rests awhile.

And as she lies there stewing, she thinks about nothing in particular. Not Layla, not Neda. Not her parents or her childhood, or her cancelled future, and what it might have looked like. If she thinks of anything, it's about the heat of the bath, and annoyance at the man beside her.

I pick at the frayed edges of the sodden bathmat. The threads come away easily, it's so worn. And if she won't think of anything, I'll think about it for her. Neda, too young to understand. She won't remember her mother. She'll grow up as the motherless kid, and when she's eight she'll start calling her stepmum Mum, and when she's sixteen her father will tell her everything. About Layla too. Neda will find the news difficult at first. But it'll be too abstract and far away, like the adverts of starving children on the television, and eventually she'll forget. Neda's father will grieve for Dalia in some small way. But he'll also feel guilty that he now has everything he ever wanted. A happy family, all under one roof.

Dalia opens her eyes, as if she can see it all. She sits up, grabs the shard of broken plate. She holds it, and turns it,

catching spectral visions of herself in the white ceramic.
She rests the sharp edge on her wrist. She turns her head
towards me, ever so slightly.

— You're not going to stop me, are you?

It's not an accusation so much as a realization. She
knows that I will sit here and watch this. I will let it
happen. I will watch her bleed, watch her arms grow weak,
watch the blood drift into the water like ink. I won't move,
she knows this. Because this is everything I am. Not a
friend or a lover. Just a watcher at her side. No, I tell her.
I won't stop you.

Now, there's a wobble of hurt in her eyes. The shard
is still pressed to her wrist, but it trembles, and her voice
changes.

— Why?

— It's not my place.

— It's not your place.

— No.

— What does that mean, Travis?

— It means I'm not here to change anything.

— Right.

For a moment she looks determined to slice her skin.
She brings her wrist closer to her face, bites her lip. But she
glances at the ceiling with dampening eyes. She swears to
herself.

— So you're not gonna say anything? You won't do
anything.

— Would you want me to?

— I don't know. I can't do it when you're watching.

206

— I'll look away.

— You're such a useless knob, do you know that? Why are you even here? What good are you? Why don't you just leave me in peace and then come and clean up the mess? Travis, will you bloody look at me?

Her eyes are fixed on me now. This anger seems to have given her some energy. For the first time in weeks, she has a focus. She points the shard at me.

— You're pathetic, do you know that? You don't give anything. You just come along and take things away. You ruin lives – that's literally it. That's all you're good for. I look at you, and all I see is this pitiful, weak man. How can you live with yourself? It must be very lonely.

— Yes, it is.

Those three words knock her off guard a bit. She blinks. She breathes. The anger wanes, just for a flicker, then returns, but it's a little forced now.

— Well, good. I hope it is. You deserve to be lonely. You *make* people lonely, Travis. That's what you are. This bath is still too bloody hot.

She leans forward and turns on the cold tap. And while it runs, she doesn't lie back down – she sits with her dark hair dripping down her back, and she sets the shard down again on the side of the bath.

— You took everything from me.

— I know.

— Do you even care?

I draw a breath to answer, but it wouldn't mean anything.

— No, of course you don't. You can't. People die every minute of every day. If you cared about each one, it wouldn't work.

She turns off the cold tap. She stares towards the tiny fogged-up window, the sun screaming through, lighting up the steam. She's thinking about what it must mean to be me. She's thinking about all of it, but she stops and shivers. Her back is goosebumped in the tepid air. She turns to me.

— She loved you, you know. Layla. She thought you were brilliant.

— I thought the same about her.

— Did you?

— Yes.

Dalia squints, still looking at me. The anger has crumbled, and in its place, a different kind of sadness. She looks at my hand on the bath. It looks for all the world like a man's hand, with hair and cuticles and fingernails. She considers holding it, or simply touching it to make sure it's real.

— If you tell me not to do this, I won't.

— I can't tell you that.

— Why not?

— It's not my—

— Right, right, it's not your place. I will kill myself, Travis. I'm certain of that. Maybe not today, but it will happen. I know it in my heart. And it scares me, but I can't live with this. How am I supposed to live with this?

— What about Neda?

— Oh, Neda is better off without me. I mean that. That's not just me feeling sorry for myself. She really is. Her dad has more money, her stepmum is more patient. Neda doesn't need to grow up with a broken mother – she deserves more. I'd rather she just forgot about me.

She didn't realize the truth of her words until she spoke them out loud. She nods, as if that's settled. And she sits in the water until it's cold, and she asks me to pass her the towel.

Dalia and I eat lunch in a dreary hut called the Sunshine Cafe. I have a black coffee and a slice of carrot cake, she has a latte and a toasted tuna panini, and as we eat, she asks me about myself. My true self. They're not questions of what's going on inside me – she knows I won't answer those; they're academic. Technical. Questions about geography and motivation and logistics. These are the easiest ques-tions to deflect, but it's a welcome distraction, so I try. For her, I try to answer each one thoughtfully, with respect, but in a manner that would sound coherent to a person who isn't me. She's not bewildered by any of it. She nods. She frowns as if to say, that makes sense. And for now, she's satisfied.

The bath seems to have awoken her appetite. She eats her food fast, and she steals the last few bites of my cake. And after lunch, we meander through town. Along the river, the jetties, through the smell of goose shit and reeds, past the embankment. A drizzly sky. The green dome of

the mosque like a hill in the rainy haze, and she tells me
things. Truths she's kept from herself until this moment,
about motherhood, about grief.

— When I was twelve I saw this picture in the news-
paper. It was a man – a father. He was crying because his
daughter was killed when they fled the war. I can't remember which war. But I couldn't stop looking at this picture.
God, his face was crushed with so much misery, so much
disbelief. It was the most powerful thing I'd ever seen –
more disturbing than pictures of aeroplane crashes – more
shocking than any photo of violence or gore – this one
father who'd lost his daughter. I couldn't imagine feeling
love like that.

We walk to the loch and we lean on the railings and
watch the brown water.

—And years later, when I'd lost the picture, but it
was branded into my brain, when I gave birth to Layla,
I finally understood it. I still didn't know exactly how
that man felt, but I understood how he could feel it.
I understood the weight of the love behind his screwed-up
face. I didn't care about anything except that little girl in
my arms.

She releases a breath that sounds almost like a laugh,
with a puff of condensation. She shakes her head and rests
her hands on the railings.

— Travis, I wish I could feel what you feel. I want to
see it all as if I'm looking through a window, and I can't
reach it, and I don't care.

— I never said that I don't care.

— But you don't. Not truly. I can see it in your eyes.
And I don't blame you – how could you?

We watch the canal boats come and go. The fan of
ripples behind them. She stands up straight, as though she's
shed a heavy burden.

She looks at me.

— I think a part of me always knew who you were.

I help Dalia wash the dishes. She scrubs, I dry, and we
don't speak. The radio plays dreary tunes, and I help her
dust the shelves, the window ledges. I wipe the toast
crumbs and the coffee puddles from the kitchen counter,
and I start making a cup of tea. The radio man says he
hopes everyone's made their New Year's resolutions,
and he wonders how long he'll keep his – probably five
minutes, he says – and while I wait for the kettle to boil,
Dalia stands in front of me. She doesn't hold me, nor
I her, but she rests her ear on my chest, and we stay like
that, and she doesn't say anything about what she can or
can't hear inside my chest, and the kettle finishes boiling.
I move, but Dalia tells me to stay. Let's just stay here a
minute. Furniture polish and tea bags. The man says, this
next song is for anyone feeling lonely at this time of year,
and it's a melancholy thing with optimistic strings, and
I feel my hands moving down her arms until our fingers
meet. We weave them. And when I start swaying lazily to
the music, she laughs. You're an idiot, she says. But she's
smiling, and she sways too, for a joke, until it's no longer
a joke, and she rests her cheek on my chest again and

we're swaying to this bittersweet tune in the kitchen with
the kettle cooling in the last few hours of the year her
daughter died.

Should old acquaintance be forgot, and never brought
to mind? Should old acquaintance be forgot, for the
sake of auld lang syne? We two have run about the hills,
and picked the daisies fine. But we've wandered many
a weary foot, since auld lang syne. And there's a hand,
my trusty friend. And give me a hand o' thine. Should
old acquaintance be forgot, for auld lang syne? And in
the first two hours of the new year, Sun-jung opens her
veins with a paperclip, wondering how the blue can come
out red. In the first two hours, Martha clutches her heart
on the stairs, Reece gives up the battle against his liver,
and Georgette sips her last few lavender breaths, wishing
farewell to her hundredth January. And there are tears
and there is singing of forgotten words passed down, and
there are beginnings and ends, there are babies wriggling
in bellies and there are crossed words and scuffling in the
street, a bottle thrown, a stubbed cigarette, yeah, you
prick, walk away, prick, and Sun-jung opens the other
wrist and sits in bed with a hot water bottle, and reads the
story her mother used to read. The bed blushes around
her, and I sit beside her and wait. And if it weren't all
so beautiful, if every tiny thing weren't so relentlessly
fucking beautiful, perhaps I'd be the one with the paperclip, but instead I'll wander through it alone, blessed with
every friend there is.

A VERY OLD WOMAN

She's folding clothes in the utility room. Dresses, leggings, cardigans. She folds them and lays them in the washing basket, and when I try to help, she bats my hand away, tells me I won't do it right, so I lean against the wall in the cramped afterthought of a room, and I watch the care she takes with every item. She looks small and tired, her white hair sticking out like pampas grass, her glasses askew. She huffs and tuts and mutters fleeting thoughts, and it's all just an interlude.

She's sure of it now – her remaining days are nothing more than hours to be filled. She has candles, but she won't light them. She has bath bombs, but she won't use them. She has music, but she won't play it. She'll just get up, get dressed, watch television, eat, wash, go back to bed – and repeat until it's over.

— Stop watching me like that. If you want to make yourself useful, you can carry the basket into the bedroom.

I do as she says, and she follows me into the bedroom and tells me to pass her the clothes. One by one, she hangs them up or folds them into the drawers.

— Don't you have other places to be?

— I like it here.

— I can't imagine why. You should find yourself a nice girlfriend instead of hanging about with an old woman.

I pass her a skirt and she clamps it in a coat hanger and hangs it up. I pass her some stockings and she folds them. She used to be protective of her underwear, even her socks – she'd make sure they were tidied before I came through the door. Now I'm passing her bras and big flowery pants and she doesn't bat an eyelid.

— Where's my blue cardigan?

— In the wardrobe.

— It can't be.

— That was the first thing I gave you. It's hanging up.

— No, I've got a blue cardigan. Pale blue. Go and see if I left it in the washing machine.

— It was the first thing I gave you. It's hanging in the wardrobe.

— Don't be stupid, for goodness' sake – don't you think I'd know if you'd passed me it? Go and check the washing machine, will you?

I stand up and walk back to the utility room, though I know I won't find anything. The washing machine is empty, the worktop is bare, and when I come back, she's holding the blue cardigan in her hands.

— It was hanging in the wardrobe.

— I know.

— Did you pass me this?

— Yes.

— From the basket?

— Yes. It was the first thing.

She sits on the bed and stares at the blue cardigan in her hands.

— I must be losing my marbles. Don't remember seeing it. Oh well, take the basket back to the utility room and make us a cup of tea.

— Okay.

She brushes her hands along the weave of the cardigan, trying to remember where she got it — did she buy it, or was it a gift? How long ago? Was it last year, or the year before? She asks herself these questions, but the blue cardigan offers no answers, it's always been there, and it'll be there until the day she dies.

In the kitchen, there's a cup of tea beside the kettle. It's an hour old, no milk. Brewed and stewed with a filmy layer on top. I pour it down the plughole.

— What are you doing?

— Pouring this tea away.

— What tea?

— It was on the side. You must have poured it and left it.

— I suppose I…

She turns her head and closes her eyes, trying to retrace her steps. Trying to remember filling the kettle, clicking it on, waiting, fetching a cup, dropping the teabag in, pouring, but there's nothing. She holds the worktop for support.

— Oh god, Travis.

I drop the bloated teabag in the bin and fill the kettle again. I fetch the milk and take my favourite cup from the hook — the one with the sunflowers — and we listen to the rumble of the boiling water.

— I knew this would happen. I knew I'd start falling apart.

— You're eighty-nine. It's to be expected.

— No, it's more than that. I can feel it. I took the remote to bed with me the other day. Got in bed, curled up, and I'm like, what's that? Bloody remote in the bed with me. Get out of the way, you can't put the milk in straight away. You need to let it brew. Come on, move.

She takes a teaspoon and stirs the bags into the water, and I watch the tea diffuse like brown smoke. She wipes her forehead with her cuff.

I tell her to go and sit down, I'll finish up here. She's about to argue, but she nods. She glances around the kitchen in case there's anything else she'd meant to do. I stir the tea, and she places her old hand on mine.

— I'm frightened, Travis.

— Why are you frightened?

— I don't want to lose myself. This is the worst thing. This is what I've been dreading. I want to leave this planet while I still remember everything and everyone.

She squeezes my hand. She touches my hair, like a mother with her son.

— Please, Travis, you've got to let me go. Show some mercy. You owe me that much.

A faint smile on her lips. She nods, urging me to do as she's asked. I spoon the teabags out of the cups and drop them in the bin. I pour the milk, stir some more.

— Today isn't the day. I'm sorry.

The old woman scrunches her eyes shut, and she looks like she might collapse. And behind the dark of her eyelids,

she imagines the final day of her life, when she barely
knows her own name, when the grandkids need to feed
her and clean up after her, and she's nothing but an empty
brain in a broken body.

Go and sit down, I tell her. I'll bring the biscuits.

The hospital building sits in the crisp air, the sparkling
black wisps of trees, frosty pavement, glitter bushes,
the upper storeys lost in fog, white sky, a robin on the
steps, and the foyer is warm and bright. The air hums
with anticipation and a smell of heaters. The this-way-
that-way of people at the entrance, like a train station,
almost festive, and some of them leave with things they
didn't arrive with, a sleeping babe, a looming knowledge
of cancer creeping up the colon, leaving, arriving, and
now Dalia arrives with her work bag and a lump of ice
in her stomach. She steps through the yellow light, the
big yellow echo-space, she rides the lift to the maternity
ward. Standing in that little metal box, feeling her weight
shift as the lift ascends, she tries to ignore her reflection
on the stainless-steel wall, she tries to ignore what happened last time she was here in this hospital, but although
she ignores it, it's right there, right behind those sliding
doors, and for one moment she almost expects the doors
to open and reveal Layla standing there in the black shaft,
her zombie make-up now real, rotting in the flickering

lights. But when the doors open, they open to the long corridor of the maternity ward, the waiting area, the reception desk.

Susan at reception spots Dalia, and she gets up from her seat and rushes around the desk to embrace her. Oh Dalia, she says. Oh Dalia, Dalia. You poor thing, my god. And Susan cries and hugs her, while Dalia stands there dry-eyed, arms by her sides, my god, you poor thing, I am so sorry. You poor sweet thing.

When Susan lets go, her pudgy face has melted with mascara, and she fetches a tissue from the box on the counter, and she passes one to Dalia, but Dalia just holds it.

— I'm okay, Susan. I just want to get back to work.

— Of course you do, sweetheart. I'll make you a cup of tea. Nothing's changed since you've been gone. Same madhouse. Ruby split up with Josh again. Sit down, I'll make you a tea.

Dalia stands in the middle of the queuing area, beside the sign that says WAIT HERE. There are no patients waiting, but Dalia can hear an infant screeching, she can hear the murmurs and footsteps, all those familiar sounds from another kind of home.

Susan comes back with two cups of tea, and she urges Dalia to sit. Dalia does as she's told, sitting on the blue swivel chair, while Susan sits on the reception desk, cup of tea on her lap. The mascara is gone, the pitying look is gone, as though she's forgotten already, and Dalia likes it. She drinks her sugary tea, allows Susan to fill her head with empty gossip. She's slipped back to one year ago, before everything.

She delivers three babies before lunch, and they're overjoyed, these families. They cry and cuddle and take pictures, they call their parents on the phone and say it's a boy, it's a girl, you've got a granddaughter, they dress the babies in their first impractical sleepsuits, and they smile like they're high on morphine. They exist in a separate world from everyone else, a fuzzy warm world all pink and blue, and they thank Dalia, and Dalia just nods. The new families load their babies into car seats, and they disappear forever. Dalia sits in the toilet cubicle and closes her eyes, trying to picture the sleepless nights, the postnatal depression. She tries to imagine the dad getting irritable, drinking a couple of glasses of whisky to help him sleep, and the mum shouting at him, saying, I can't do this on my own. And the dad says, I've got work in the morning, and maybe the dad moves into a flat on the other side of town, and the mum screams at the baby who hasn't stopped crying since they came home from the hospital – and Dalia imagines all of this in the toilet stall, and it calms her. There are no perfect moments.

Another healthy baby, another happy family. This stupid smiling family, gazing goofily at their suckling son. They don't know. They don't know what some parents have to endure. They haven't seen the panic, the tearing flesh, the blue lifeless alien – they haven't had to break a baby's arm to get it out, or tell a mother their baby needs to be taken to the NICU. They've seen nothing. Oh, it's so easy, isn't it? Not a care in the world. The dad half sits on the bed, with one arm around his wife and the other holding the baby's hand. A big stupid grin on his face, this perfect easy happy family forever and ever.

Dalia watches, smiling on the outside. She pinches her eyelashes between her thumb and forefinger, plucks a few, brushes them on her tunic.

Within an hour, the baby is dressed in a sleepsuit and loaded into his car seat. Dad carries it, while Mum shuffles along like she's had triplets and an episiotomy. Dalia shakes her head and goes to make a coffee. But while she stands there waiting for the kettle, she thinks more about the stupid family and she rushes out into the car park.

The dad is loading his new boy into the car. Mum leans on the wing mirror, waiting for some help. She spots Dalia and waves.

— Did we forget something?

— No, no. I just wanted to say, I think you did amazing in there.

Dalia catches her breath. She's not sure why she's here.

She peeks in through the car window at the sleeping boy.

— Aw, thank you. And thanks for being such a good midwife. Best day of our lives.

— You're so welcome.

— Makes it all worth it, doesn't it?

— It really does. He's beautiful.

The dad shuts the baby's door, then comes around to help his wife into the car. She winces as she sits down. She straps herself in.

— Maybe we'll see you again when we have the next one.

— Maybe you will.

Dad walks back around to the driver's side. He stops, waiting for Dalia to say whatever it is she came to say. Dalia knows he's tired. They just want to get their perfect stupid baby back to his perfect home.

— Anyway, take care you two. I wish you the best of luck. And if Baby has any problems with those lungs, you make sure to come back and see us.

— What's that?

— Lungs? What about his lungs?

They both look at Dalia – the mother in the car, the father peering over the roof.

— They didn't say anything about his lungs.

— Oh god – didn't they? They're so useless sometimes! It might be nothing to worry about. I shouldn't have said anything. Maybe they'll send you a letter.

— Tell us. What's going on?

— He has a condition called myovascular bronchiolitis. Affects about one in a thousand babies. As I say, it could be nothing, but it can turn sinister if you're not careful. Just something to be aware of.

— God.

The mother turns to look at her sleeping boy. His perfectly normal snore is now a wheeze of impending death in her mind.

— I can't believe they didn't tell you. I'm so sorry. They have so many other babies to attend to, you see – healthy ones. Anyway, well done in there, guys. Take care.

Dalia strides back across the car park, her legs like rubber tubes. She tries not to laugh or cry, and she doesn't look back at the confused and frightened family.

Before Dalia goes home, she goes to her locker. She rifles through the boxes of pills she's pocketed throughout the day: white boxes with white stickers, medicines with alien names full of Zs and Xs. She stows the boxes in her bag and slings the bag over her shoulder.

Make sure you wrap up warm out there, Susan says. It's like the Arctic. Susan stands in her puffy rose-gold jacket with the fur hood, that sympathetic gawp again.

— You will be alright, won't you?

— I've made it this far.

— If you need us to take Neda or anything, so you can have a bit of peace, you know where we are. Terry won't mind.

— I know.

— I'll see you tomorrow.

— See you tomorrow.

And in the car, while she's driving, Dalia closes her eyes at five-second intervals, and she reaches across to the passenger seat, unclips her bag and glances at the boxes of pills.

As she drives, she fiddles with the seal on one of the boxes; she fiddles until the box opens as if by accident. And when she stops at a traffic light, she fiddles with the plastic tray, and she pops two pills onto her palm and holds them in her fist until they're clammy, and the light turns green.

Dalia places the pills onto her tongue. Before they even hit her stomach, she's overcome with relief. Because she knows they'll soothe her. She took similar pills when her brother died, and they made the world a little softer around the edges, a little warmer, like that first glass of red wine, that new pair of socks, that lavender bath bomb. And her breathing steadies. Her hands stop trembling.

She drops one more pill into her mouth and crunches it. Bitter and chalky, dissolving into her gums. Soothing waves rush through her, and she doesn't feel angry when the driver in front hesitates at another green light.

It's dark now, and the headlights catch lonely flecks of snow. Dalia picks up Neda from crèche. They tell her she's been good as gold, and they start telling her what she's been up to, but Dalia ignores them, carrying the toddler to the car.

At home, she cooks some pasta, but it's too much, and she pours some out of the window and it steams on the patio. She chops Neda's pasta into tiny chunks and mixes it with tomato sauce, and while Neda eats it, Dalia eats a couple more pills. I'm sorry, baby girl, she says. I'm going to try harder. I promise I'll try harder. And as she watches her oblivious daughter, Dalia begins to melt. Her breath comes out so easy, so soft, like she's wrapped in a squidgy blanket, her rubber limbs, her trickling honey blood, and the room is half a mile away, Neda is half a mile away with her orange sauce, and it's all hushed, mfffffffffffffff, mfffffffff, Dalia tips her head back in the chair and stares at the dark white of the ceiling.

∾

Winter thaws, the trees drip with ice water, the ground softens and releases a smell like stewed plums. Green buds breach their heads through the gnarly ends of sleepy twigs, and it all stretches, yawns, the warming earth, the new breaths into the cool air, it all shakes itself from its dream, the grass stands on end like hairs, the conifers shiver and the skeleton trees creak and groan, is it time to wake up already, just another hundred years, please, just another hundred. A pause, a reset, now return to the beginning of the circle, same as the first circle, ready to do it all again, and the mayfly nymphs are hiding in the pond.

At the allotment, we cut the last of the rhubarb stems and dig up the last of the potatoes. They're all black and rotten where we left them to die, but Dalia says she'll keep on top of it this year. That'll be my resolution, she says. She asks me what mine is. She says, let me guess, you don't have one, and she's right. She says, you need to think of one.

And we leave the allotment and walk through the town. She's wearing a black parka with grey fur around the hood, and I can only see her nose poking out and her white breath. We buy some sugared doughnuts from the van and we eat them on the bench near the underpass. She salutes a magpie.

She says, see if you can eat a doughnut without licking your lips, and I try it, and I fail immediately, and she laughs, her features framed by the fur of her coat. I like hearing her laugh.

She wipes the sugar from my chin. And as we sit on the bench with her fingertips on my face, her eyes flitting about my features, the breaths of steam, hers and mine, and the infinitesimal push of my fingernails and hair — as we sit with my stomach grumbling, my toes poking through the holes in my socks inside my shoes, my blood running warm, I have never been more aware of all these human frailties. And this is when I know I must leave her alone.

She visits Layla's dad on a Sunday morning, and when he answers the door, he's drunk and gaunt. He stumbles away from the door to let her in. She steps inside, hit by a stink of ammonia. He's moved his bed into the living room, and he's hung towels over the windows to black them out, and when Dalia pulls the curtains away, he shields his eyes. In the sharp white light, she sees a skeleton. Wispy hair. His lips are cracked, his neck is all sinew and shadows. He looks ten years older than when she'd seen him just a few weeks ago.

— Jesus, Nick.

The place is crawling with cans and bottles, with tissues and underwear. Dalia steps through it to open the window.

— Have you eaten? When did you last eat?

He shrugs. He barely seems to know where he is.

— Sit down. I'll make you a sandwich.

— I don't want a sandwich.

— Tough. You need to eat. Sit down. I'm here now.

Nick hesitates, but he sits on the mattress on the floor, and Dalia goes into the kitchen and opens some cupboards. A few condiments. Mouldy bread. There's nothing in the fridge but beer and a slice of ham. She goes back into the living room, where Nick sits cross-legged on the bed.

— I'm nipping to the shop. I won't be long.

She's not expecting an answer, and she doesn't get one.

Long before Layla was born, Dalia would console Nick in the long nights, listening to his stories of being abused by his dad and his uncle, stories full of bodily details that made Dalia sick and gave her nightmares. He'd tell her stories of being homeless, and the cold, of how he'd clawed his way back into a job and a home, and she always admired him for that – his resilience. She'd seen him relapse into drink, she'd watched the paramedics force a tube down his throat to pump his stomach, she'd washed his clothes, tidied his house and mopped up every conceivable fluid from his floors.

Now she brings bread, butter, ham, cucumber and a small pack of energy drinks. In his kitchen, she makes some sandwiches, and she's thinking of nothing except the

softness of the bread, the pop of the butter lid, the sweet
watery scent of the cucumber. She sets one plate atop the
other, sets them both on the pack of drinks.

— Here we go. You like cucumber, don't you?

She rests the plate on his lap, and he doesn't look at it.
He's off somewhere, his head lolling gently on his neck,
and Dalia sits on the floor beside the mattress and bites into
her sandwich.

— It's cold out there. I think it might snow again.

Nick closes his eyes, rests his chin on his chest.

— You need to eat that. I'm not leaving until you do.
And I got some energy drinks because you look like you
need it. I should have brought you a glass of water as well,
really. I'll go get you one.

She stands up.

— Dalia.

— Yeah?

— Dalia, why are you here?

— What do you mean?

— Why are you here? Now?

— I wanted to make sure you're okay. And you should
be glad I did. You're a mess.

— You've barely spoken to me since Layla.

— Well, no, I couldn't.

— She died.

— Yes. She died.

His sunken blue-grey eyes, so defeated, so lost, like
he's wishing for nothing more than to die too, and soon.
He says it again. She died. And this time, his face breaks

and his lip judders and the tears pool in the bony sockets. Dalia sits on the mattress and holds him. His sobs are high and breathy, and she strokes his back, and she wants to say, it's okay, it's okay, but she can't bring herself to say those words, not even for him.

— She was so beautiful.

— She was.

— Do you remember when she'd get angry, she'd always—

— Let's not talk about those things. I'm here to look after you. I don't want to talk about those things.

— Okay.

She sits back on the floor, and Nick holds his sandwich like he's forgotten what food is. He raises it to his lips, sniffs it. He bites it, and chews it for five minutes like a cow on cud before he reaches into his mouth, pulls out the beige bolus, places it back on the plate.

— Sorry.

— Don't be sorry. Why don't you try a bit of cucumber on its own?

He looks at the sandwich again. Lifts the slice of bread. Pinches a slice of buttery cucumber between his thumb and forefinger and drops it into his mouth. He chews, swallows, smiles at her.

— That's it.

She cracks open an energy drink and passes it to him.

He holds it but doesn't sip.

— Dalia?

— Yeah?

— Have you been okay?

— No, I haven't. But I'm getting there. I have to, don't I? Neda needs me. You need me.

— Okay.

He sips the drink. She can hear it fizzing on his tongue before he swallows.

— Dalia?

— Yeah?

— Thank you.

❧

A STRONG MAN

On a frosty morning, I walk up the grand driveway of Keith Rotherham, former strongest man in the world. His salmon-coloured driveway is lined with plastic topiary and mini Greek-style pillars. His double front doors are shaded by a great stone awning, and when he sees me from the threshold, his red face glows.

— Travis! Wondered when I'd see you again. Come in, kid.

I step into the echoey entrance hall with my briefcase, and he pats me on the back with exaggerated force. Keith is bald and bearded, with a cartoonishly broad body beneath his vest. He hobbles on his crutch beside me – six foot five – and he asks how I've been.

— I've been well.

— Talkative as ever.

— How have you been?

— Oh, you know. Dying slowly.

He drapes an arm over my shoulder, and we walk past the paintings and plant stands, past the grand staircase splitting left and right. He offers an arm towards his study, and I step inside and sit at the desk. This room is smaller, and dim. Dark wood and leather. Keith sits at the other side of the desk, in front of his trophy cabinets.

I open my briefcase, hand him some paperwork. He clicks his pen and signs the papers without even looking. He passes them back to me.

— There we go. Is that it, then?

— That's everything.

— Cheers, Travis. I really appreciate what you've done. It's nice to know everything's in order when I go. How about a drink to celebrate?

— Yes, please.

— Water?

— I'll have a rum.

— Rum? Blimey. Well, I guess you're off duty now, aren't you? Dark rum alright?

He stands up, shuffles to the drinks globe and bends down to reach the glasses. He groans and places a hand on the small of his back. I can see he's wearing a wide black weightlifting belt. He tries two or three times to reach the glasses before I stand up and fetch them for him, and he pours a scotch for himself and a rum for me. He swills the drinks around in their glasses, as though this will make any difference, then slides mine across the desk and sits back down.

He scrunches his big fingers through his beard.

— Do you want to see it, Travis?

— See what?

— The cancer. The flaming cancer.

Before I can answer, he pulls his vest up over his head. His torso is both muscly and flabby – a vast round belly, square chest, thick black hair all over. He turns and shows me a spattering of brown lumps all over his shoulders and spine. Each lump contains its own spattering of darker spots, some of them reddish, others blue. He pulls his vest back down.

— What do you think of that? You ever seen anything like that?

— Have they told you how long you've got left?

— Oh, every time I speak to them it's a different number. They said three months six months ago. They don't know what they're on about. But it's coming soon, I know that much.

— Are you frightened?

— Me? Nah. No, why would I be frightened? I've never been scared of death – I've done everything I wanted to do. I've had a good life.

He fans his hands over the trophies either side. Most are gold statuettes of Atlas with the globe on his shoulders, shiny as the day he won them.

— Yeah, I would have liked to go a bit older. But my daddy died young, and his daddy. Nah, I knew this would happen. Everything's in order, thanks to you. Everyone will be taken care of. The kids won't believe their luck, I've never told them what I'm worth. They'll probably piss it up the wall. But at least they'll spend it.

He sips his scotch and I sip my rum. He points his drink at me.

— You got a girlfriend or what?

— No.

— Gay?

— I don't know.

— You don't know? Christ, Travis. You're worse off than I thought. My daughter would have liked you, I think. Maybe you should speak to her when I'm gone.

He leans back in his captain's chair, peering at me like I'm a magic eye picture, trying to see something. And we sit there looking at each other across the desk, and slowly his face changes in a way I've seen countless times. The squint softens. The mouth loosens. He clears his throat.

— Tell you what. Come with me.

Keith stands up, grabs his crutch, and I follow him through a side door into the garage. It's a clean garage – white walls, every tool in its place. And in the centre sits a gleaming black Lamborghini.

— There. What do you think of that?

— It's very nice.

— Nice? Flowers are nice, Travis. This is a *machine*. One of the most beautiful machines man ever created. A true feat of engineering. They only made a hundred. Climb in – she's unlocked. No, no, driver's side. That's it.

I open the door and sit behind the wheel. The seat is low, and it's dark and cramped as a coffin. Leather and air fresheners. Keith climbs in the other side and closes the door. He looks squished in the little cockpit. He's hunched, the back of his head almost touching the ceiling.

— Shut your door, kid. That's it. So come on, what do you think? Feels powerful, doesn't it? You feel like a strong man now, don't you? A man in control of his life.

I tell him yes, to make him happy.

— I've only driven her a couple of times.

— Why?

— Dunno. I always wanted a car like this, ever since I was a kid. I'd dream about it. At school they'd always take the piss out of me for being fat, and I thought, you know what, one day I'm gonna be the strongest man in the world, and I'll buy the most expensive car I can find, and then you'll see. I'm the one who's laughing now, aren't I?

Keith takes a little device from the dashboard and presses a button. The garage door clangs, then pivots, revealing the vast bright driveway and the rows of topiary. I squint into the light.

— Well go on, kid, turn the key. Take her for a spin.

— I'm okay.

— Come on. Just round the driveway.

— No, I'm okay.

— Alright. That's alright. I didn't think you would. Y'know, when I was doing all those competitions, lifting those bastard tyres and logs and boulders, I never thought about the weight, I was thinking about this car. I'd be tugging a lorry on a rope, and I'd say, come on Rotherham, put your fucking back into it. You want that car, don't you, Rotherham? Tug harder. Lift higher. Throw further. And then, on my thirtieth birthday, I bought her.

He glances around the interior, nodding.

— Do you know what I felt when I bought her, Travis? Nothing. In fact, it was worse than nothing. I drove her home from the showroom. The seat didn't go back far enough. Brakes were squeaky. Windows didn't go down all the way. I thought this car would fix some things, but it didn't. Probably why I've hardly driven it.

He pats the dashboard.

— Ah well, my daughter will get the car now. She'll like it more than I did.

And he smiles and releases a rumbling breath from his barrel chest, and he holds his hands in his lap like a little boy. He looks at me.

— I know who you are, Travis. I see you now. And yes, alright, I am frightened. I thought I had everything in order. I thought I was ready, but I'm not.

— People rarely are.

I reach across and rest my hand on his bare shoulder. It's firm and warm, with a tattoo matching his trophies – the man with the world on his back. On his other shoulder, Sisyphus pushing the boulder up the mountain. Both tattoos are fuzzy from the speckled moles, and as I stroke his back I can feel the lumps and ridges.

— Be honest, kid. How long have I got?

— Not long. Hours. Minutes.

He inhales again, short and sharp. His red face turns redder.

— I wish I'd done more for them. For the kids. I gave them everything – money, clothes, whatever they wanted – but sometimes that's not enough, is it? I wasn't there. I was too busy travelling around the world. They hardly visit me now. They look at me, and all they see is this big fat cripple in a big fat house, a man on his crutches, a man who can barely lift a bag of shopping. Where did it all go wrong? Tell me that, kid. Tell me that. Christ's sake, look at me. Blubbering like the world's strongest baby.

— Cry all you need. I'm here.

— I appreciate that, I really do.

I glance through the windscreen. The topiary and pillars leading towards the giant monogrammed gates. I turn the key. The engine bellows like some great hulking god behind us, and I inch the car out of the drive and up the path.

— Yes! Now we're talking, kid.

Keith roars a war cry from deep in his belly. He drums his fingers on the dashboard, and I ease the car down his driveway, through the gates and along the tree-lined road.

— Keith?

— Yeah?

— Tell me what else you've lifted.

He roars again, laughing, smacking my knee.

— Oh, kid, what *haven't* I lifted?

Keith Rotherham – 68 years, 11 months, 1 day

Every Wednesday evening she drives Nick to his alcoholic meetings, and instead of driving home she waits in the enclosed dark of the car. It's so dark she can't see herself in the mirror. Neda sleeps gently in the back, and Dalia just sits with her hands on the wheel, watching the traffic, the passers-by with their umbrellas in the orange light of the street lamps. The windscreen fills with spots of rain and condensation until she can see nothing but orange and black blurs, and it makes her sleepy, but she doesn't sleep.

This hour, this one small hour, is her peace. This in-between world where real life pauses, where she doesn't exist, this is her favourite. And when Nick opens the car door and sits back down, she asks him how it went. And every week he says the same thing. It was good, he says, what have you been doing?

Faye packs her bags, and now she's leaving the house where she's lived her whole life. She's nineteen, and they're moving south, and a new family will live here. These rooms will mean nothing to the new family. To them, it'll just be an ordinary house, ordinary rooms, but Faye knows everything. She knows the way the living room door brushes along the carpet – the carpet with the wodge of plasticine stuck in the corner. She knows the Lego piece that fell down the crack in the wooden floor in the dining room. She knows the way you have to pull the string of the bathroom light just right, otherwise the thing will come off the end. She knows where she kissed a boy for the first time. She knows every birthday, every Christmas, every argument. It's all still here, and the new family have no choice but to live amongst it.

But the loft. The loft has always been foreign to Faye. It's sat above her head all her life, but when she pokes her head through the hatch, it's like another house, a topsy-turvy unfinished other-space. Faye spends her whole afternoon in the loft. Her final afternoon in this house. She sits among the rafters, the insulation, the draught, the bricks, the slightly damp smell, and she soaks it all in. She feels guilty for not spending more time here. It's not a remarkable loft, just a storage area, but somehow she feels like she wasted it. Like an old friend she never spoke to. And when she leaves the house that day, with her mother and father and her younger brother, she rubs her bare wrist and she knows her bracelet will always be up there in the loft – a piece of her left behind, nestled beneath the fibreglass.

Patricia spends more time with the dead than the living, and she wants each of them to look their best. Today she applies make-up to an old woman who died of a stroke on Thursday. She applies lilac eye shadow to the wrinkled eyelids. A subtle dust of blush upon the mottled cheeks. Sometimes she speaks to them, or sings. Today she sings.

There's nothing morbid about it, she tells her friends. It's just a mark of respect. I can't let you leave this world looking like corpses, can I?

Giselle stands naked before her floor-standing mirror in the bedroom. She's surrounded by macramé and monstera plants, hanging moons and watercolour foxes. She sighs. When she was in her twenties, her body was tight and smooth. Now it's saggy and lumpy as an old cushion. A bulge here, a stretchmark there, a wrinkle, blue veins. Her nipples are large and extended from three lots of breastfeeding. There's a pouch between her crotch and belly button that never used to be there. That's the part she hates the most. This gelatinous pouch that doesn't seem to shift no matter how many hours of Pilates she does. She's approaching fifty now. She sighs again, staring at this unfamiliar suit of fat and skin. She's disgusting.

Her husband walks from the en suite into the bedroom in his boxer shorts. He's drying his hair with a towel, his face hidden, and she uses this chance to sneak a look at him. He's still trim, a little grey. If anything, she thinks, he looks better than when they met. When he sees her, he wolf-whistles, kisses her cheek. He squeezes her sagging backside. And she smiles and throws the crochet blanket back over the mirror.

And there's a family doing family things, and nothing hap-pens, and it's beautiful. There's no moment, no event. Just a family watching television. There's a family eating dinner

around their dinner table. And they talk, or don't talk, or
maybe they argue but it's a small argument, silly matters,
money, work, but mostly they are a family and the mum
tucks them in and reads a story, and the dad sits with them
and says goodnight, or maybe there's a bath, or a lullaby,
and there's a family, and there's a family, and it's perfect and
it hurts and I can never stop watching, never stop peeking
like an urchin through a sweet shop window, and I'm not
there, but I am there, I'm with them, I'm on the sofa, I am
a silent guest at their dinner table, I'm sitting at the end of
the bed, I'm there with them, and I suck it all in through
my mouth, I open my eyes so wide to let in the light, these
big silver eyes shining like film canisters, and I watch in the
homely black rooms, and I dress in the father's clothes, I kiss
the mother, I switch on the nightlight for the kids, and I'm
crawling up every wall, hanging over every ceiling like black
spotted mould, this looming presence, and they forget, and
they ignore, and they pretend, but I'm here and they're
there and I love them and I envy them and I don't know
who I am but I wish I were someone or anyone, and I watch
them, the families, every family in every house in every
time where there are people in houses, and spray-painted
hieroglyphs on roughened roads denote the water pipes, the
gassy pipes, and the chattering wires with signals sparking
every home alive, please let me in, it's dark out here, please
let me in, tap tap tap on the window pane, please let me in.

And there are joyous moments. The boy with the itchy
leg where his cast was removed, and he scratches it, and it's

bliss. Or the girl with the certificate for excellent reading, after struggling for half a year. There's the blind woman with the new dog, and the man whose cancer disappeared into the shadows, and the other man who paid off his first house after being told he'd never amount to anything, and the woman who finally found the courage to step outside her house. There's an escape here. It's all here, it's here.

Stuart has the worst day of his working life but he smiles when he walks through the front door and hears the kids calling Daddy Daddy Daddy. James sits on the end of his bed with his school trousers around his ankles, making sure he knows how a condom works because of Kelly and the camping trip on Saturday. And as he tears open the squidgy packet, his big sister Charlotte has a miscarriage in the bath. Beneath the house, a family of mice makes a nest from shredded magazines. One of the articles is titled 'My Husband is a Ghost and He's Cheating on Me', and outside there's a man in a tatty jumper and jeans, and he's wandering these restless streets.

When Nick visits Dalia's new home for the first time, he walks around the rooms checking the light switches and taps, as if he has a clue what he's doing. Dalia lets him get on with it. She knows he's only trying to make himself useful, maybe as a thank you for her help over the last few

weeks. He raps his fingers on the walls. Now he's in the
bathroom, running his finger along the grout between
the tiles.

— You're starting to get some mould here.

— Yeah?

— You'll need to be careful or it'll take over. I've got
some spray at home. I'll bring it round.

Dalia stands in the bathroom doorway, arms folded.
She watches as Nick turns on the hot tap, holds his hand
beneath the running water and looks at his watch. He nods,
dries his hands. Dalia laughs.

— What?

— Just you.

— Just me, what?

— Do you actually know what you're doing?

— I'll have you know I'm a nearly qualified plumber.
You won't be laughing when the toilet breaks.

— I can fix a toilet, Nick.

— Yeah, alright.

They both smile, and Dalia is glad he's looking healthier. More shape in his cheeks, less sunken around the eyes.
She asks if he wants a cup of tea.

And while the kettle boils, he tells her about his appren-
ticeship at the plumbing company, he lays out his plans for
the next five years, about starting his own company, hiring
a couple of people – he's even come up with the name.
Nick's Plumbing.

Dalia passes him his tea.

— It sounds brilliant. I'm happy you're doing better.

— How about you? Are you alright?

— I'm alright.

— You know, if you ever want to talk about things, about what happened, I wouldn't mind having someone to talk to. You're the only person in the world who knows what I'm going through. I've been thinking about it a lot.

— There's not really much to say.

Dalia considers sitting with him on the sofa, seeing what words come out, but instead she leans against the kitchen worktop and sips her tea. She watches Nick, as he watches her, two grieving parents with a million things to say and no way to say them.

The country park is a haven in a quiet spot of town. A protected land of public footpaths and lakes, a couple of cafes, some wooden playgrounds, a miniature train ride. The air is sharp and smells of pine.

Nick pushes Neda in her pushchair, while Dalia walks alongside with her salted caramel coffee, and they don't speak, but they enjoy the views of the woods, the lake with the wild island in the centre, the swans. They take the long route around the largest lake, hopping a fence and cutting through a field of cows that stare at Nick, forcing him to pick up his pace, and Dalia laughs, and they walk across the mini railway crossing to a play area of wooden see-saws and swings, a plastic tunnel through a man-made hill.

— How are things with you and Travis?

— I'm not sure. I think he's avoiding me.

— Oh.

And he puts Neda in the baby swing and pushes her. She looks bored, so he pushes her harder, and there's a moment where she gets scared, then she giggles. Dalia sits on a concrete boulder and smokes a cigarette, watching the other families, watching a little girl on the zipline. She watches a mother chase her daughter through the tunnel, and she wonders, did I ever do that? Did I ever chase Layla through a tunnel? Would I even have chased her through a tunnel if she'd asked me, or would I have said, not today baby, it'll be all dirty, I've got a coffee, I don't fancy running around today. She sips her coffee. She's been trying to avoid thoughts like this. It's a sharp sweet torture, like digging your fingernails into your cheek – but no, ignore it, we're having a nice day, Nick is really trying. Look at him with Neda. He's looking so much stronger. Listen to her giggling. This is a nice day, and you don't need to torment yourself. Just enjoy today.

— Do you want to push her?
— No, you keep going. She likes it.
— Can I take her down the slide?
— That one? It looks a bit big.
— She'll be alright. I'll put her on my lap.
— Alright.

Dalia watches as Nick carries Neda up the muddy hill to the top of the long metal slide. He sits her on his lap and they descend, slow and squeaky from Nick's boots, and Neda doesn't look impressed.

When they reach the bottom, Nick straps Neda back in her pushchair, and they're off again, away from the playground, past the field where families try to fly kites, but it's not windy enough, and along the twisting gravel path where geese honk, and there's a swan caught halfway between its adult feathers and its grey baby feathers, and there are signposts pointing to the cafe, the car park, the nature trail. Toadstools grow like scales on the rotting fallen tree. Black earth, banks of stinging nettles. Magpie eggs, cracked, discarded. A forty-year-old crisp packet, its colours washed away by sunlight and rain but for the cyan. There's a scent of ducks and algae, and for the first time in months, Dalia can breathe.

They stop at the cafe, and Dalia orders another coffee and a milk for Neda. Nick buys a slice of carrot cake and a water, and they sit by the big windows. He takes his boot off and rubs his toes.

— My feet hurt like shit. I think these shoes are too small.

And they gaze out over the lake, at the families in the pedal boats, the dinghy tied to the jetty.

— When I was at my alcoholics meeting the other night, I was thinking about how life can be good, and then just be awful.

— You're not wrong there.

— I always thought life was a bit like a house.

— Right?

— People buy a house and they spend their whole lives trying to make it perfect. They decorate the rooms the way they want them. Make it a happy place to be. Make it somewhere they could die in. That's what I used to think.

244

And he stares across the lake, eyes glistening, finding the words.

— But life isn't a house, is it? It's more like a hotel. And there are good hotels and there are bad hotels, but it's okay because you only stay in each one for a little bit. Maybe you're staying in a nice room with a comfy bed and good food, but the next one could be horrible. Or maybe you're in the horrible one, but you know the next one might be better. And you're constantly moving, and things get better, and things get worse. But no matter what – it's not a house. You can't stay there forever.

Dalia looks at him, this recovering alcoholic, talking about hotels and houses. This man she shared a child with, this plumber's apprentice with the patchy beard and bad breath.

She grabs a fork and reaches for a chunk of Nick's cake. He holds her fingers.

— Dalia, I hope you're okay.

— I am. I'll get there.

— I hope so. I really hope so.

— I am, I promise.

— I hope one day you'll forgive yourself.

— Forgive myself?

— For Layla.

— What do you mean?

— Well, just for what happened. It's not your fault, but I know you wish you'd done things differently. Taken her to the hospital sooner and stuff.

— Of course I do. What's made you say that?

— No, nothing. I just know how I'd feel in your position, and it must be so hard. Especially with something like meningitis, you have to act fast.

Dalia puts the fork down.

— You think it's my fault.

— I didn't say that.

— Oh my god, you do, don't you?

— It's no one's fault. That's what I'm saying.

— Fucking hell, Nick. Fucking hell.

— What?

— You blame me for what happened.

— No, I don't, I really don't. I was just—

— I didn't take her to hospital because I didn't see the rash, alright? She was wearing zombie make-up, which you'd know if you ever bothered to be there.

— You didn't wash the make-up off before bed?

— I thought about it, but I didn't.

— Why not?

She looks at him, this boy, this scruffy excuse for a dad. His dopey eyes. He's been waiting to say this, he's been waiting to blame her, she knows it. He's always thought it was her fault.

— Because she was poorly. Okay? I didn't wash the make-up off because she was poorly and I didn't want to disturb her. And you're right. I should have known, I should have done more. You're right – it's my fault. She had a sore neck, her muscles were aching – I should've checked. So yes, thank you, Nick. Thank you. It is my fault.

Dalia looks at him. He tries some half-sentences but gives up.

In the lake, two families collide softly in their pedal boats. They laugh, and one of the dads nudges the other family away with the heel of his boot.

❧

These days I ride the bus for the smell of it. For the reek of people and their lives. Every person on this bus would rather have stayed in bed – it's five in the morning and the world outside is black – black enough for the big rectangular windows to reflect our misery back at us – and it's bright in here, and yellow, with a cold metallic tang, and a superficial warmth from the vents behind our ankles. The bus rattles and clatters like an old projector, the filmstrip of windows with the dust and scratches of a world flickering by, black and white, and no one says a word but for the little boy to his father. The boy is six, and he's asking questions about electricity, and the father is tired and he responds but realizes he doesn't know all the answers, and maybe no one knows. The old woman crochets a scarf using a video on her phone – the scarf is absurdly long, but she won't stop until she runs out of wool. The woman beside me has a bag at her feet and one on her lap, and she's wearing two coats and a red beret. She's googling her symptoms. When she looks at me, I look out of the window, but there's nothing, just our mirror images, and this is our shuttle of sleepy strangers, and the boy says, but *where* does it go when it's not in the wires?

❧

AN OFFICE MAN

Barry Lightfoot has never needed a piss so badly as he does right now, in the monthly manager's meeting at the hotel. A white conference room with a smell of carpets. A large table, a laptop plugged into a projector – an accountant reeling off figures from a spreadsheet – and Barry's bladder pressing against his belt buckle like an overripe peach.

He would ask to be excused, but he's already dipped out twice in the last hour – once for a phone call from his ex-wife, and once for another piss which he rushed so he'd have time for a cigarette. Only twenty minutes until lunch, he tells himself. Might as well hold it.

A co-worker asks if the minuses on the spreadsheet are good or bad. The accountant scrolls up and down the spreadsheet before deciding it means good. Means we're under budget. So red is good, the co-worker asks. In this column it is, she says.

She brings up a pie chart that looks how Barry's bladder feels – big and round and mostly yellow. She brings up line graphs that make Barry think of long cathartic streaks of piss across a pristine white bowl. He can feel his pulse in his waistband. The sweat building at his temples, around the arms of his glasses. He squirms in his seat.

— You alright there, Baz?

— Fine, fine. These rooms get stuffy, don't they?

Barry tries leaning forward to release some pressure, but this only lets his bladder fill more, so he leans back, and it's somehow worse – stretching everything out, feeling the liquid slosh around. He stares at the digital clock in the bottom right of the projected computer screen, but it doesn't display the seconds, and every minute is impossibly long, cruel, even.

Twelve minutes until lunch. Then there's the thirty-second jog to the toilet – no, not a jog, a kind of glide. We don't want to bounce the bladder. Thirty-second glide, then three seconds to unzip and aim. Imagining that sweet release almost makes him release it there and then.

— Barry, what do you think?

Barry hasn't heard a single word of the conversation that's been taking place in front of him, so he delivers his trusty go-to line.

— I think it's all about margins.

A few murmurs of approval, some nodding, and the conversation flows from there. It flows like a trickling stream. A stream so clear you can see the pebbled bed. Barry imagines his bladder like a great yellow demijohn heavy with home-made cider, only instead of apples it's fermented from instant coffee and the espresso back at the office. *Expresso*, Sheena had called it. Not the brightest PA in the world.

— Shall we call that lunch, guys?

— Is that alright, Barry?

— I suppose so.

They all stand up from the table, moving at half-speed, nobody wanting to appear too eager to leave, but Barry pushes past them and makes the world's longest trip down the hotel corridor to the toilets. Smooth strides, Barry, smooth strides. Maybe if you start releasing it now, by the time you're standing at the urinal it'll be ready to flow.

Around the corner, past the little buffet table, into the toilets. These toilets smell more beautiful than any Barry has ever remembered smelling – disinfectant and urinal cakes. By the time he's at the urinal, his belt is loosened, his zip is undone, his penis is out.

It takes a moment. Pent up for so long, his body has forgotten how it all works, or the piss has solidified into yellow calcite – but no, here it comes.

The relief shudders through him, hot and glorious – the longest piss of Barry's life. Certainly in the top ten. He releases an involuntary moan, and it was almost worth it for this catharsis. And it's done. He's empty.

He gives it a shake. Composes himself. Stands at the mirror to wash his hands. And as he catches sight of the bald porky man in the reflection, that's when Barry Lightfoot has his first massive heart attack.

When they discharge him four days later, and when his mum has stopped fussing over him, Barry goes home and cooks a curry. He fries the chicken and chops the onions

before realizing he doesn't have a jar of sauce, so he orders
a kebab instead. While he waits for the delivery, he sweeps
the chopped onion into a Tupperware box and wraps the
chicken in foil. And when the food arrives, he eats it in
front of the nine o'clock news with a can of cider, and the
kebab is fat as a yule log, stuffed with doner meat, mayon-
naise, salad, chilli sauce, and wrapped with care by the lads
at Super Kebab & Chicken. Barry opens the polystyrene
tray of chips and dumps them on the plate.

His home is quiet but for the drone of the journalists,
the intermittent fanfare and gongs to accompany the
headlines. His skin looks blue in the wavering television
light.

He finishes the kebab and chips, licks his greasy fingers,
carries his plate to the kitchen. He takes the pint of ice
cream from the freezer, another cider from the fridge, and
he sits back down with a cigarette while the newsreader
talks about a former world's strongest man who died in his
home on Sunday night. Barry taps ash onto the brim of the
can.

I watch him, this grisly creature on his grisly sofa.

I've always prided myself on my impartiality. Even with
the worst of people – people far more nefarious than Barry
Lightfoot – it has never been my place to judge or interfere.
But sitting here now, a part of me is sick. I'm trembling as
I watch him.

— You haven't looked after yourself, have you, Barry?

Barry jumps, spilling cider on himself. It fizzes into his
polo shirt. I'm in the armchair in the shadows. He looks at

me, horrified. He wants to ask who I am, but he already knows. They all know, at the end.

— How are you feeling, Barry?

— Much better. I'm better.

— Do you think so?

— Yes. They said I am.

— That's good. That's good. Is that all they said, Barry?

— It's none of your business. I think you'd better leave.

— What did they say? Tell me what they said.

— They just said I need to take it easy. Stop getting so stressed at work.

— What else did they say, Barry?

— To stop smoking and drinking. To eat better. To do some exercise, get some fresh air. All the same old shit. I'm not stupid. I know these things. But who's got the time? And I'll try, I've said I'll try, but flipping heck, I'm fifty, I can't change my ways now.

— No?

— No, I don't think so.

— You might be right.

He spoons up some cookie dough-flavoured ice cream. He brings it to his lips, holds it there for a moment, then drops the spoon back into the pot.

— Are you just going to sit and watch me eat?

— What would you like me to do, Barry?

— I don't know. It's rude. You're being rude.

— I'm sorry.

I turn my head to the television, and we both sit and watch the weather – spring sunshine is on its way – and

Barry doesn't touch his ice cream. He doesn't put it to one side, either. He sits with the pot on his lap, letting it melt, and he smokes his cigarette and drinks his cider.

— I bet I'm the unhealthiest bloke you've ever seen.

— I've seen far worse.

— I only have a couple of cans a night. If that. And the ciggies help me relax. They help me sleep. There's a bloke at work, his dad has smoked twenty a day for fifty years, and he's ninety-eight, still going strong.

— I know.

— I have tried to stop. I will try harder, alright? I'll try harder. That's a promise.

— That's good.

I think of Layla and Dalia, and my fingernails cut into my palm.

Barry stubs the butt of the cigarette into the top of the can, and he fiddles with his wedding ring. She divorced him eighteen months ago, but he couldn't bring himself to take it off. What would she think if he died? She'd be sad, probably. Even after everything they went through, they're still friends. They'll always be friends.

Barry mutes the television.

— Are you even here, in this room, or are you in my head? It's those hospital drugs. I'm probably talking to myself. But whatever, either way, I get it. Alright? I need to change. I understand.

— That's good.

— No more smoking. No drink. I'll eat better. Walk to work.

He unmutes the television. I stand up and sit beside him on the sofa, our thighs touching, and I can see he's uncomfortable with me sitting so close, like a sudden chill. He tries to ignore me, but his eyes wander. He looks at the cushion pressing beneath me. He looks at my face. I draw a slow breath.

— Barry, in ten minutes you're going to suffer another heart attack.

— You're lying.

— This one will kill you.

He says no, and he turns his head slightly, but he still stares at me. He says it again, no, and his eyes shimmer in the glow of the TV, and he shakes his head.

— I've told you, I'll change.

— It's too late, Barry.

— Rubbish. Anyone can change. Look.

He reaches into his pocket, pulls out the box of cigarettes, scrunches each cigarette in his fist until the tobacco sprinkles over his lap. He tosses the crumpled carton across the room. A defiant face. Tight lips and a high chin. He's made up his mind – he will not die.

— You didn't look after yourself.

— I just let things slip. I got myself into a rut.

— You're a waste. You're disgusting.

— No, I'm a good person, I just need to sort myself out.

— You're a pathetic creature. You deserve nothing.

— This is a wake-up call. Alright? You've got me. If you were trying to scare me, consider me scared. Congratulations.

— You have nine minutes, Barry. What are you going to do with them?

— Please, I swear. I swear I'll change it.

Now he's sweating. He unbuttons his polo shirt and sits up straight, glancing around for something to save him. He pops the lid back on the ice cream and places it on the arm of the sofa. He stands up and drops his cider in the bin. He opens his arms as if to say, there, is that good enough? He's wheezing.

— Better not get yourself worked up, Barry.

— What do you want me to do? Why are you here? If you're not going to change anything, why are you here? What's the point of it?

— You'll see in eight minutes.

Barry bounces on the spot. He glances at pictures of his kids on the walls, pictures of them as toddlers, and graduations, and weddings. Their whole lives flit through his mind – every single thing he wishes he'd said and done. He grabs his phone from down the side of the sofa and calls his ex-wife.

— Sonia? Sonia, I'm not feeling good.

She says some things, she asks some questions.

— Just listen, Sonia, I don't think I've got long. I just wanted to say I'm sorry. For everything. I'm really really sorry, Sonia. I was stupid. I'm a stupid man. Always have been. Tell the kids I'm sorry too. I'm so sorry, Sonia. If I could take it back. God, I'm sorry. And thank you. I lost sight of things, but thank you. You were always there. You— Hmm? No, I don't think there's time. I'm okay though, Sonia. I'm okay. I didn't look after myself. I didn't look after myself. I'm sorry.

Barry ends the call before she can respond, and he looks down at me from where he stands. I sit with my hands on my knees, looking up at him from the flickery shadows of the screen behind him, and he drops his phone into his pocket.

— How many minutes?

— Five.

— Not long, is it?

— No, Barry, it's not long.

He glances around the room again, at all the nothingness. The things of his life — an expensive lamp, a drinks cabinet, the painting of a waterfall — they'd meant something once. He opens a drawer in the Welsh dresser and pulls out a black DVD case covered in dust. He wipes the dust away, opens the case, takes out the disc. And he puts the disc in the player, and he sits back down beside me, and we watch it: a thirty-year-old Barry, a little thinner in his grey suit, dancing with Sonia in her white dress. She's six months pregnant.

Barry sits on the edge of the seat, and I watch him instead of the video. He looks like a man remembering something he'd long forgotten. A man surprised that he'd ever forgotten it. A man who lived underwater for twenty years and has finally come up for air.

His chest begins to tighten, his breathing slows.

Do it now, he says. While I'm watching this.

— While my eyes are on her. Do it now. Please.

There are two minutes left, and Barry lives every second of them. The wedding video ends, a black screen, and Barry Lightfoot dies on his sofa, though he's somewhere else entirely.

Barry Lightfoot — 50 years, 0 months, 26 days

In the night-time she sinks to a place inside herself, all cushions and fizz, all tingles and nothing, all blurry and mffffff, deep in a hole, and the world is far far up there in the circle of light, and she can hardly feel her fingers as she grasps the plastic tray of pills, pinches off the punched-out pill-shaped cap of foil attached to the packet, holds it in front of her eyes, this two-dimensional capsule of foil with the cut-off black writing, and when she bends the foil between her fingers it stays bent, and she folds it, and folds it again, a sharp little speck of silver, and she presses the point to her fingertip, a distant pleasant pain, and she drops the foil to the floor. She's sitting on the carpet with her back against the sofa, and she peels off each loose bit of foil, then punches another pill from the tray and nibbles it until it's soggy in her mouth, and she swallows it and washes it down with a glass of red wine. This isn't an overdose, she tells herself. I haven't taken enough to overdose. This is just me climbing out of the hole I've sunk into — and that's good, isn't it? This is me sitting on the edge of a cliff with

no intention of jumping, and if the breeze weren't so cool
up here, if the sea air were not so fresh, maybe I'd go and
sit somewhere else, but I'm happy here, I'm no one here,
and she sips the wine and presses the empty pill casings
inside-out like bubble wrap, and she presses herself inside-
out. She eats the pills from the hospital, and she opens the
box of paracetamol.

And I must witness this. I must watch her dissolve,
and although I am not there, I wonder if she can feel
me, and although I am not there, I urge her to stand up,
to put the medicine in the bin, to cancel this and see what
tomorrow looks like, but she cannot hear me, or she does
not listen, and soon I will show up and do my duty, but
I don't know if I'm strong enough, I don't know if I can
be the one to extinguish her, to watch her fall limp, I don't
know if I can. Dalia, I wish you wouldn't die. Please. Stand
up. Stand up and be strong so I don't have to.

In the centre of the Earth there's a star raging white hot
and rumbling, a searing chamber of heat and light, and
I curl in my ball like a foetus in an egg and the gravity
crushes me into something that won't fall apart, my bones
that resemble bones, my stomach pouch, my lung sacks, my
ear tunnels, the miniature trunk between my legs, the purse
of ripened fruit – I want to melt and crumble in the eye
of that blazing star beneath the sea and crust and oil and
clay in the middle of the world that bore them all, every
one, and this one, this woman, midwife, mother, why
must you occupy some special place within me – no – you

do not – I reject it – I do not care what you do – come,
die – open that box of medicine and pour them onto your
tongue, crunch them into bitter paste and swallow them
with bottle after bottle of wine until you are as big as the
moon, and I will space-walk on you and plant my harpoon
flag between your eyes and say, look, I was here. This is
who and what I am, and though you have wobbled me you
will not topple me, so do it, get it done, let's complete this
transaction, hurry up. I refuse to intervene. Why would
I make an exception for you? I have been coming for you
every day since you came out of your mother, and I will
not leave until I have you, every one of you, so yes, come
on, do it.

But there's something about your face that seems like a
waste, something about your soothing voice and your
simple nature – you are not particularly beautiful or wise
or funny – I cannot point to one trait and say, you intrigue
me because of this or that – instead it's a subtle accumula-
tion, it's a specific set of intangible qualities that make up
'you' – the points and lines that form a shape, a shape that
happens to tessellate with mine in a way that is pleasing
and inconvenient and unwarranted, and the sour irony, the
hilarious truth about all this is that you – you, dear Dalia –
might just be the death of me.

And when she hears the knock at the door, it's blurry,
underwater. The knock has no meaning – except, a knock
means someone is knocking – a knock means someone

wants you to answer – a knock means you need to answer. Knock, knock, knock. He's coming. He wants to come in. She looks at the door. Perhaps it's not the door – perhaps the knocking comes from inside herself – but she stares at the door anyway, knock, knock, knock, knock, knock. Someone says Dalia, and she knows that's her name. It sounds like the man who visits her sometimes in her worst moments. The tall man with the holes in his socks and the unbrushed hair – he's come to see her again. She remembers the day her father died, and she tries to remember, was the tall man there that day? Was there a strange visitor in the house, making small talk and drinking tea, visiting her father in the quiet hours? It's possible. He has one of those faces. She feels as though she's seen him on every street corner, in every shop, in every school, library and pub, just looming, waiting. Knock, knock, knock, knock.

She pushes her pills beneath the sofa and stands up. The room is a football field, but she crosses it, her soles brushing the carpet, and she unlocks the door and opens it. But it's not the tall man, it's the other man. The man she once had a baby with, and then the baby died. That man.

— Are you busy? Can I come in?

— No, no.

— No?

— No, I'm not busy.

She steps away from the door, and she tries to steady her eyes. Her words come out like her mouth is full of paper, so she walks to the kitchen and pours some water from the tap.

— Do you want any water?

— No, I'm alright.

Nick looks at the empty bottles on the side, but he doesn't say anything. Dalia sips her water. It makes her gag.

— Are you okay, Dalia?

— I'm fine. Why are you here?

— I'm not staying long. I just wanted to apologize. For the other day in the cafe. Travis said I should apologize, and he's right. I'm sorry for what I said. It was horrible, and I'm sorry.

— Travis said that?

— Yeah.

— When did you see him?

— About an hour ago. Bumped into him on the street.

— I haven't seen him for a while.

— Well, I just wanted to say sorry.

— Thank you.

Nick looks at her, but she looks at her feet. She leans near the sink with her glass of water, and she looks drained, half asleep. Nick stands beside her.

— I shaved the beard off. What do you think?

— Hmm? Oh. I hadn't noticed. It looks good.

He rubs his sore cheeks with his palms. The stubble is already growing back.

— I had a really nice time the other day, walking around the lake and stuff. I hope we can do something like that again.

— We will.

— I liked seeing Neda.

— She liked seeing you too.

He holds her hand. She can barely feel it.

The tap drips onto the stainless-steel sink.

Drip. Drip. Drip.

— I've been feeling a lot better.

— Have you? You're done grieving, are you?

— Well no, course not. I guess you're never done grieving. But I feel clearer. Like I can start living some kind of normal life.

— That's good. That's really good.

And they stand there, the two of them, the one full of wine and pills, and the sober one, there in the kitchen, the tap still dripping. Dalia makes a noise. Nick holds her, and she breaks down in his arms. He strokes her spine and tells her it's okay, shh, it's okay, and she says some words, but they come out as gibberish and she tries again. I'm scared, Nick. I thought I was making things work, I thought I was okay, but I don't think I am. I don't think I'm well. You have everything together, Nick. How are you doing it? How are you doing it? And he says, it's okay, I'm here. I'm here. I'm here.

And it's all there, the hidden life – all the teeth and tongues, every sock in every drawer and all the books under the beds, and I am tired, so tired, but it never stops, it never shuts up, and if I could die then I would die, but I can't and

I won't, and it's all there, every plate in the cupboard, all
the junk, every scrappy drawer packed with batteries and
screws and Blu-tack and string and instruction booklets
all falling down the back, and it's there under every set of
stairs, in every loft, down the side of the sofa, under the
oven, under the carpet, under your fingernails. It suffocates
in that same gruelling way, the way without ending, a
rising pitch that never falls. I was there before you knew
anything, I was there when it started, all of it, and I will be
there in those few cold quiet moments when everything
that can ever be done will finally be done and I can rest,
because I adore it and you, but if I could only rest that
might be nice, after all, you can, why can't I – but it's okay.
It's okay. Yes, it's okay. It's okay. It's okay.

Curl naked in the copse with my thumbs in my ears,
middle fingers pressing on my eyelids, mouth shut, the
itchy grass around my neck, my waist, my buttocks, my
ankles, perhaps if I stay here it'll all grow around me,
the little shoots and roots will dig inside and through
me, maybe I can decompose. I am done. I reject the
responsibility. Let me sink back to where it began, let me
become a part of it again. Maybe I can rot, my fingernails
sprouting buds and flowers, my eyelids bearing fruit,
succulent earlobes, mossy underarms, maybe these toes
will claw into the soil and suck moisture from the good
earth, my skin will drink the sun, you stupid stupid
thing, I am a baby in the mother's nest, the Big Mother,
the Old Mother, the Great Mother, the Green Mother,

the Milky Mother, the Sweet Mother, her baby in the
clutch, suckling, the leafy sprog in the cradle of blackened
leaves, the baby pushing back between the mother's legs,
the Home Mother, the Light Mother, the baby with its
branchy arms, sappy tears, that's it, sob into her heart,
curl up tighter if you think it will help, has it ever helped,
has it ever stopped? How about you continue the work,
the sequence, the paths leading out like woody fingers,
lightning forks and mollusc trails, and how about it, how
about it? But hush, stay awhile in the brush with the
snails and the ants, stay with me and the woodlice, I can't
do it, not yet, I cannot take her, hush, yes I can, I will,
I always have, the Warm Mother, the One Mother, hush
now, hush.

And on a bright pink morning, I visit her grave. I'm not
one for visiting graves, but this morning I do. It's a small
white headstone, rectangular, and there are flowers, but
they're dead. I take the dead ones. They crumble in my
hands, and I don't know why I'm here, but I crouch and
study her headstone, the name in gold cursive. Layla
Preston. The year she was born, and the year she died, the
same decade, and the numbers seem too close – the text
itself looks crowded, like a joke – and it says daughter,
and it says sister. And her body, that tiny body she drove
around in for a few years, it's there in the ground beneath
my bare feet. I didn't bring flowers, it didn't cross my mind.
I brought nothing. Some people speak to the gravestones,
I know that. Some people cry. But I don't do either of

those things. I lay my hand on the top of your headstone, Layla, I close my eyes, and in the dark I wish you a happy birthday.

∾

And in the spring the storm drains overflow and bubble with rain and raw sewage. It's a mild morning when she walks to the allotment and cuts ten fresh daffodils from the soil. The daffs are still closed up in their yellow petals, but in a few days they'll open. Dalia takes them from the allotment, past the council houses and the parish and the field where the lads play football with their coats as goalposts. She takes the flowers to her daughter's grave. She'd almost forgotten what it looked like. She'd barely glanced at it at the funeral and hasn't been able to muster the courage to visit it since. But she kneels beside it now, poking the daffodils into the metal holes, and she looks at the white marble – the dirt and the flecks of green and the splat of bird shit. She picks the mess away with her thumbnail, then wipes the green with her cuff until the whole thing shines. She'd like to say some things. All the normal things, she thinks. Sorry and thank you and I miss you and I love you, but the words fall short as they always do, so she stays quiet, and this feels right, this quietness. She traces her fingers over the recess of the child's name. She closes her eyes and breathes.

*

In the flat, I pack up my photographs, my tools, my brushes and glues, my bottle of deionized water. I dump them into sacks until the room is a white shell with a white cat. I pick up the cat and cradle her, and she enjoys it at first, but then she squirms and I carry her across the hall to the man who lives there now. He answers the door in a dressing gown and furry slippers and he will die by drowning. I tell him, you must look after this cat. He asks why, and I say, this cat doesn't have an owner and I'm going away and this cat needs a home. I lay the cat in his arms and it pounces straight to the floor and sniffs around at the last few scent-traces of a girl it used to know. And I leave the man with his new friend and I carry the sacks of rubbish to the bins and I don't look back.

And when she stares at the grave, something's out of place. She plucks three daffodils from the plinth and carries them to the other side of the cemetery where another headstone waits. She's only visited this stone once. The name is Samuel Preston, a reckless soul, a risk-taker blessed with so much life it burst from him, this rolling boy, this brother beneath her feet. And although she's been angry with him since the day he died, she remembers him now as a loving thing: a brother who would listen, an uncle who would tease. He was there when Mum died, and Dad, and although he was stupid and brazen and he could have killed someone, he only succeeded in killing himself — and that, in itself, is a kind of redemption. She lays the three daffodils at his grave.

She stands up, peering across the field of stones. Now her mind is clear.

$$\sim$$

As Dalia drives away from the city, she remembers the streets where she grew up, before her father got bored and moved them to a quiet rural village. She was seven then, her brother barely a year old. A small country house with a couple of outbuildings, and a workshop where he could fix his cars. The closest neighbours were the barns and garages on the horizon, and she would spend her weekends wandering the fields, climbing fences into meadows that didn't belong to her, finding dirt tracks and ditches and thickets.

All through autumn, Dalia would watch her father in his workshop. She would sit on the bench with her legs swinging beneath and watch him build new shelves for the workshop, and she'd smell the sawdust, the motor oil, the sugary scent of two-stroke petrol from the quads he rode around the field for the fun of it. She always thought he'd rather be somewhere else.

Sometimes her father would lift cars on his old forklift, and he'd spend hours tinkering around in the guts of wires and pipes. Dalia couldn't imagine how one person could understand it all. It looked like a giant mess.

And she hated that forklift. It was yellow and patched with rust and crackling paint, and its chain was brown. Her father would lift a car twice the size of the forklift itself, and he'd stand in the car's shadow, a tonne of machinery over his head, just a chain keeping it from crushing him. He didn't seem frightened, not even a little bit.

Sometimes she said, Dad, I don't like you going under there. And he'd say, what, under the forklift? And he'd smile, handsome, bearded, skin slicked with oil. More than once, he told her to come and stand under the car. And she did, crouching slightly, as if this would allow her more time to escape when it inevitably came crashing down.

But it never did. That would have been a quick death. The forklift lasted another twenty years before being sold for scrap. Her father's death was the much slower kind. Wasting away one day at a time, in the middle of nowhere, quiet, simple and always a little bored.

❧

A MOTHER

You drive two hundred miles out of town, along motorways and through the winding villages that feel like another country because they're pretty and quaint, they're hilly and old-fashioned with flower boxes in the windows and paper birches in the gardens, and you drive to a building site surrounded by a tall chipboard fence.

There are no sounds of construction, only the clucks and chirrups of birds on the fence.

There was a hospital here, once. You were born in it. But they tore it down a few years ago, and the ward where you were born is now just a floating point in the air. You imagine yourself up there, in the sky, inside your mother's body on the hospital bed, your father excited at her side. You imagine being pushed out and delivered, and you wonder if you could have become someone else. From that moment you entered the world – if only you'd said a different word here, made a different decision there, you might have lived a whole other life. If you'd gone home all those years ago, instead of kissing Nick on the dance floor, you might not have had Layla, and maybe if you hadn't had Layla you wouldn't have had Neda – but then, you wouldn't know it, so you wouldn't have missed them. Maybe there are infinite children you didn't have, but could've had, and you would've loved them just as intensely – and if that's the case, what does it really mean, any of it? If only you'd been a better mother. Wiped off Layla's zombie make-up. That fucking make-up. If this, if that.

You think of Neda, and what she might be doing right now, with her dad. He'll be playing with her, or reading to her – he was always good like that. Even when she was first born, he never complained about the mess or the late-night feeds. Maybe you were the problem all along.

And you start the car again and drive a few miles to a small house behind the sycamore trees – your first home.

You lived here for three years, and only fragments
of memories remain, but I remember every tiny bit of
it. I remember them bringing you home. The tingle of
anticipation and fear, the two of them standing and staring
at you for an hour before retiring to a sleepless night
in bed.

You want to knock on the door, say hello, I used to
live here, can I look around, but you drive fifty miles to
the next house, in the city. A housing estate. You remember this one. You remember the layout of the rooms, the
furniture, you remember your school and your friends
before you moved to the countryside. And you drive
to that house in the countryside, and there's a different
car parked in the driveway now, and the workshop is a
different colour, and your chest burns with nostalgia for
all the beautiful years that didn't seem beautiful at the
time, they just felt normal, and you can see all the after-
images of all your past selves running about in the field
with your brother, and you remember Christmases, and
you try to remember each birthday cake for each year you
lived here, and then we drive to the first home you lived
in alone, as an adult – a dirty flat where you met Nick.
Where you went out dancing and you kissed him and
he tasted like cigarettes and he taught you to smoke, and
you brought him to your flat and had sex with him on
the floor. You remember the pregnancy test, and sitting
in the abortion clinic, running away at the last minute,
and you didn't see Nick for three months, and when you
saw him he stared at your stomach with the eyes of a

petrified boy, and you said, it's okay, you don't have to do anything, so he didn't.

And we drive to the flat where you lived opposite a tall man, and this was Neda's first home, Layla's last home, and we look at it, this ugly multi-storey building looming over the busy street. And we drive to your current home, but you don't stop the car, you drive past it, through the town, away, to the rural roads where every house is a mile from the others, little beacons on the horizon.

You park your car on the bend of a gravelly back road. Fields and ditches. Clusters of willows. The car is quiet now. Without the rumble of the engine, the silence is heavy and soft as a weighted blanket, and we both sit and stare at the plain fields. The sun will set in an hour, and you don't speak to me. You open your window a crack and watch the breeze roll over the cropped acres.

— Dalia.

— Be quiet, please.

You step out of the car, fetch the hose and funnel and gaffer tape from the boot. I watch you in the rear-view mirror, and from every angle, as you attach the funnel to the exhaust, wrapping layer upon layer of tape to keep it in place. You squish the hose onto the end of the funnel, then feed the hose around the car, through the open window.

You sit in your seat again, shut the door, and close the window until it stops at the hose. You tape up the gap in the window. And without a moment's hesitation, you start the engine once more.

You close your eyes. Rest your head back. We're facing east, unable to see the sun as it falls. All we see is the shadow it leaves, inching across the flat golden land. A silhouetted flock of starlings bursts from a tree, then swoops back into it.

— Dalia.

— I said shut up.

The air ripples over the fields, turning the grass to silver ribbons, and with each ribbon you try to recall another one of your birthdays. The one with the burger cake. The one where you broke your arm. The one with pass-the-parcel when your dad let you win the final surprise.

These memories reel inside you, but you don't let it show. You feel to me now like the sea, and the surface of the sea roils with every memory, every word, each face, but beneath it all is a deep stillness, a heavy screaming nothingness. I watch you until my eyes lose focus, and I peer out over the field with you.

— Dalia, I know you don't want to hear from me. I know your mind is made up, but if you're doing this, I need to tell you some things.

On the horizon, a tree stands alone. The tree is tall and bare with yellow-grey bark and bronze branches bending in the breeze.

— People amaze me. All of you. Every single one of you amazes me. The things you're capable of. The pain you're capable of enduring. I have witnessed moments that perplex me, moments I would have thought impossible. You are resilient. Adaptable. Capable of so much love, it astounds me. I would give anything to feel what you feel.

— Then what do you feel? Nothing?

— I don't know. I feel a great many things. Maybe everything. But that, in itself, is a kind of numbness. I'd like to be smaller. I would die for that.

— Do you mourn them? All the people you take? Do you mourn any of them?

I gaze back out at the burning sky. The tree in the distance. Something spooks the starlings again, and they flutter from the branches and settle back down. I look at you.

— Every single one.

I hadn't expected you to cry, but you cry at that.

Your eyes are white with the reflection of the sky, and your mouth hangs with the unfairness of it all. You glance about as if to find an answer in the air. The voice of a woman running out of time. Every breath is a conscious effort, a decision.

— How do you do it, Travis? How can you bear it? All those people. How can you keep all that inside you? I'm struggling with just one.

I see the desperation in your eyes. The answer seems of vital importance – you want me to spill the secrets, some ancient wisdom to set everything right, as though my next words could make or break you.

I hold your gaze for as long as I can, then I look at my hands because it's a question I'm rarely asked, and I hate it, and I have no words. How *do* I do it? How do I take a young mother like you, sweet Dalia, and a child such as Layla, and seep into your lives, rotting you, tearing you down like old apartments? How do I stare at the rubble from afar before moving onto the next poor home, and the next? How do I keep it, and hold it, and remember it, and repeat it, without destroying myself in the process? I look at you again.

— I wander.

You gaze out over the fields, the pinkish light, the orange sky.

You watch the shadows of the clouds glide along the land.

And as the car fills with invisible poison, I wish I could choke on it, I wish I could sleep. I'm thinking of you and Layla and Neda, and that one perfect summer, that interlude I spent pretending to be a part of your family, when you let me in – a dinner here, a playground there, a performance for you and a fantasy for me – and you're yawning, your eyes are closing as your lungs fill and your head spins and floats away.

In a few minutes, I will do what is in my nature – I will place my hand upon your skin and release you from your body – and you will not know, but I will know, and it is not my place to change your course, and even if it were, could I change it? Is there a simple thing I could say or do? Perhaps I could ask you not to do this. Perhaps if you only heard those words, from me, they'd be enough – but no, that is not my role. I cannot and will not speak. Things are as they are.

Still, when I look at you, sitting in your seat with
your eyes closed, there is a squeeze in my centre. I see a
mother full of so much pain, a woman who invited me
into her life, a woman who ushered lives into the world
while I ushered them out — a woman who grew rhubarb
and daffodils — a woman who deserved nothing more than
a happy healthy family, yes, there is a squeeze, a knot, a
foolish twisting in my gut, because perhaps this woman
meant something more than the others, meant something
to me, and in all my selfishness I'd like to see her remain
in this body a while longer, maybe to watch her heal and
grow towards a more fitting end — but no, I can't. It is not
my place. This is not my place.

— Dalia?

You don't stir. Your eyelids don't flicker.

Toxic blood, suffocating brain.

— Dalia.

— Mmm?

And there's a lightness in me, a weakness, because
I know what's coming. I am an addict who knows he's
about to relapse, and it's terrifying, but it's a rush of giddy
relief all through my body, because there's no more fighting it.

And I say, Dalia. Dalia. Please don't do it.

Please don't do it, Dalia.

Dalia, please. Dalia.

Dalia, please don't do it.

A POND OF NYMPHS

The mayfly larvae huddle in the silty shadows, waiting for the Special Day. They don't know when it will occur, or why it is special, they only know that it is special. They've waited all their lives. Each nymph is an orphan – no knowledge is passed from parent to child, no information about the Special Day. Only rumours. Whispers. They feel it in their fibres – one day something will happen, something so big it defines our lives – and we will never be the same again. They huddle in the dark, evading the rainbow trout, the dace. They peer up at the rippling firmament, wondering why it changes colour, wondering about the visions of flying things, about the edges of the world. Had their ancestors lived, they might have explained. They could have passed on their wisdom in stories and songs. Instead, the nymphs are an infant culture, a barren collective, learning each thing anew. Season after season, they huddle in the black. Some of them are snatched up by hungry mouths, some die of boredom waiting for the Special Day. But most of them wait. A quiet anticipation, building, building, building inside them. When will it happen? When everything is right. How do we know it's right? We'll just know. But I'm ready now. It's not time, brother. It's not time, sister. The oldest among them, the one who prophesied the Special Day, even he begins to

doubt. He'd had vivid dreams of a great festival, a weight-
lessness, a joyous frenzy. He'd dreamt of his forefathers
and foremothers. He'd dreamt of spinning thread in the
moonlight and living for a thousand years after the Special
Day, fostering the next generation and the next, passing
their stories through the ages, so they might never be
infants again. But the dreams have slowed. The dreams
cease altogether. And Elder Nymph doesn't know what this
means – does the Special Day approach, or were the dreams
only ever dreams? Maybe we were doomed to lie here in
the mud, blind and heavy and stupid. The nymphs huddle
in the dark, dreaming of a special day.

A VERY OLD WOMAN

When she wakes on the morning of her ninetieth birthday, she rolls over and stares at the calendar on the wall. There's no sense of pride at having reached nine decades. There's no wave of relief or comfort, or whatever a ninety-year-old is supposed to feel. Just a hollowness. The number 100 looms at the end of a long corridor, goading with its empty eyes – too far to reach, but the only destination. Eighty-nine felt like the end of something. Ninety feels like another beginning, and all these numbers curdle in her mind – ninety, one hundred, eighty-nine – and all the numbers on the calendar sit heavy in her stomach like too much jelly and ice cream. Not another ten years. Please not another ten.

She wakes at six but stays in bed until eleven, her eyes drifting over the nothing on the wall. This bed is her waiting room. This is the world where nothing happens.

She twists the engagement ring on her finger, and she wonders, do I remember? Do I *truly* remember him putting this on my finger? Do I remember what he said, or where he said it? What did he wear – something smart, maybe – or was it one of his tatty old T-shirts? Did he get down on one knee? Do I remember anything, or is it all just memories of memories of anecdotes of memories, is my head full of half-truths and delusions?

She tries to remember his face, but it's a blind spot. Even the photographs seem absurd, like a photo of a stranger in a magazine, and he looks too young, and she feels too old, and is this how it is? Losing the chapters of your life like a book shedding pages until you're just an empty cover whose front touches its back, with nothing but a crusty spine holding it all together? She twists the engagement ring again, this promise, this reminder, and it all seems like a joke with no punchline.

At half eleven, a knock at the front door. She ignores it, but they knock louder, so she sits on the edge of the bed and waits. Wait, wait, wait. When they knock a third time, she sighs and makes that slow walk across the house and answers the door.

It's her youngest grandson, Mason. He's holding a bunch of flowers and he's smiling. Mason kisses her cheek, wishes her a happy birthday. He takes her hand and says, come on.

— Come where? Mason, I've just sat down.

— Time to get dressed, Nan.

— No, no, I'm fine in this.

— You can't wear a nightie on your ninetieth birthday. Come on. Won't take long.

— Oh, for goodness' sake.

Mason pulls her to her feet. He rests a hand on her back all the way down the corridor, into the bedroom. He helps her pick out a smock and a cardigan, then he leaves her alone. He speaks at her through the door.

— You alright, Nan?

— No, I'm not.

— Why not?

— Because I'm ninety.

— I know. It's a special day.

— Is it?

— I hope I make it to ninety. It's impressive.

— What's impressive about clinging to life like a bloody barnacle?

— Nan?

Mason opens the door and looks at his grandmother.

— I mean it, Mason. I'm tired. Sick and tired. I've been here too long.

He's heard her speak like this before, but never so seriously. He sits beside her on the bed. She looks tiny in her baggy cardigan.

— So you want to die?

— Yes. I've lived my life. I don't know if I'd care to repeat it. But it was a life, and now I'm done. There's no reason for me to be here.

— What about us?

— Who?

— Your family.

— Ha! You lot don't need me. And that's fine. I don't want to be needed. I just want to leave with dignity.

— You will, Nan. When the time is right.

Mason takes her hand again and leads her back to the living room. He's looking concerned now, his angel face all creased and hardened. He helps her into the armchair.

— Oh, here they come!

— What? Who? Mason – who's here?

He stands at the window and watches the rabble walking up the driveway. She can't see them, but she hears them: her daughter, her daughter's husband, their two boys in their twenties, three friends from the book club. She can hear them all chatting and laughing.

— For god's sake, Mason. I said I didn't want any fuss.

— It's not fuss – it's your birthday.

— I don't care what pissing day it is.

They come in without knocking, all rustling with presents and balloons, the boys first, the son-in-law. Her daughter carries a white box that could only contain a cake. Mason stands in the corner, sheepish, putting all the flowers in a vase.

— Hello, Nan!

One of the boys leans over, almost falling on her, kissing her cheek. She hugs him. He smells of aftershave. He smiles, handsome, but she can't return the gesture. She wants to go back to bed. The son-in-law gives her a kiss.

— Ninety, eh? Bloody hell, girl.

— A proper old biddy now!

— You gonna make it to a hundred or what?

— Hey, open my present first. It's drink. I'll have one.

— You alright, Mum?

— I'm alright, I just didn't want all this fuss. I told you I didn't want all this.

— But you're ninety!

— So I keep bloody hearing.

— You've got to have a little do on your ninetieth birthday.

They pile the presents and cards on her lap. Another grandson perches a plastic tiara in her hair. They all stand around gawping like she's some curiosity, some artefact – a zoo animal – waiting for her to move or speak. She doesn't speak. She distracts herself with the cards: saccharine watercolours of lilies and foxes, sickly poetry written by no one, the same old gags about being old and worn out.

She opens her presents, appreciating each one, but they're things she'd rather not own – a new cardigan, new slippers, chocolates. It all rings of a life waiting to happen, waiting to be used.

Mason lights the candles on the cake. Nine of them. And when he holds the cake to her face, she tries to see each candle as a decade – school and college, kids and marriage and lingering heartache. Nine tent posts, right here upon the white icing. She blows them out.

Make a wish, Mason says, and she does. She wishes it hard.

He takes the cake away and says he'll cut it, and everyone else stands about in the living room like it's a wake, murmuring, checking the time, as though they're waiting for something. Mason comes and sits on the arm of the chair. He holds her old hand and brushes his thumb over the baggy skin, the blotchy blue veins.

— Sorry, Nan.

— It's not your fault.

— Is there anything I can do?

— No, it's done now. I know you were just trying to do something nice. We'll have this cake, and then I'd like to be left alone, please.

— Okay.

Her daughter comes back with slices of cake on kitchen roll.

— There you go, Mum. I cut you a bit with a flower on it.

— Great.

And the room is quiet, but for the tacky sounds of people eating birthday cake and the wump of car doors outside. Everyone looks at her again.

— Will you lot tell me what's going on? What have you got planned now, hmm? A marching band? A stripper? I told you I didn't want all this fuss. I said it. I said—

The front door opens. Her granddaughter, Cara, steps in with her fiancé. And when the very old woman sees what's in his arms, she rests the cake on the table.

The fiancé, Tom, smiles.

He says, happy birthday, Dalia.

He says, Dalia, we'd like you to meet someone.

And he lowers the tiny thing into your arms.

Before you can look at her, you glance around at your family. This is what they were waiting for. And they're all smiling at you, especially your daughter Neda, who looks like she's about to cry. You draw a deep breath and look at the baby in your arms. Your first great-granddaughter.

She's sleeping. A little pink sleepsuit.

Crimson lips and wrinkled skin, like yours.

— We've decided to call her Layla.

You squeeze your eyes shut, your head flushing hot, and you sit there with your eyes closed for some time, just feeling the weight and warmth of the child cradled in your old arms. Four generations in one room.

When you open your eyes again, the world is blurry. You wipe your tears and look at her again – this new life, this little Layla. The tiny child opens her eyes and gazes up at you. Bright and full of life. You hold her fingers.

You're perfect, you tell her.

You're perfect.

That night, when everyone's gone home, you switch off the lights and make your way back to the bedroom. It was a good day. A good day. You feel weak with love, exhausted. You think of the beautiful baby, and her mother, and hers. It's the longest walk to your room, and when you open the door, a man waits on the chair beside the bed.

We smile at one another, and you climb onto the bed, atop the covers. You sit against the headboard and turn your head to me. You reach out and touch my cheek.

I look different now. I have a new face. New skin. A new name. But you know, with all your heart, who I am. Everyone knows, at the end.

I lay one final present on your lap. A photo album. Inside are photos of you as a much younger woman. Photos of you, even of me, photos of your girls – Neda and Layla. Almost all of them taken by Layla herself. Even now, you remember those moments. Even now, you miss her.

And for the rest of the night, we talk about days past, we study the photos of a different time – it seems so long ago, yet it's so clear. We look at our different faces. We wonder how things might have been different. We laugh, we hurt, we remember.

And that night, you stand up. You take my hand.

I stand with you, and you hold my waist, and although there is no music, we dance. Although there is no music, we hear it, the symphony of a life lived, and we dance to it, you and I, in this little room. You rest your head on my chest, and we dance. We are both so young and so old in the lamplight, and I am honoured to be here with you, at the end.

As we dance, you tell me you wish you could go back. Just twenty minutes. Just a normal day with your girls. You wish you could go back and live it again.

You tell me not to be lonely. To surround myself with the living, and to embrace them. You kiss my cheek. And when you're ready, you lie back down. I hold your hand one final time. You say thank you. Thank you. Thank you for making me wait. You smile once more. Thank you. You close your eyes, rest your head. And you leave this world, a mother, a great-grandmother, a very old woman.

Dalia Willard — 90 years, 0 months, 0 days

A DANCE OF MAYFLIES

And the sun is wavering red through the surface of the above-world, a shimmering halo, a signal. The nymphs can feel it. Each of them tunes their micro minds to the frequencies of the world, each of them is still and quiet, anticipating the moment. They are one, watching the sun. Smelling the water. Dreaming of the future times they'll spin silk threads in the moonlight. An invisible countdown like the bells of a New Year's Eve. They wait. Wait for something, wait for nothing. Wait for the unknown cue they've waited for their whole lives. The pond nymphs. The sun.

The first nymph sprouts its wings.

Others look on. Do I get wings?

Why does he get wings? I didn't know we had wings.

The second nymph sprouts its wings, and the third. The eleventh, the twelfth. The hundredth. These water nymphs burst with the secret they've held even from themselves – and when the wings arrive, they feel natural. Yes. This is what I've been missing. This is what we are. I knew there was something. A part of me knew it

all along. I remember. We were not meant to swim but
to fly.

So fly, one of them says. No, you go first. No, you.

Fly, angel. Fly up through the thick atmosphere we live
in, and breach the barrier, soar into space. Go on. I'll be
right behind you. No, you first. No, you. They are ready.
These winged astronauts, thousands, ready, on the edge
of something novel, a colony of travellers on a frontier to
a new land, these pioneer aviators, they are ready. Go on,
you first.

They all go at once, like fireworks. They shoot up through
the water, leaving their world behind – they breach the
surface and are overcome by a freshness, a thinness. The
veil has been lifted, the reins removed. The nymphs race
into the sky, higher than they ever dreamt, and it's so fast,
so smooth up here in the real world. They beat their wings,
and they dance, these mayflies in the meadow.

A watcher from the bank might see a cloud. A morphing
brown cloud over the pond, through the reeds, in the
weeps of the willows – but looking closer they'd see that
the cloud is a million tiny creatures with threads for tails,
weaving, darting, the day they got their wings.

The sun dips over the trees, the light is red, the light is
gold, the crickets buzz at their new intruders. The frogs

scurry from their hovels and burp and lick – is this dinner?
Is this the great feast, here, already?

And the mayflies realize a forgotten truth. A knowledge
lost from generation to generation. This day. This first day
they flew. This is their one day, their last day.

The mayflies, sweeping as one through the air, testing out
their loops and dives, they realize this is it. This is what it
was building to, this whole time. This one day. These few
hours. We are here to dance, to meet, and then we're gone.
We have no mouths from which to eat – we were never
meant to last. We are here for this one sacred moment.
That's all it ever was.

And the mayflies, these tricky mayflies, they slow down.
Just for a minute. Slow down. Can we go home? Can
I give my wings back? I'm not ready. Please don't let
this end.

Come, one of them says. If this is it, then let's sip every
splash of sun from the air, let's rinse every drop of life
from our bodies, let us dance and love and collide to make
new nymphs just as we were made, so they can learn
everything we learnt, all over again. Yes. Let's do that. And
the mayflies are ecstatic once more. Spin with me, show
me how fast you can go, how high. This is our ballet, our
opera – spin with me, spin.

Two mayflies collide and a human baby takes her first breath. Two mayflies tangle in the golden curtains and twin brothers unwrap matching bikes on Christmas Day. A mayfly weaves through the reeds and a father hugs his son for the first time since the coma. A mayfly rockets up up up until the meadow is a miniature, and a young woman graduates from university after leaving her homeland seven years past. Two mayflies tussle, and a father traps his daughter's fingers in the car door. Three mayflies ring-a-rosie over the pond and a man kisses his new husband in the library after dark. Four mayflies skim the water's edge and a little girl starves to death on the dusty road. Five mayflies are snapped up by frog tongues. Six mayflies kiss with wings and tangled tails in the fiery sky and every inch of air is an inch of life and it all twists and unfolds in impossible fractals, these beautiful-agonizing minutes, these frightening-lovely hours, slipping, fading, rushing, a cloud of insects, unholdable, uncapturable. They fly with their special birthday wings.

The sun pushes through the blur, an opalescent haze, these shimmering rainbow mists hanging over everyone, the burning of the pond. A place so bright and so dark that every detail vibrates with the scratches and grain of an over-exposed photograph, and the brightness stings and the brightness soothes. And the brightness stings and the brightness soothes. And it is violent and it is real.

A TWENTY-MINUTE GIFT

Imagine for one moment that you're in the future. Your future. These are your last moments before death. You're in your own bed, surrounded by flowers and cards and people you love. And there, in the corner of the room, like a shadow, is where you finally meet me. Now, imagine I give you a final gift. You're allowed to go back. Just for twenty minutes, you're allowed to go back to the exact moment where you're reading these words – you're back. Here you are.

This is your twenty-minute gift. Do not waste it. You can't change your life in twenty minutes, so don't try. No – do the thing that you'll wish, on your deathbed, you could have done one last time. Something precious. Kiss your partner. Play with your children. Wander in the world.

You have nineteen minutes remaining.

ACKNOWLEDGEMENTS

Thank you to my agent, Laura, for believing. To James, Margo and the team. Thank you to Caroline at the Bath Novel Award for making this happen. To Chris, Luke and Tom for reading my novels since we were at school. To Sam, Alan, Daisy, to my mum and Jon, dad and Wendy, to Auntie Wendy and Uncle Ron, to everyone at my day job. To my beautiful children, Eila and Eli, who always understand when I need to write. And to Kelly, for never giving up on me. This is for you.

BEN REEVES lives in Peterborough with his wife and two children. He won the Bath Novel Award 2024 for *Everything was Beautiful and Nothing Hurt*. When he's not writing, he paints, makes music and works as a web designer for a book printing company.